Chow Down

Second Edition

Chow Down

Second Edition

Mike Faricy

Library of Congress Control Number: 2023913120
paperback ISBN: 979-8-9880826-7-5
e-book ISBN: 979-8-9880826-8-2

    MJF Publishing books may be purchased for education, Busi-
ness, or promotional use. For information on bulk purchases,
please contact the author directly at mikefaricyauthor@gmail.com

Published by

MJF Publishing
https://www.mikefaricybooks.com

To Teresa
"Feck 'em all and let's
just get on with it."

Acknowledgments

I would like to thank the following people for their help and support:

Thanks to Roy, Steve, and Julie for their creative talent and not slitting their wrists or jumping off the high bridge when dealing with my Neanderthal computer capabilities.

Last, I would like to thank family and friends for their encouragement and unqualified support. Special thanks to Maggie, Jed, Schatz, Pat, Av, Emily, and Pat for not rolling their eyes, at least when I was there, and most of all, to my wife Teresa whose belief, support and inspiration has from day one, never waned.

One

Craig Cullen gripped the wheel tightly as he fish-tailed off the paved road and splattered mud along the side of his BMW. He raced down the gravel road to the processing plant and skidded to a stop next to the black SUV parked in front of the building.

Terry Taggert slammed the rear hatch on the SUV, smiled, and thought, *Oh shit.*

"Hey, Doc, didn't expect to see you all the way out here." Taggert's eyes blinked and darted from side to side like a cornered rat.

"We have to talk," Craig said.

"Just delivering our first box of steaks. Want to take some home?" He almost had to yell to be heard over the noise from a hundred-and-fifty cinnamon-colored Chows barking in the kennels behind the building.

"Good God, no! Are you crazy? It's one thing to try and pass the pelts off as exotic fur, but steaks, my God! You aren't really planning to go through with this insane scheme, are you?"

"What'd you mean insane? You were all for it. You came into this with your eyes wide open. Hell, you even thought it was kinda funny. As a matter of fact, your wife, Marti, begged me to let you in on the ground floor, give you a little taste of the action. You sure as hell loved the old projected profit ratio on them fur coats."

"That was then, before—"

"What? Now all of a sudden, when things are about to happen, you're getting cold feet? A conscience? Far as anyone knows, we're just a little old import company, Doc, nothing more, nothing less."

"The coats… well, yeah, that was okay, maybe. But this meat thing, I mean, come on. Look, I want nothing more to do with your 'import company'. The idea of jail time doesn't really appeal to me."

"Does Marti know you're out here? Did you check this out with her?" Taggert asked.

"No! I don't have to check with her. I make my own business decisions, and I just want my investment back. We'll call it even. I'll just go away and not say a word to anyone. I promise."

"Hmm-mmm, well, as long as you promise, Doc. Not much I can say except sorry things didn't work out. Come on into the office. I'll cut you a check. You sure I can't talk you out of this?"

"I'm quite sure." Craig shook his head, relieved things had gone this well. He followed Taggert into the cinder-block building. The office was actually more of a grimy lunchroom, the counter littered with dirty coffee cups and empty fast-food containers. A table strewn with pornographic magazines stood at a haphazard angle to the counter. On one corner of the table, a cup of coffee steamed next to a land-line phone.

Tilted on the rear legs of a chair sat the rumpled figure of Luther Suggs, his psychotic face hidden behind a foldout and a two-day beard. He lounged in a grimy, blood-stained lab coat. A white baseball cap emblazoned with 'Chow Industries' was perched backward on his head.

"Luther, look who came to visit," Taggert said, eyes darting from side to side, signaling there might be a problem.

"Something in your eyes?" Luther asked, looking up from behind the foldout.

"Let me see, Doc. We were gonna cut you a check," Taggert said, emphasizing the word check as he raised his eyebrows. He gave a palms-up gesture, suggesting Luther remove his size-twelve feet from the table.

"Mind if I use that chair a minute and cut the Doc here a check?"

"Huh?"

"Move, damn it."

"Oh, yeah, just reading an article here."

"Did I just hear the phone?" Taggert asked, inclining his head in Craig's direction.

"The phone?" Luther asked, now vaguely aware he might be missing something.

"I thought I heard this phone ring. Hello?" Taggert said, picking up the receiver. "Hmm-mmm… Oh yes, just a minute, he's right here. It's for you, Doc," he said, holding the phone in Craig's direction.

"Me, who would—"

Taggert slammed the receiver across Craig's left temple with a dull thunk. Thunk, thunk, thunk. He hammered until the receiver shattered across Craig's skull.

"Ughhh." Craig groaned and dropped to the concrete floor, pulling Luther's mug of scalding coffee down on top of him.

Taggert quickly followed with his loaded thirty-eight, hammering on the top of Craig's head. "Luther! Damn it. I could use a little help here."

Luther watched passively for a long moment, then reached down with a massive hand, grabbed Craig by his perfectly coiffed hair, and slammed his head a couple of times against the cold concrete floor. The third slam made a noticeably different sound, like a ripe melon falling off a truck.

"There, now he ain't going nowhere."

"It's about damn time. What did you think I was doing?"

"Sorry, man, I was busy."

"Take his keys and wallet and pull his car behind the kennel. Then dump him in the grinder. Grind him up a little at a time, so there's no trace. I doubt anyone knew he was coming out here. I was with that pain in the ass wife of his last night. She would've said something if she knew. I'll call her and set something up. Damn," Taggert said and rolled his shoulder, then kicked Craig's body for effect. "I think I tore a rotator cuff."

Luther grabbed Craig Cullen by the heels and dragged him across the floor, out through the door, to the processing area and the large stainless-steel meat grinder.

TWO

DJ gasped in a futile attempt to push him off. "Come on. I can't breathe! Oh, God. Dickie, I'm not kidding, get off me!" Eventually, Dickie Mullins rolled onto his back and gasped for air.

"You know, Dickie, it's a good thing for me, I'm not picky about who I climb into bed with." She laughed, then crawled out of bed and put her glasses back on.

"No complaint from me," he said.

"Hey, what'd you do with my underwear?"

From his angle on the bed, Dickie watched the reflection in the full-length mirror as she crawled along the floor. In the relatively close quarters of his thirty-foot houseboat, there was no room to spare, and her bare hip made a squeaky sound as she brushed against the full length mirror.

"Oh, Jesus," she said, grabbing the errant garment from under the bed. She stepped into the thong and then stopped, thumbs hooked in the straps around her thighs. She peered at the photo of his police academy graduating class. The light streaming through the small window cast golden highlights off her thick auburn hair.

"Looking for anyone in particular?" he asked.

"Yeah, my favorite arresting officers," she said, snapping the elastic across her hips. "Just looking. Hey, you were quite the stud back then. Oh, can you spot me twenty bucks? Oh, come on. Don't give me that look. If you're gonna make a Federal case out of—"

"Relax, there's twenty bucks on the dresser."

"Forty would go further."

"Twenty. Sure you can't stay?"

"Very sure. Look, I got an early day. See you around," she said, stuffing the twenty in a front pocket. She bent over Dickie and gave him a quick peck on the cheek before grabbing her cotton top and strolling out the door to the small deck area.

"Hey, put your top on for Christ's sake." He stepped out of bed, hopped across the floor and into his boxers.

"Good morning, Vernon," she said.

"DJ, always a pleasure." Vernon smiled, stared, and sipped some coffee from the deck of his boat next door.

"You know, Vernon, what do you think about an ex-cop who lives on a boat with a view of the city jail?" As she spoke, she gazed at the early morning reflection of the downtown buildings across the surface of the Mississippi.

"Real nice," Vernon replied, ignoring the river.

Dickie stepped out the door clad in Hawaiian print boxers.

"My God, that's too much to take in at this hour," Vernon said and covered his eyes.

"Dickie, put something on because you're scaring poor Vernon here. See ya later," DJ said. She pulled her top over her head, stepped onto the wooden dock, and walked toward the Wabasha Bridge.

"Dickie, Lord knows you sure as hell don't deserve it, but you're one lucky son-of-a-bitch," Vernon scoffed.

Dickie silently watched DJ climb up the marina steps and disappear before he went back inside.

His houseboat consisted of a room paneled in cheap knotty pine with a double bed, kitchen counter seating for one, a sink filled with dirty dishes, two cupboards, and a very small refrigerator. He poured a mug of coffee from the pot DJ had started and stepped back outside.

He sat on the tiny deck in a faded, folding aluminum chair. Every time he bent his elbow to sip some coffee, the chair creaked. He had almost finished the cup when he caught DJ's figure in the middle of the bridge, making her way to the downtown side. She was a computer geek who walked dogs for a living. It didn't seem to make sense, like just about everything else in his life.

He absently ran his hand across his midsection, where his t-shirt rode up, and his boxers wedged down, revealing an ample spare tire. He planned to lose twenty pounds last summer, get back into some semblance of shape. He'd have to lose closer to thirty now, starting to-morrow. Once he picked up the surveillance case from Darcy.

Dickie had been on a disability pension from the police department since 2013. Some guy coming out of a liquor store at high noon. Who robs a liquor store at noon on a Monday? The dirtbag came out, and his car wouldn't start. First squad on the scene calmly pulled behind the fool's car, blocking it. By the time Dickie and his partner showed up, they were just watching the show.

Some department shrink talked the idiot into giving up. The poor guy, dressed in a cowboy outfit with a black ten-gallon hat, sat in the front seat of his car with a six-shooter in his lap, crying.

They had him surrounded on one of the first nice days of spring. Sunny, warm, and the only question was what kind of paperwork would have to be filled out, an arrest or a coroner's report.

Eventually, the shrink talked the fool into tossing his weapon out the car window, which he did, unfortunately, with the hammer cocked. The damned thing discharged, ricocheted off a parked snowplow, and clipped Dickie's left hip before exiting his rear.

He was just minding his own damn business, thinking about how great it felt to be in the sun, warm, safe, and glad he wasn't the lead officer on this cluster when—BOOM! Just like that, quick as you could say, "What the hell!" Dickie ended up retired and on disability.

It wasn't long after that, once he had completed his correspondence course, that he had started his private eye gig. About a year after that, he got the brain fart to buy a bar and restaurant, the Emporium of Dance. It was a local meat market, for lack of a better term. Now, with the economy the way it was, he'd been working overtime just to keep it afloat. He glanced at the clock, six-thirty. He had an appointment at eleven, which gave him almost three more hours of sleep if he hurried.

He crawled onto the pile of leopard print sheets, reeking of spicy lubricant. A hint of DJ's perfume still lingered around the pillow as he fell asleep.

Three

Dickie slowly opened his eyes as a female voice, frighteningly familiar and way too cheery, called from the door. "Knock, knock, knock, Sleepy Head, rise and shine. Come on. I brought you coffee. Mmm-mmm, here smell, Baby. Fresh black coffee, just the way you like it." The voice was suddenly next to his bed.

According to the digital, it wasn't quite eight-thirty, and Dickie could only hope he was in the midst of some strange nightmare and not really hearing his ex-wife's voice.

"Come on now, Baby. Up and at 'em. Come on." She bent down, letting her blonde perfumed hair brush lightly across his neck, chasing away the final vestige of sleep.

Dickie had always been convinced his ex-wife, Rae Nell, held on to his last name just to piss him off. She was the youngest of four sisters, Rae Jean, Rae Dawn, Rae Lynn, and Rae Nell. They had been called the *Sun*

Rae's by their mother, and by the time of his divorce, Dickie thought of them as the *Death Rae's*.

Rae Nell divorced Dickie six years ago in search of her *freedom*. Following the divorce, Dickie got the house payment, Rae Nell got the house, along with the *freedom* to pursue any get rich scheme that piqued her interest, which seemed to be most of them.

She sniffed as she stepped back to the kitchen counter. She picked up an oily hint of spicy something from somewhere.

"New aftershave you're wearing?"

"I don't suppose it would have done any good to lock the door," he groaned.

"Not really, Hon, you gave me a key. Remember? Besides," she said, snooping in the bathroom, "it's not like you have anything worth taking."

"Well, you'd know all about that, Rae Nell, since you already took everything. So what do you want?" Dickie said as he sat up in bed. He blinked in an effort to accept the brightness and rubbed whatever two scant hours of sleep might have deposited in his eyes.

"Oh, don't be such a sore loser. Here, just the way you like it, black, not too hot," she said, prying off the plastic lid.

"Mmm-mmm," Dickie groaned, then rolled out of bed and stumbled the five feet to the counter.

"Wow, there's a lot more of you to love, honey," she said, sounding genuinely surprised. She gave him the once over from head to toe before handing him the cup of coffee.

"Rae Nell, darling," Dickie said with an inflection, not quite suggesting warmth. "What in the hell are you doing here at this hour of the morning?"

"Well, aren't we just Mr. Crabby. A girl can't even bring you a nice cup of coffee without being yelled at."

"I didn't yell."

"Could have fooled me. For your information, Crabby Appleton, I was just in the neighborhood, and since I hadn't seen you for at least half a year, I was wondering how you were getting along, that's all. If you're going to be a poop, I'll just leave."

"Okay," he said and sipped.

"Honestly, Dickie, I just wondered how you were doing. Gee, I can't be concerned without you getting upset? What's that all about?"

"I'm touched you're so concerned, Rae Nell. I really am. But, you have to admit it's only right I'm a little gun shy. Let's see, there was that wrestler you were dating, you remember? You told him I was stalking you. That was great. He showed up at the Emporium of Dance with two other clowns the size of semi-trucks intent on wrecking the place."

"The Emporium of Dance? Oh, please, Dickie. It's a weekend meat market. You serve up one-night stands as the house specialty with a side order of too much to drink."

"Hey, Rae Nell, you don't have to describe what you did last night. I'm just a little leery about your so-called concern, that's all. We could discuss the stockbroker, you remember him? Had you selling stocks to me without a license, the inside tip on the clapper for computers. Clap it on, clap it off." Dickie clapped his hands.

"Remember? Securities and Exchange parked out in front of your house, attempting to serve you a subpoena. So you hid out here for a week and a half while I was vacationing out west. I come home relaxed and all jazzed from seeing Mount Rushmore, and you make me get a hotel room because you couldn't possibly be inconvenienced."

"Well, excuse me. I thought I was doing you a favor by giving you three more nights away from this scow! Besides, you were dating that underaged child, if I recall."

"She was twenty-four."

"Exactly."

"Then, there was that guy who was mad at you and your imported pearl business, so he took a baseball bat to my car!"

"That orange Geo Metro? That dreadful thing? Oh, really, Dickie, it belonged in the scrap heap, if you could even find someone to dispose of it. My God, talk about toxic waste. I can't believe the state even allowed that death trap on the road."

"It was a classic, Rae Nell, a classic."

"Classic junk is more like it, Dickie. It leaked, just for starters. Did you ever get rid of the bean bag you had for a passenger seat?"

"The passenger seat was reinstalled," he said, declining to mention the fourteen-inch gash across the leather.

"Whatever."

"Well, we might discuss the shipping container of honey you imported from Thailand and had dropped off at the rear of the Emporium of Dance last summer. That was beautiful. I don't know the thing is coming, and they punch a hole in the container with a forklift before leaving it by my back door. I had to shut down for three days because the wasps and bees were so bad. Neighbors started a petition against me, and I'm still battling with the Department of Health."

"Yeah, that one was kind of goofy. Okay, I admit that," she said, shrugging. "Look, enough crying over spilled milk."

"Spilled milk, I—"

She held up her hand. "I didn't come here with fresh coffee, so I could get yelled at and listen to your attempts to start another fight. Honestly, I just wondered if you would like to come over for dinner tomorrow night. You know, see the old place. I mean, after all, you're paying for it. We could maybe just catch up. You know, touch base."

"Why? What do you need?" Dickie asked cautiously.

"Why do I have to need anything? Why can't I just do something nice without you complaining all the time?"

"Maybe, Rae Nell, because it's just that when you try to do something nice for me, I always end up getting royally screwed."

"Look, do you want to come over for dinner or not? You can leave as soon as we're done eating and get back to that Brothel of Dance place if that's what you're whining about. I'm sure you wouldn't want to miss out on all the haggling for price and services that's bound to go on."

"It's the Emporium of Dance, as you know. You promise I can leave after dinner and you're not going to ask me for any money? You're not going to ask me for any favors? You're not going to complain about…"

"Dickie, when did you get so cynical? I promise I won't ask you for any money. I promise I won't ask you for any favors. My God, I'm just looking to catch up, that's all. You're free to leave whenever you want. Jesus, I have to say, after extending the olive branch, I honestly thought I would get a little better reception than this."

"You sure?"

"Girl Scouts honor. Say seven-ish?"

He let out a long sigh, closed his eyes, reminded himself this was really stupid, then nodded helplessly.

"Okay, seven, but I'm warning you, Rae Nell. The first time you ask me for a favor, any favor, I'm out the door. Okay?"

"Okay, Crabby," she said, then gave him a peck on the cheek and quickly made her exit before he had a chance to change his mind.

"Hello, Vernon, you're up bright and early," Rae Nell said.

"Just enjoying the early morning views around this place," Vernon said.

Four

Dickie cautiously backed his Jeep Wrangler into a parking space a half-hour late for the appointment with his accountant and friend, Fenton Larkin. His car had seen better days. The duct-taped windows leaked, and the interior was just a tad moldy from the summer rain. Earlier in the year, an irate stripper wielding a nail file had slashed a fourteen-inch gash across his refurbished passenger seat. The doors had a tendency to slam the unsuspecting before they had completely climbed in, and the infamous body had been reshaped a few years back by a boyfriend of Rae Nell's wielding a Louisville slugger.

He'd been seated in the lobby for a few minutes and was aggressively attacking either a chili or spaghetti sauce stain, he wasn't sure which, on the sleeve of his navy blue sport coat. Finally, Clairese, Fenton's secretary and receptionist, had enough. She charged out from behind her desk, armed with a towel and a bottle of club soda.

"You know, Dickie, you could just get this thing cleaned or, better yet, throw it away," she said, then grabbed his sleeve and poured club soda over the stain.

"Hey, watch what you're doing there."

"Oh, sorry, I didn't realize this coat never had anything poured on it. Give me this," she commanded, yanking his arm back in front of her.

"You could stand to get those trousers pressed too. Looks like you slept in them more than once. And maybe a shirt and tie instead of the golf shirt."

"You think maybe there could be something between the two of us, Clairese?"

"Nothing but distance."

"Want to think about it?"

"I don't see enough lowlifes in here every day? I need to take up with someone like you? I don't think so. Besides," she continued, snapping the wet towel at the golf shirt stretched tight as a drum over Dickie's stomach. "Someone like you rolls over on little old me in the middle of the night, they'd have to scrape me off the bed with a spatula."

"You could take tops."

"Please, I'm barely two hours past breakfast. Unless you want to see strawberry yogurt and All-Bran on that coat of yours, you'll think of something else entirely."

"Dickie," Fenton called from his office, "nice of you to finally drop in. Get the hell in here."

"Some other time, Clairese. Thanks for the wet spot on my coat."

Clairese just shook her head.

"Jesus, Dickie," Fenton sounded more frustrated than usual as Dickie stepped in. "You had better start getting back into shape, pal, or I'm going to have to ask for cash upfront. At this rate, you won't be around to get my invoice."

"Just more of me to love," Dickie said as he slapped his midsection.

Fenton peered back over the top of his reading glasses.

"You're an early heart attack just waiting to happen, my friend. Start eating right, start getting some exercise, or you become a liability. I'm not kidding here."

"Okay, okay. Did you get up on the wrong side of the bed this morning? Relax. I'm starting a new regimen tomorrow."

"It's always tomorrow, isn't it? Here," Fenton said, tossing a file in Dickie's general direction before turning back to his computer screen. "Things are looking pretty good, that is if your goal was to reach ground zero. You don't have any money to move around or protect, no working capital, no assets except for the Emporium, well, and that raft you live on. Basically, you're broke. I can't believe you're even keeping books. You taking cash out every night? Based on the figures you gave me here, you're not cutting it. Oh, hey, by the way, where'd you get that program?"

"Program?"

"Yeah, and you just answered my question. You have no idea, correct? Whoever you got doing your books has a nifty little program they're using. Just as a test, we ran it off some of our systems here. The thing just whistled through each and every one of them, spreadsheets, charts, ratios, whatever we wanted. Look, find out where they got it. I'd like to get copies in all our offices. It even worked on the overseas stuff."

"Yeah, my bookkeeper, DJ. I'll mention it to her. But back up a minute, I'm broke?"

Five

Andre carefully ran his hand against the grain of two cinnamon fur coats. "I have to admit, this is highly unusual quality, Mr. Taggert.""Unusual, highly unusual. As you requested, Sir, we lined and monogrammed both coats. If I might offer a suggestion, the detachable tag affair here, Sir, behind the sleeve, black leather with the chrome buckle and the little studs. It looks an awful lot like a dog collar, Sir, and well, I wonder if your average lady might not be a bit put off."

"Thanks for the advice, partner. I'll be sure to keep it in mind. Course, these are just what you call your prototypes. We're cranking up one of them marketing campaigns. Get the word out there for the Christmas season."

"Really, Sir, interesting." Andre secretly cringed, as if what was left of the fur industry didn't have enough problems.

"I'm thinking of some sexy gal with one of these here coats wrapped around her ass. You know, an ad that appeals to the naughty side of everyone. Big old letters across the bottom of the ad, Chow Furs." Taggert gestured in the air with his hand as if reading the copy on a giant billboard.

"Amazingly unique. I'm quite sure no one has ever conceived of an ad campaign quite like that, Sir."

"Yeah, we'd most likely be the first."

"Certainly the first, Sir," Andre said, thinking *unbelievable*.

"Yeah, well, look, partner, appreciate all your work here," Taggert said, not wanting to give away any more of his marketing campaign.

"Yes, Sir." Andre smiled weakly.

Six

Over lunch, Marti Cullen was replaying her morning conversation. She'd been in bed, propped against a mountain of silk pillows, watching Craig get dressed. "You know, Craig, this may come as a surprise to you, but I can do something besides spend money."

"Look, Marti, all I'm saying is you seem to be rather unhappy of late. Now, I would like to pursue this further, say over dinner tonight. I can't think of a better topic to discuss than why you're feeling unhappy *this* week. But right now, I've got an early morning meeting and then surgery. I don't have time to discuss this any further. At least, not now."

"Surgery, Jesus, Craig," she groaned, falling back on the pillows. "My God, like you're some kind of brain surgeon or obstetrician or something. Craig, you're not a doctor, you big phony. You manufacture lingerie. You create feats of engineering for women. That's what you do. You make underwear for God's sake, Craig, underwear!"

"I am a doctor."

"Oh, God, Craig, let's not quibble about this again. A doctorate in Medieval English Literature does not entitle you to elite medical status. Yes, you have a doctorate; no, you are not a medical doctor, okay?"

"Easy for you to—"

"God, I still cringe at the awful memory of that flight to New York when you booked our reservations as Dr. and Mrs. Cullen. That poor little man with the heart attack and you, you big phony, you go back to look at him with the stewardess and then tell her there's nothing you can do. My God! Of course, there was nothing you could do unless he wanted a story read to him while he sat there and died somewhere over Ohio. What the hell were you thinking? We're lucky they didn't arrest the two of us when we landed at JFK. So please, do not give me the surgery routine. You're just building underwear for some surgically enhanced bimbos to show off the latest pair of medical marvels. It's just underwear, Craig, underwear!"

"You and your Foundation Development Corporation. Good Lord, it sounds like you're raising money for the International Children's Fund or the Ronald McDonald House instead of selling lingerie to ridiculously enhanced strippers!"

"Well, you'd certainly be the authority on surgical enhancement, Marti."

"Oh, that is ridiculous. A few nips and tucks, a slight firming, a couple of lifts, my enhancement insertions have absolutely no relationship whatsoever to—"

"Sorry, but right now, I have to run. I'll be happy to discuss your own personal tale of medical reconstruction at the end of my day."

"Fine, but I'm out with umm, with friends tonight, so don't wait up."

Seven

Dickie was attempting to start the Jeep and not meeting with much success. The meter had expired a half-hour ago, and the stupid engine groaned in response to his attempts.

"Son-of-a-bitch," he shouted, then slammed the steering wheel, hoping the vehicle would feel the pain shudder down the steering column.

His cell phone rang. He patted himself down, searching for it, cocked an ear, and followed the tone to the glove compartment.

"Yeah."

"Christ, you even got that thing on? Jesus, I was beginning to wonder. You forget about our lunch date a half-hour ago? I've left three messages. You get any of them?" Darcy's tirade suddenly reminded Dickie of their luncheon appointment.

"No, sorry, something came up, and I couldn't get back to you until now," Dickie said, doing his best to grovel.

"You forgot. Don't bullshit me, man, and you didn't get back to me. I called you. That's what I get for making the appointment with you in the parking lot after a Twins game."

"I'm not kidding, man. Something came up. I figured you'd understand. You had to eat anyway, right?"

Darcy Dalton, attorney to the stars, according to his self-promotion. He handled high-profile divorce settlements, prominent possession cases, and the occasional murder.

Dickie had thought he was in good hands when he had Darcy represent him in his divorce from Rae Nell. Now he found himself sleeping in a used houseboat in the St. Paul Marina while Rae Nell walked away with everything but the Jeep, which she hated and didn't have room for in the garage, anyway.

"Look, Richard," Darcy continued, knowing Dickie hated being called Richard, "we were going to meet, if you recall, to discuss you investigating a divorce case. Are you still interested?"

'Not really,' Dickie thought but said, "Yeah, Darcy, sure I'm interested. Can we reschedule?"

"Possibly."

Dickie waited a couple of beats.

"Sorry, just checking my calendar. I'm in trial the day after tomorrow. Suppose you've heard about the Carter case."

Of course Darcy would be representing a creepy prominent dentist who jacked up his dates on nitrous oxide. At least until one drowned throwing up in a sink, and suddenly the floodgates opened with a dozen women filing charges against the guy. Heard about it? Dickie was one of the few people in town not claiming to have been raped by the guy.

"Yeah, I maybe remember something. Hey, Darcy, if you want my help on that, much as I'd like to, I better take a pass. Probably wouldn't be able to get on it for at least a couple of days, and doesn't your trial start the day after tomorrow?"

"It's not about Carter, and can you meet me tonight? It won't take long. Can you meet me at seven?"

"Okay, how about Lenny's?" Dickie said.

"Lenny's?"

"Yeah, steak joint, corner building, white with brick—"

"I know the place. Okay, just be on time," Darcy said and hung up.

The phone rang again.

"Yeah."

"Oh, so you finally have your phone turned on."

"Hello, Rae Nell."

"I've been calling you for the past few hours. Where have you been?"

"Meetings. What can I do for you?"

"Just checking. You're really coming tomorrow night, right? You wouldn't stand me up, would you?"

"No, I wouldn't stand you up. Look, I said I'd be there. I will. Tomorrow night, seven-thirty."

"Seven! Okay, I'll see you then. Don't be late. Bye, bye, bye." Click.

"Shit!" Dickie said. She had something up her sleeve. He could feel it.

Eight

After shopping for a set of 'event' underwear, Marti Cullen spent the rest of the afternoon being pampered. An overall body massage followed by a manicure, pedicure, facial, and hair appointment, then driving home to nap before seeing Terry Taggert.

She met him just over a year ago, bowled over by his lingering glance, ruggedly handsome good looks, and a body that wouldn't quit. Add to that his incredible performance stamina, and she'd hit the jackpot.

He had told her that he played for the New Orleans Saints, laughing at her when she mentioned she knew nothing about basketball. He called her the moment he came to town, never in the same hotel twice, always the best suite of rooms. They would have a fun night, fantastic sex, and those 'small tokens of affection.' Diamond earrings; she checked, and they were real. A gorgeous tennis bracelet, the cocktail ring, money seemed to be no object, and she'd be a fool to pass it up.

Taggert was a good ten years younger than Marti, which made him at least twenty years younger than Craig. She rounded that up to an even quarter-century. Now that was a piece of meat worth sampling.

Nine

Dickie picked up his phone, "Hello."

"Well, at least you answered this time. Where the hell are you now?"

"I'm in the parking lot, Darcy. Calm down. I'll be there in just a minute," Dickie said, exiting off the freeway ramp, late for dinner. He stopped at the light to wait for traffic before completing his turn. If he made all the lights, he could be at the restaurant in five minutes.

"Well, hurry up. I'm starving, and I'm wasting billable time in this dump you picked."

"Grab a table. I'm just about to get out of the car now."

"I've already got a table waiting. It's bad for my image to be seen sitting alone, especially waiting for someone like you."

"I'm almost in the door," Dickie said, barely creeping forward at the traffic light.

"Hurry up."

Ten minutes later, Dickie entered Lenny's barroom and found Darcy hunched in a dark corner. His back was to the door, nursing a cosmopolitan. His slicked-back hair was wrapped around his tanned face like a helmet.

"Darcy, what are you doing back here in the dark, man? This can't be good for the old image."

"Dickie, you said one minute, and it's been about thirty. Where the hell have you been?"

"Look, sorry, ran into some old clients in the parking lot, and they wanted to thank me and chat for a minute. Old schmoozer like you should know how that goes."

"All I know is the only thing any old clients of yours would want to do is run the other way. Look, I don't care. Let's just get to the table, so I can order, and we can get going on this thing, okay? I don't like being seen in this place any longer than I have to be."

"What? Lenny's?" Dickie shrugged. "Hey, sorry, I picked a place with great steaks."

"Like I explained before, it's part of my image, Dickie. It's a big part of the legal business, clients like a winner. Look, never mind. Let's just eat, okay?"

They walked through a small arched doorway that led to the dining room.

"Hey, Dickie, good seeing you, man. How's it going?" A burly guy with a shaved head and a black handlebar mustache grabbed Dickie's hand, pumped it up and down, then slapped him on the shoulder. The sleeves on his white shirt were rolled up, revealing massively muscled forearms. The white, ankle-length apron wrapped around his black trousers masked thighs the size of tree trunks.

"Going good, Perv. How's Carol?"

"She's good. You know, chasing the kids every-where, that whole routine. She's here on weekends, Dickie. You should stop in and see her. She'd love it."

"Oh, hey, sorry, a friend of mine, Darcy Dalton. Darcy meet Perv. Darcy here is a lawyer. You're ever in trouble, give him a call. He needs the business."

"Yeah, right, who doesn't love lawyers, Dickie." He shook his shaved head and laughed. "Hey, look, your pal here had a table reserved, but I didn't know you were joining him, Dickie. I got a better booth for you guys, nice and private like, back there in a corner. Maybe be better since he's a lawyer and all, you know?"

"Nice to meet you, Perv. About that booth?" Darcy said.

"Oh, yeah, right, here you go, gents," he said, taking two laminated menus from under the counter and walk-ing back to a far corner of the restaurant.

"I'll have one of the girls back here in no time. Dickie, nice as always, and pleased to meet you, Darcy." He nodded, then flicked a small lighter. Something akin to a six-inch flame shot out as he lit a ruby-red globe on the table.

Darcy slid into the booth and watched their host re-turn to the front of the restaurant.

"Perv? You introduce me to some guy named 'Perv' working in a restaurant? How wonderfully appealing!"

He adjusted the paper placemat in front of him. It was embossed with the purple outline of the building. 'Lenny's' was scrawled in cursive script across the front.

"Relax, that's Lenny, and it's a long story. Some mix-up years back with a couple of women and hand-cuffs, that's all."

"That's all? Dickie, you just sketched out an event that is most likely foreign in the day-to-day workings of normal people. Never mind, I've already got too much information. What's good here?"

"Well, it's a steak place, so I'd stick with that if I were you. Let's order, and then you can tell me what's so important it can't wait."

"Yeah, well, it doesn't look like you're the first one to push away from the dinner table on most nights." Darcy nodded.

"I'm working on it, so relax and just pick a steak. I'm starving."

"Okay, but I'm buying. I don't care what you say." Darcy waved his hand dismissively.

"Fine with me."

"That screwy bar working for you yet?" Darcy asked.

"The Emporium of Dance," Dickie corrected. "Yeah, I'm about to turn a corner, I think. Just back from the accountant's this morning. Things are starting to hap-pen," he said, not mentioning bankruptcy as one of the possible options.

"Care for a beverage, gentlemen? Before you—Dickie?"

"Hey, Barb, how are you? Long-time no see."

"Well yeah, it's going great, Dickie, real well. Gee, I just, well, you caught me a little by surprise, all of you. I mean, both of you guys here, you know? Yeah. So can I get you something to drink before you order?"

"May I see your wine list?" Darcy asked.

"Yeah, sure, right here." She pointed with her pen to the lower corner of the menu. "Five-fifty for any glass. Bottles run fifteen to twenty, depending." She cocked a hip and waited for Darcy to decide from one of the four offerings as she rolled her eyes toward the ceiling.

"Charming," Darcy sighed. "We'll have a bottle of the d'Abruzzo, thanks," he said, flashing a quick smile.

"I'll be right back with that, Sir. Great seeing you again, Dickie," she said, looking him up and down one final time before departing.

"Okay, so what's so hot with you it can't wait?" Dickie asked, watching as Barb wove her way through the tables. The past year had been good to her. He quickly flashed back to a summer of fun weekends at her lake place before their relationship fizzled with the coming of fall. He remembered the fun they'd had, playing house at her lake cabin, no pressure, no interruptions, no expectations, and then one day, no relationship. There was never the big break up. Things had just naturally sputtered and then seemed to die of their own accord.

"...finally gotten to the point where she decided she's had enough, and as her legal advisor, I fully concur. In fact, in all candor, I feel she's been far more patient than most. Now, of course, just the obvious question remains, and that's where you come in."

"Oh, thank you." Darcy ceased droning and sat back as Barb delivered an open wine bottle and two glasses. Dickie wasn't sure how long he'd tuned Darcy out while daydreaming of Barb and the lake.

"Well, at least the bottle was opened," Darcy said.

"It's a twist-off cap," Dickie said.

Darcy poured a little into his glass, swirled it around, stuck his nose in the glass, and then took a sip. He rolled the wine over his tongue and eventually swallowed.

"Meet with the master's approval?"

"Surprisingly, not bad, not bad at all," he said, filling his glass then Dickie's.

"Look, Dickie, let's get things back on the right foot," he said, raising a glass across the table. "You've obviously moved on from your divorce."

Dickie gave Darcy a look for just a half-second, the wound not yet completely healed.

"And," Darcy continued, "after what I just told you, you can understand why this is so damned important and what it could mean for both of us. So here's to the beginning of a solid business relationship, if you think you can handle it. I mean, I do need to know if you're up to the task. If it's too much, I think we know one another well enough that you can just say so. We can still have dinner and part as friends. Fair?" he asked and extended his glass to toast.

Ten

Barb suddenly appeared from out of nowhere, pen poised. "Ready to order, Gentlemen?"

"Do you have a suggestion? By the way, this wine is excellent, wonderful tannin," Darcy said, then began studying the menu selections.

"Yeah, it's uncomplicated with a nice finish. Tonight the small filet is probably your best bet. It says small, but it's not. Corn fed, tender, comes with a salad and garlic toast." She snapped a small wad of gum on the left side of her mouth then waited.

"Very well, the small filet it is."

"How would you like that done?"

"Just the slightest bit past medium." Darcy gestured with a movement of his hand, suggesting 'very slight.'

Barb pulled the menu from his hands. "Dressing? We got French, Thousand Island, Italian, she pronounced it eye-talien, Blue Cheese."

"The Blue Cheese."

"Dickie?"

"Just a dinner salad, Barb. Italian dressing."

"You sure?" Barb and Darcy exclaimed.

"I'm buying!" Darcy reminded.

"Just the salad," Dickie replied, resisting temptation. In a flash, he remembered DJ gasping for air beneath him, Rae Nell's comment, Fenton's warning, Darcy's look, and finally, Barb's poorly disguised shock just ten minutes ago.

"Okay," she said, then took Dickie's menu and shrugged as she walked off.

"I thought you said you were starving. What? My offer floor you?" Darcy asked.

"No, just watching things, getting back into shape. So tell me again about this deal."

"You weren't even paying attention, were you? Okay, you ever hear of Helen Hardy?"

"The automobile heiress?"

"Half-right, actually auto parts was the most recent guy, Winston Hardy, her third husband. Before him, a fortune in offshore oil with a guy named Sonny Delaney. Her first husband invented the computer or some damned thing. She's actually a pretty nice old gal, once you get to know her. Anyway, she's outlived three husbands."

"She went for something different this last time. Number four is a real peach of a guy by the name of Terrence Taggert. Claimed to be from New Orleans. Of course, tough to check very much since a good portion of those records were destroyed with Katrina. Anyway, there's about a forty-five year age gap between the two of them."

"Forty-five years?"

"I drew up a prenup, protecting her fortunes, so she's safe there, but he's got a taste for ladies on the side, and she's past ignoring it. She wants to catch the guy red-handed. You know, photos, receipts, all that sleazy stuff. Of course, I thought of you right away."

"Thanks."

"Don't mention it. Anyway, this clown was a some-time jock. Nothing big, bounced around a couple of minor league farm teams until he hosed that up. He did some male model gig for a while after that. He dated one of those chicks with a name we're all supposed to recognize, only she never did anything, so who really cares?"

"Client of yours?" Dickie asked.

Darcy ignored the comment. "Anyway, Terry Taggert was a waiter when he met Helen, a love at first bite thing. One night, he's walking around with a tray of canapés, then three weeks later, she's flying back from the Caribbean with stars in her eyes and this clown on her arm."

"That was about sixteen months ago. True to form, Terry Taggert has already screwed the golden goose. I almost got the bastard last week, but he jumped off a second-story balcony, bounced across the hood of a car, and bolted. Bastard paid cash for the eight-hundred-a-night suite, so no credit card receipts, no photos, and therefore no divorce. All I've got to show for my effort is one pissed off, rich, old lady threatening to pull all her business."

"Who'd you have doing the investigation?"

"Someone else who didn't work out. That's all you really need to know. I'd prefer not to mention his name. Besides, it's not important."

Dickie guessed it was Darcy himself who had screwed things up.

"Your filet, Sir, garlic toast, and salad," Barb said, setting a tray down next to their table, deftly shoveling a sizzling steak platter, toast and salad in front of Darcy as if she were dealing a hand of cards.

"Damn it!" Darcy yelped, shaking his right hand in the air.

"Careful, Sir, that platter's hot."

"God damn it!" Darcy whispered.

"And your dinner salad, Dickie, with Eye-talian. Anything else, guys?" she asked, ignoring Darcy examining his fingertips. She departed when Dickie shook his head.

"Darcy, you didn't hear that thing sizzling? What'd you think you were doing? She told you it was hot."

"That was after the fact. I should sue this joint. They're liable, nothing but gross negligence. I wonder how many times that happens on any given night."

"Probably never, since you're the only one stupid enough to grab a sizzling platter. So back to your close personal friend, this Taggert guy. You said you need photos?"

"Exactly!" Darcy said, continuing to examine his hand for a telltale blister.

"Look, I've done a few of these deals before. It sounds fairly routine," Dickie said, stuffing lettuce into his mouth. "You don't need shots of the guy in the sack with some woman. Get them coming in and going out of the room, a digital time setting in the corner of the shot. Maybe a good-bye kiss in the hallway or the parking lot. That's all you'll need. He'll fold."

Darcy pondered that for a moment as he took a bite of steak. "Nope, we need the action shot. Hey, this steak is great, perfect. And this wine, fantastic," he said, slurping.

"How's the hand?"

"I guess I'll live, but Jesus. Your salad?"

"Just what the Dr. ordered," Dickie said and then gazed longingly at Darcy's steak.

"If you say so."

"Look, Darcy, if I'm going to get the action shot, the problem is I'll have to know where he'll be well in advance. I'll have to get in there ahead of him. I won't have any warrants, so if it goes to court, the image or video will be tossed out. By the way, it ain't gonna be cheap. I'll give you a deal, don't worry, but just so you know." He forced down another bite of his salad.

"Money's no problem. Man, mmm-mmm, what's better than a steak?"

'Music to my ears,' Dickie thought.

An hour later, Dickie looked longingly at the two or three bites of steak Darcy left on his plate and said, "It sounds pretty damn screwy, Darcy. You want the action shot. I'm not saying 'No'. I'm just telling you it makes the mission about a thousand percent more difficult, and for what? It's not going to make your case any stronger. Well, maybe the shock value. Just show the guy the photos, and he's toast."

"Helen needs the photos."

"Look, Darcy, relax. I'll nail him. Come on. You know guys like this Terry Taggert character, they just disappear." Dickie ran his fork along the edge of his empty salad bowl, hoping he might capture a morsel of garlic, the hint of tomato, maybe some small crumb he missed on a previous pass.

"You said the guy signed a prenup, right? So I'm guessing he's going to end up without a cent when he gets nailed. Course, I'll do whatever you want. But I'm just telling you, the old action shot makes it a hell of a lot more difficult, and you'll be no further ahead."

"You sure you don't want to grab some dessert or an after-dinner drink? Something? Anything?" Darcy asked.

Dickie shook his head, gripped the table leg, and hoped he could hang on before blurting out he wanted a twenty-four-ounce steak and a loaf of garlic bread to go.

"Man, I gotta say, I'm impressed with your discipline. Check!" Darcy waved at Barb. "Look, I'll get the file on our boy over to you tomorrow morning. Give me your office address," Darcy said, pulling a fountain pen out of his suit coat.

"How 'bout I just pick up the file tomorrow? That'll give me time to think this through."

"Okay, suit yourself, man. Great idea coming here. I knew it would be good the moment I walked in the door," Darcy said.

Eleven

Terry closed his eyes and took a deep breath. "Oh, man, baby, that feels so good. Ahhh, yeah, right there, oh yeah, oh, baby."

"Look, Terry," Marti Cullen groaned, rolling off his back after thirty seconds. "You want a massage, hire a masseuse. I'll wreck my nails if I keep that up."

"Come on, Baby. I just rubbed your back for about fifteen minutes. My shoulder's killing me. I told you I hurt it at practice last week. Now be a good girl and give me a rub, right there," he pleaded, rolling his shoulder.

"Ughhh, all right, all right. But I hate doing this. I wreck a nail, and believe me, there will be hell to pay."

"Hey, come on."

"Well, hey," she imitated Taggert's accent in a whining tone. "This is different. You don't have nails like me. Besides, if your shoulder hurts, it's your own fault. You should learn to be more careful."

It was dinner time, and Taggert's stomach growled. His face remained down in the pillow, as he thought, *It suddenly wasn't so fun being with this woman.* Unlimited millions of dollars to tap into, compliments of his old bat of a wife, Helen Hardy, and he was risking it all on some self-absorbed, washed-up model who wouldn't even give him a back rub. Too bad she didn't have a clue she was a widow as of this morning.

He thought back to that night just a week ago. That was no room service waiter knocking on his hotel room door— some guy with slicked-back hair and a camera hanging around his neck. Taggert hadn't ordered room service. So he did the only sensible thing and bailed. He pulled on his jeans, then out and over the damn balcony, hurting his shoulder as he landed on the hood of that car. Now he couldn't even get a damn back rub from this pain in the butt. Sometimes life just sucked.

Twelve

ickie took his time walking out to the parking lot, feigning a trip to the men's room in order to give Darcy a head start. He didn't want Darcy watching him open the broken door on the Jeep as he stuffed himself behind the steering wheel. He didn't want Darcy seeing him grind away, cursing when the car didn't start. He didn't want Darcy to see the duct tape around the windows.

"I think that's you," the kid next to him said. They were staring straight ahead at the glazed brick wall sixteen inches away, whizzing into a stainless steel trough filled with ice.

"Christ," Dickie half-grumbled, nodded his thanks to the kid, then zipped up, stepped back, and patted himself down, searching for his phone.

"Yeah," he answered.

"Catch you at a bad time?" Rae Nell cooed.

"No, no, go ahead," Dickie said, pushing his way through the swinging door, nodding to Perv and mouthing, 'Thank You' as he headed into the parking lot.

"I was just checking to make sure we're still on for tomorrow night. I'm preparing something very special."

"Special?" Dickie asked.

"Well, yes, it's going to be a very special evening, but you'll just have to wait and see. You won't change your mind now. Promise, please!" she said in the little girl voice Dickie had initially found charming and now served to do nothing but aggravate.

"Rae Nell, I told you I'd be there. So, I'll be there. Special?"

"You'll see, Dickie. See you tomorrow night. Bye, bye, bye," she said, sounding disgustingly bubbly.

Amazingly, the Jeep started on the second try, and on his way to the Emporium of Dance, he took a four-mile detour, cruising past his old house where Rae Nell lived. He couldn't explain why he drove past, unless it was to make sure she hadn't dug a pit with sharpened punji sticks in front of the steps.

Instead, cruising past the two-story stucco home, he caught a glimpse of Rae Nell walking out of the kitchen into the dining room. She carried plates and silverware, setting the table for tomorrow night's dinner. Things seemed to look normal, which made him all the more suspicious.

He drove to the Emporium of Dance. Unfortunately, with just a half-dozen cars in the parking lot, he was able to pull up and park almost next to the front door. Three of the cars belonged to staff.

Inside, his worst fears were confirmed. No one was dancing at the Emporium of Dance. In fact, almost no one was there. Three single guys, reeking of aftershave and lost in thoughts of days past, sat alone at the bar. Empty stools were spaced between them. They sat with their hands folded, looking neither right nor left, just staring blankly ahead. Their untouched beers had sat for so long that the perspiration on the now room temperature mugs had disappeared.

He knew one by name and called, "Hi Jerry." Jerry Baxter, an old Vietnam vet, retired as a city inspector. Nice enough guy, quiet, unless he was over-served, then fireworks or just a crowd could set off a flashback.

At the sound of Dickie's voice, Jerry glanced over, nodded, and then returned to study his hands.

Dickie's footsteps echoed across the wooden floor. Empty tables sporting flickering candles, folded napkins, and clean silverware announced another money-losing night.

"Beer, Dickie?" Noel, the bartender, asked. He reached for a beer glass, ready to pull the tap and pour Dickie sixteen cold ounces of pleasure at the first hint of a nod.

"No, I think just a diet coke tonight."

"Really?"

"You okay?" Laurie asked, looking up from her paperback. She was the only server on duty and bored out of her mind.

"Wish I was. Has it been like this all night?" He grabbed the diet coke and took a sip.

"Actually, it's picked up. No one was here until these guys showed up about forty-five minutes ago." Laurie indicated the three silent customers.

"Ughhh," Dickie groaned. He smacked his lips in an attempt to banish the taste of a non-alcoholic drink.

"Okay, look, you guys shut down at eleven unless a heavy drinking, free-spending crowd barges in here by mistake. I'm going home. This is too depressing," he said and set the diet coke back on the bar.

Once back on his houseboat, he phoned DJ, hoping she could come over, but he ended up leaving a message.

"DJ, when you get a minute, call me. My accountant wanted to know about the software you're running my books on. He liked it, wants to get some. I might have some work for you, too. I need your help on some computer stuff. Oh, yeah, and I don't have one, a computer."

He looked around the cluttered galley, decided to wash the dirty coffee mugs and drink glasses. He straightened up as best he could, wiped down the counter, then took a deep breath, and, armed with a green trash bag, opened the refrigerator door.

There were a half-dozen different Styrofoam containers stacked one on top of the other. He had no recollection of placing any of them in the refrigerator. He tossed them into the bag after wisely deciding not to open them. Next, he tackled the freezer, two half-eaten tubs of ice cream, one with a spoon still stabbed into the center of a rich chocolate vein, three frozen pizzas, a box of stuffed jalapeños, and a box of maple-flavored Deep Fat Fried Bacon on a stick. He quickly shoveled the lot into the trash bag.

He rifled the galley cabinets, adding three packages of cookies, a tub of caramel corn, two jars of chocolate sauce, and a bag of lime-flavored tostada chips. He knotted the trash bag and walked down the dock, tossing the whole affair into the marina dumpster.

Back on his boat, he groaned out seventeen pushups before collapsing. He vowed to stay away from the cooler of warm beer. Thirty-five minutes later, he fell asleep on top of the clothes he had piled on his bed.

DJ woke him as she crawled in bed alongside him.

"Got your message…charming…not."

"Sorry, but at least it got you to come over. Sorry, been a pretty tough day."

"We can talk about that in the morning. I've got a better idea for right now," she said and kissed him.

He woke sometime after four. DJ was snuggled against his chest, with one leg draped over his. She was breathing deeply with the slightest hint of a smile across her face.

If he were really honest with himself, it was times like this, with DJ snuggled against him, that he felt safest. His potential bankruptcy, no business at the Emporium of Dance, Darcy's pain-in-the-ass proposition, even Rae Nell's reentry into his life, none of it mattered at the moment because DJ was here next to him.

Thirteen

Dickie's stomach growled him awake around six-thirty. DJ had tip-toed out at some point, and he was alone in bed. Light sifted through the curtained porthole just above the bed and hinted at the promise of a pleasant day, at least weather-wise. He felt like he would kill for a breakfast of double cheese and sausage pizza. He sighed at the memory of the calorie-loaded treats he'd discarded the night before during his fit of self-righteousness. Then he glanced over at his reflection in the mirror and grew more depressed.

Stretching out on the cramped deck in catsup-stained sweatpants and a too-small St. Paul Saints jersey, he groaned and grunted his way through sixteen pushups, then grabbed a bottle of water and decided to start the day with a jog to the convenience store.

Twelve minutes later Dickie pushed a carton of milk, a box of oatmeal, and four yogurt containers across the checkout counter. He resisted the urge to demand a half-dozen Snickers bars and the tray of caramel rolls.

"Hey, Dickie, I didn't think you did mornings, least not this early. Just coming in from last night?" Robert asked.

"No, just the new, responsible me. This'll do for now, Robert. I'm doing roadwork."

"Suit yourself, man. Eight-forty."

"Eight dollars and forty cents for this healthy shit?" Dickie said.

He gathered his little shopping bag and walked back to the Marina, figuring the distance to be about a mile and a half each way. He was feeling pretty good crossing the parking lot when he saw the pack of dogs camped on his small deck. One of them, a scrawny little white mutt with black spots, was in the process of lifting a leg on his chair.

"Hey, hey, you mutts. Get outta here. Go away, shoo, shoo!"

"Dickie, that you?" DJ called from inside. "I was taking these guys for their walk. I've got some coffee going. It'll be ready in a minute."

She wasn't wearing makeup, and with her hair pinned up on top of her head, her freckles, and those green eyes behind her glasses, she was absolutely beautiful.

"Hey, it looks like you cleaned the galley a little. I was going to put in a pizza. I figured you couldn't have gone too far with that crappy car of yours still up there, but your cupboards are really bare. Not even leftovers, no crumbs for the crumb."

Dickie flopped onto the railing surrounding the small deck.

"Sweatpants?" She said, peeking out the door. "What are you up to?"

"I was out doing my roadwork and picked up a couple of things I needed for breakfast."

"Roadwork? You? Get serious. Since when did you start doing roadwork?"

"I've been doing it."

"Yeah? Since when, yesterday?"

"No, I started today, but I've already done about four miles," he lied.

"Oh, that's great. I'm so proud of you. Where did you go?"

"Up to the Holiday store," Dickie answered absently, attempting to wade through the pack of dogs, step over leashes, and avoid the warm puddle at the base of his chair.

"The Holiday store? What route did you take?"

"Route? What are you talking about, route? I just walked there. You know, pretty much a straight line."

"That's your four miles? Dickie, it's maybe a quarter-mile there and a quarter-mile back. You'd have to do a dozen laps around the parking lot just to make it an even half-mile. Four miles, get out of here!"

"Yeah, well it felt like four miles, and I caught one of these mutts, that little one with the spots, pissing on my chair." He pointed at the small, spotted dog, suddenly wagging its tail and sticking out a bright pink tongue.

"Yeah, right. I'm sure that's the first time anyone's ever done that on your deck. You want some coffee?"

Over coffee and between yogurts, Dickie attempted, without much success, to explain Darcy's job offer from the night before, hoping to enlist her help getting information on Terry Taggert.

"Actually, I do understand what you're saying. It's just that it won't work," DJ patiently explained, pouring more coffee. "You want to find out about this guy, we can get public record information on him. Anyone can. It's no biggie. It becomes a little more difficult to find the things you're suggesting. It's not public record stuff. It's against the law, for starters, secure databases, police stuff, not to mention the old privacy act, so it could take a little time."

"I thought you were supposed to be the genius on this stuff, the computer geek. Can't you just *goggle* this stuff?"

"You mean Google?"

"Yes, I can, and I will. I'll be glad to teach you, as a matter of fact. That's the public record stuff I was referring to. But, in the meantime, you think of what it is you want to find out, specifically. Look, I'll take these guys home." She waved her arm at the pack of snoozing dogs. "Give me at least an hour and a half to get rid of these guys and get my stuff, then pick me up. That should be just about enough time for you to get your car started."

"Very funny."

"Call me just before you leave," she said, gathering leashes as the dogs reacted in a swirl of frenzied activity. She twisted and turned, stepped over one or two, and then they were suddenly all off in a pack, over the side, onto the dock, and heading toward the stairs.

"And I'm proud of you for doing your roadwork, no matter how far you went. Keep it up," she called over her shoulder.

Dickie stepped inside to gaze in the mirror, disgusted he didn't look thinner.

Fourteen

Dickie was seated at his kitchen counter in front of DJ's laptop. "All right," she cooed into Dickie's ear, guiding his hand on the mouse.

"See, you type in the subject there. Okay, Terrence Taggert, like this, and then click on search, right here. Yeah, okay, and it does the rest. See, now, what's so hard about that?"

"Man, nothing. So that's it?"

"This gives you a number of options. Now, we have to glance through them and see if any are the Terrence Taggert you're looking for. If you had a middle initial, or a location, something that would narrow your search, that would help. See this number here? That means you have over eight hundred and seventy-nine options, various items where the name Terrence Taggert showed up. See what I mean about narrowing your search?"

He nodded.

"Click here, Dickey. It shows you the first ten of eight hundred and seventy-nine, and you determine if it's of any use to you."

"Man, is this information available on everyone? Even me?" he asked.

"More or less," she said, placing her hand back over his and guiding the mouse. "There, now double click here, and you'll get the full set of information. Might be a paragraph, might be ten pages."

She was speaking softly, so close he could feel her breath blowing on the sensitive skin of his inner ear. He heard her lips smack as she spoke, felt the firmness of her breasts against his shoulders.

"Okay, so grab yourself a beer or whatever you want while I read this stuff. You can get me a diet coke."

"Dickie, I'm proud of you for sticking to this diet thing. It may be just your second day, but that doesn't make it any easier. In fact, I think it makes it harder," she said, then slid a can of diet coke toward him. She opened a beer for herself and pushed up against him ever so slightly.

"Here's a disorderly charge out of New Orleans." He clicked on the site and then read through the two paragraphs of information, a six-year-old article from the *Times Picayune*.

"Seems your boy was relieving himself against a wall in a French Quarter alley. He turned when he heard something and splashed the boots of New Orleans' finest. The officer took exception to the poor aim and hauled Mr. Taggert in on a charge of indecent exposure, pled down to disorderly with a six-day sentence of community service."

"Another one, possession, pled down, more community service." Dickie seemed to be getting the hang of it, clicking back and forth, skimming the information quickly before returning to the main menu.

"Public intoxication, pled down. Possession with intent, pled down. Propositioning, pled down. Aggravated assault, dismissed, pretty lucky there. He sounds like a someone unwilling to learn from past screw-ups. That seems to fit what Darcy was saying."

"Hey, how about I go get some skinless chicken breasts, salad makings, and cook a healthy dinner for us here? You can keep researching. We can have dinner tonight," she said.

"Sounds great, but I can't. Thanks, honest. Believe me. I'd much rather be with you than what I have to do." Dickie cringed inwardly, wishing he'd never agreed to dinner with Rae Nell. He didn't dare look at DJ. Instead, he continued to stare at the screen, afraid he may have already said too much.

"What exactly are you up to?" she asked, suddenly curious, pressing against his back ever so slightly.

"Oh, not much, just a meeting… asset management, stuff like that. Boring accounting stuff, mostly."

"Assets, huh," she said, sounding unconvinced.

"Asset management. Can I get a rain check for dinner tomorrow night?"

"We'll see," she said. "Go ahead and hang on to this computer. You remember how to turn it off when you're finished?"

"Yeah," Dickie said, thinking, *What the hell, I'll just unplug the damn thing.*

"Okay, as long as you don't just unplug it. That screws up my software."

"Which reminds me, don't forget what I said about my accountant, Fenton. He was really interested in where he can get the programs you were running my stuff on. And he isn't that easy to impress. At least, I've never managed to do it."

"Okay, in the meantime, behave yourself at dinner. Have a glass of water before you sit down at the table. It'll fill you up, Dickie."

Fifteen

Rae Nell was beginning to worry about her dinner plans, looking out the dining room window, scanning up and down the street for Terry's SUV. If he didn't show, and soon, the whole reason for having damn Dickie over would be ruined. She was just about ready to microwave some chicken breasts when she saw the black SUV turn the corner. She quickly retreated to the kitchen and looked busy.

"Come on in," she yelled in response to Terry's knock on the door.

"Rae Nell?"

"Back here. Hey, perfect timing, Terry. Here, let me take that. How's the shoulder feeling?" she asked, grabbing the package of large steaks labeled Chow Meats.

"Okay, considering," Taggert said and grimaced. "How's my top sales lady? Got time for a little bonus plan?" He playfully cupped his hands across her rear and squeezed.

"Let me put these down, and 'No', to answer your question. Not that I wouldn't want to, but I've got to get this stuff ready for tonight."

"You sure?"

"Oh! I'm just so excited. I'm doing a test on a local restaurateur tonight. I'll have him do some market research, and I know he'll pay for product, so don't you worry, no freebies. Then we can start to tell your story, and in no time at all, we'll have the whole city clamoring for Chow steaks."

"Sounds super."

"I'm thinking the food channel for starters, then radio interviews. I've already contacted the newspaper. I just love your meat. The steaks, I mean." She blushed and crinkled her nose.

"By the way, that was sure weird, you going off the balcony like that the other night. What—"

"Oh, yeah, look, I just hate the damn paparazzi. You know," he said. "That National Enquiry, The Star, New York Times. They're always chasing me 'cause I'm a star, trying to follow whatever I do. It's one of the reasons I got into this business. I couldn't go out for a steak with a gorgeous woman like you, Rae Nell, without them following me around, snapping their damn pictures and all. It just gets crazy."

"Wow, sounds exciting. I can't wait. So that's why you jumped off the balcony onto that car? Just so that creep couldn't take your picture?"

"Yeah, pretty much." Taggert winced and rotated his shoulder for effect. "You sure it wouldn't make sense to hop in the sack just for a few minutes, maybe take my mind off this shoulder?"

"No, now go on, you get out of here and let me get back to work before my guest arrives." She shooed him out of her kitchen then gave him a long, wet kiss at the front door.

"I know everyone'll like them steaks, Rae Nell. Appreciate you doing this."

"Remember, I'm your number one salesperson," she called.

You're the only one, darling, he thought and gave a little wave and climbed into his SUV.

After delivering the box of steaks to Rae Nell, Terry Taggert drove back out to the farm to check on Luther and pick up the gift for his evening's entertainment. He pulled alongside the low building and found Luther in the processing room, dumping a bin of meat into the hopper that fed the industrial stainless steel grinder.

Taggert waited until Luther was finished and turned off the grinder. The whine of the electric motor seemed to hang in the climate-controlled air for a second or two before Taggert spoke.

"Any problems with the good Dr.?"

Luther snapped the fingers on his latex gloves and discarded them with a practiced ten-foot toss into a bin.

"Oh, you won't have to worry about the Dr. He's made his last house call. Get it? Made his last *house call?*"

"Yeah, I get it, Luther. What'd you do with his car?"

"Locked it in the equipment shed. I'll take it into town later, leave the keys in the ignition. Some kids will take it, drive around, and either total the thing or get picked up. You don't think the old Doc's wife is gonna figure anything out?"

"What's to figure? He didn't tell her he was coming out here. She'll never put it together. Far as she's concerned, I'm just a little old football player with a hard-on. Still, it'd probably be a good idea to keep her occupied tonight and tomorrow, so she won't push any panic buttons. I'm gonna drop a fur coat on her. Then, I've got that flaming porn photographer set up to take some pictures tomorrow. By the time she's finished doing the photoshoot, she'll be too shocked to think straight for another day or two."

Sixteen

Dickie shook the last of the soap out of the plastic bottle, tossed it out over the top of the shower curtain, and listened as it bounced on the linoleum floor.

He had driven along his walking route and clocked the distance. He drove the long way around the marina parking lot instead of cutting across diagonally as he'd done on foot. He wasn't a quarter-mile from the Holiday store as DJ suggested. It was more like a half-mile if you rounded up, and he did, shamelessly. Generously pegging his route at three-quarters of a mile each way gave him a mile-and-a-half round trip, and he was sticking with that figure— still, a far cry from the four miles he had suggested yesterday.

He had gone one better today, pushing past the Holiday store, guessing he had walked at least two miles. Wishing along the way, he'd been within reach of a cigar and a cold beer. He toweled off, scanned the mirror, and desperately searched for some indication he was losing weight.

He decided on a dark blue pair of trousers, cordovan loafers, matching belt, and just to yank Rae Nell's chain, a fresh out of the package, white golf shirt emblazoned with Emporium of Dance, St. Paul, Minnesota. He combed his hair, slapped on aftershave she wouldn't be fond of, and glanced at the clock. He'd be at least twenty minutes late.

On his drive over to Rae Nell's, he thought about the various things she could possibly want. Their infrequent meetings over the past six years had been anything but pleasant and, in the end, always seemed to cost him. The run-ins with Rae Nell's various boyfriends and the Department of Health on the infamous honey deal immediately came to mind. Of course, the bogus stocks she had talked him into. He was playing the smuggled pearls debacle over in his mind when he turned onto his former street.

"Oh, that damn Dickie, so help me," Rae Nell screamed in her empty dining room, then blew out the candles. "If he forgot about tonight, I'll kill him, so help me, God."

She turned at the nightmare sound of a car coughing and groaning up the slight incline on the block. She watched through her dining room window as Dickie wiggled and groaned his way out of the Jeep. He held an undoubtedly cheap bottle of wine, wrapped in a brown paper bag.

She quickly relit the candles, undid another blouse button, straightened her tight white shorts, and pasted on her best smile. Ughhh, the things she did for a sale.

"Well, hey there, Dickie. I was beginning to wonder if you'd forgotten."

She stood with the screen door open and flashed a big smile, hoping it would help keep the cutting edge out of her voice.

"Stopped to pick up a bottle of wine for you, Rae Nell. Figured since you were cooking dinner, it was the least I could do," Dickie said, delighted his tardiness had pissed her off.

"Wine, no kidding. Gee, the guy at the liquor store must have freaked when he saw you weren't buying cheap beer. Holy cow, it even has a cork."

"Yeah, but once that's out, you can still drink it right out of the bottle."

"That the way they wear it down at your meat market?" She nodded at Dickie's untucked golf shirt hanging out over his belt.

"Hey, like what you've done with the dining room," he commented, not letting her get to him. He haphazardly bunched his shirt back into his trousers as he looked around, knowing full well the dining room, the table, six chairs, right down to the switch plates on the walls were exactly the way they'd been six years ago.

She walked out to the kitchen, relegating his bottle of wine to the most distant corner.

"I'll think of you when I serve this," she said, her tone suggesting she would either pour it down the drain or over pancakes. "Now, don't you get comfortable," she added, tired of sparing and going in for the kill. "I'm putting you to work outside at the grill. Here, take these steaks out there. I'll have mine just a little past medium. You remember how." She smiled perhaps just a little too sweetly, and indicated 'a little past medium' with her hand, almost the way Darcy had the night before. "Everything's ready to go whenever you finish the steaks. I've got one or two items to take care of in here before I join you outside. You want a glass of wine?" she asked, opening the refrigerator and handing him the Saran-covered platter with two large, thick steaks resting in a puddle of their own juice. The edges of the thick steaks hung heavily over the sides of the platter.

"Or, I've even got a couple of cold beers in here, somewhere," she said, bending over, reaching into the far corner of the refrigerator, arching her back in a way she knew made him crazy. She made sure her hot pink thong had a chance to show off its attributes through her white shorts. She counted slowly before looking back over her shoulder, letting her hair fall, smiling sweetly. "See anything you'd like?"

Dickie quickly looked down at the platter of steaks. He may have been caught appraising, but it also convinced him there was an agenda for the evening. He didn't know what, but Rae Nell wanted something.

"How about just a glass of water," he said, sounding slightly depressed.

"Water? You sure, Dickie? Everything okay?" Rae Nell straightened up from the refrigerator, genuinely surprised, and quickly calculated she might have a much tougher sale on her hands than she originally thought.

"Yeah, trying to watch my figure," Dickie said.

"That's a lot to watch," Rae Nell countered absently. She filled a glass with ice and water from the refrigerator door and handed it to him.

"You remember where the grill is out back?"

"You bet," Dickie said, escaping with the platter and his water to the relative safety of the backyard.

The grill looked like it hadn't been uncovered since the last time Dickie had used it six years ago. But it flamed to life after just a couple of clicks from the ignition spark. Of all the many material things Dickie had lost, this had been one of the dearest.

He had always referred to it as the Cadillac of grills, big, brushed steel with chrome trim highlights, eight gas range controls, even a warming oven, and shelf. He had once cooked steaks and corn on the cob for sixteen people and barely broke a sweat. It was gorgeous, and the only reason he hadn't slithered back in the dead of night to steal it from Rae Nell's backyard was because it would never fit on his houseboat.

He lifted the Saran Wrap and sniffed the beautiful cuts of meat. There was a smell, not at all unpleasant, but somehow different, not the same beef odor Dickie expected. Rae Nell had spiced the steaks just the way he liked them, using Wee Willie's dry rub, the Number One, not too much, and he picked up the marinade scent on the steaks. *'Screw the diet,'* he thought, setting the platter down. The gorgeous pieces of meat seemed to call to him. He placed his left hand over the grill palm down while he adjusted the flame with his right. He patiently let the grill heat a bit, so it would sear the meat, seal in the moistness, for the perfect steak. When he deemed the grill ready, he threw Rae Nell's on first, giving her steak an extra minute on each side. The meat sizzled sensuously as an intoxicating scent wafted up.

Rae Nell looked out the window and wiggled her shorts down. She sipped her glass of wine, reminding herself to take it easy, or she'd never get what she wanted tonight. She had no intention of joining Dickie out in the backyard. That's all she needed, mosquito bites. So, she planned to time her arrival at the grill just as he was ready to remove the steaks.

There were two things that could make this better, Dickie thought. He gauged the steaks, estimating perhaps another forty-five seconds before he took his off the grill. He sipped his water, thinking, *A stiff drink or a cold beer would be a vast improvement in the beverage department, and then if DJ were here instead of Rae Nell.*

Rae Nell watched him looking at his watch, knew he would pull the steaks off in less than a minute, and strutted out to join him.

"Mmm-mmm, they smell delicious, Dickie. You're always the best when it comes to steaks. I can hardly wait. I'm absolutely famished. How about you?"

"Yeah, starving. Say, I gotta tell you, these are gorgeous pieces of meat. Where'd they come from?"

"Well, you know, I ran into this place. They just sell to restaurants, but I was able to work a deal with the guy and got some steaks. Everyone absolutely raves about them, and well, I'm not going to say another word. I know you love steak. They look great, so let's just see how they taste, okay?"

"We'll know soon enough. They're done. Perfectly, I might add. You get the door, and I'll bring these in. Here," he said, handing her his water glass. "I'll take a refill."

It was something she had just said, the *work a deal with the guy* that had Dickie thinking. *Wasn't that how she had first described her bogus stock offer? Or had it been the pearl scam?* He couldn't recall, but he was suddenly wary.

Seventeen

Over dinner, between parry and thrust, they played catch up. Dickie told her about his mother living outside of Corpus Christi, his brother in San Francisco, while he savored each and every bite of steak. He couldn't recall when he'd had such a tender piece of meat. It was literally melt-in-your-mouth.

Rae Nell droned on about her sisters, Rae Jean, Rae Dawn, and Rae Lynn, the Death Rae's. Then moved on to her brother Jack, the only sibling Dickie had actually liked, now estranged from his sisters and openly gay. Dickie was not in the least surprised, knowing all four of the Death Rae's had made their brother's personal life hell with their nonstop interference. As she chatted away, Dickie tuned her out, savored his delicious steak, and looked around the dining room.

Eventually, his eyes wandered across the entryway, through the wide arch, and into the living room. The one wall he could see was painted a warm red, not garish, but comfortable, and framed on the wall was a large painting of Minnie Mouse.

Rae Nell had a thing about Minnie, always had. Dickie had fallen in love with the four-inch tattoo on her rear, Minnie lifting her dress and mooning. It served as a lifetime reminder of a now distant Florida spring break Rae Nell had taken as a college girl long before she met Dickie. She usually dressed up as Minnie Mouse on Halloween. She had, or at least used to have, king-sized Minnie Mouse sheets and pillowcases, a Minnie Mouse toothbrush for traveling, and a Minnie Mouse key chain.

"…Dance? Dickie?"

"Huh?" he asked, refocusing from his distant gaze.

"Honey, weren't you listening? I asked you how things were going down at the Emporium of Dance." Rae Nell's eyes flared as she lifted her head and shook her shiny blonde hair back over her shoulders. She gripped her wine glass tightly and took a very big sip.

"Pretty good," he groaned inwardly, remembering Fenton's rather grim bottom-line assessment, *Basically you're broke, Dickie.*

"I think I'm about to turn a corner there any day now."

She must have picked up something in his tone, took another healthy sip, and said, "Hmm-mmm, that doesn't sound too good." She set her wine glass down and looked directly at Dickie. "Isn't it working? I mean, you've had the place for three or four years. Forget my teasing about it being a meat market, a knocking shop, a sleazy, tawdry little pick up—"

"I get the idea, Rae Nell."

"Hey, forget all that stuff, that's just me. Well, and everyone else in town," she added half under her breath.

Dickie nodded dumbly, thinking he would kill for a Jameson right now.

"I've driven past a couple of times on a Friday or Saturday night, and it looked busy, kind of. Obviously, I've never been inside."

"Yeah, the weekends are doing okay. But, to tell the truth, you could shoot a howitzer through the place Sunday through Thursday and not hit anyone. I have to keep at least a skeleton staff on those nights, keep the kitchen open, insurance, licenses, taxes, bartender, wait staff. It all adds up. I got a lot of overhead costs, not to mention all the remodeling I did."

"What's your menu like?" Rae Nell asked, thinking, *God, I can only imagine.*

"It's pretty good— cheeseburgers, fries, onion rings. I tried an all-you-can-eat taco night, but that didn't really catch on. My catfish night absolutely flopped. All-you-can-eat chili didn't work very well. Course, all those beans turned out to not be the best idea. I don't know, the food end just doesn't seem to be clicking." He shrugged.

'God, all-you-can-eat tacos? Catfish night? Chili with extra beans?' Worse than she had thought.

"Maybe if you upgraded the menu, then have an open house for a couple of nights. Get a new clientele to come in and sample. They might get a feel for the place. You personally know tons of people. All the folks on the police force, high school pals, guys you played softball with. God, Dickie, half of St. Paul would show up. If you have even a halfway decent menu, they'd come. I know they would." She sounded genuine, and actually, she was, at least for the moment.

"Speaking of which, I gotta tell you, Rae Nell, these steaks were good. Good? Hell, they were fantastic. In all honesty, they are probably the best steaks I've had in a long time. Unique, I'd even say, and you know how I love steak."

"Did you really like them? I used that Wee Willey's rub you like. It wasn't too much, was it? I let them sit for a couple of hours the way you taught me." She fluttered her eyes ever so slightly.

"They were perfect, and not just the seasoning, but the meat itself, rich, thick, tender, delicious. Folks talk about melt in your mouth steak, but these really did. Never had anything like them before. I never used my knife. Corn fed? Where'd you say you got them?"

She took two large gulps, draining half her wine glass, tossed her hair back, and thought, *Here we go*, and faced Dickie with a concerned look on her face.

"That's exactly what I wanted to talk to you about."

"Oh, God! I knew it. I knew you wanted something. This has all been another one of your setups, Rae Nell, hasn't it? Get together. I should have known. You got those vanilla-scented candles lit upstairs in the bed-room?"

"Oh, Dickie, how crude. Why do you always do this?"

"Me?"

"Yes, you. Why do you always assume I have some ulterior motive?"

She jumped up from the table and grabbed the empty plates, their wedding china, and carried them out to the kitchen. She put some ice in a tumbler, grabbed the fifth of Jameson she'd stashed behind the blender, and returned, setting the tumbler and bottle on the table in front of him.

"Will you just calm down and listen? If you don't like what I say, leave, the door is open. I want to help you. I know about these sorts of things. Why not just try to listen for once and see if we can't figure something out? I know how much that shitty, sleazy, Godforsaken, little dive means to you, and I just thought I might be able to help."

He cautiously eyed the Jameson, aware he was suddenly in the middle of a minefield.

"Well?"

"So, what's your idea of help?"

"Much better," she said, standing a little closer. She pushed the glass in front of him, cracked the cap on the Jameson bottle, and poured a healthy amount into his glass. Then she refilled her wine glass and sat down.

"Okay, look, based on the little you've told me to-night, and from what I've *heard*, you need to change some things."

Dickie looked at her, reached for his glass, and belted down a good amount, thinking, *Screw the damn diet.*

"Maybe change is not quite the right term," she said, quickly backing up and taking another long gulp of wine to fortify herself. She took a deep breath and then recited her practiced lines.

"So, Friday and Saturday night people come in to dance, meet other people, right? I mean, it's a destination. They don't just happen in. They're in there for a specific reason," she said, not going any further in her description. "So what you have to do is come up with a reason for people to go there Sunday through Thursday, right? That's what you said, and you tried the taco night thingy and the catfish." She shuddered. "All you can eat chili didn't work, either. So, maybe you have to try something else, maybe, gee, I don't know, something a little classier?"

Dickie took another long pull from his Jameson. *Here it comes,* he thought. "And let me guess, Rae Nell, you just happen to know what's gonna do the trick, right?"

"Maybe, maybe not, but I think it might be worth a try. One thing is for sure, whatever you've done in the past and whatever you're doing now isn't working."

He drained the Jameson and waited for whatever lay in store, mirrored disco balls, some stupid decorating scheme with dried flowers, yoga lessons, wicker chairs. God, just say it and get the painful part over with. Finally, he just shook his head in defeat and reached for the bottle of Jameson.

"Well, is it working?"

"No, nothing seems to be working," he grumped.

"Did you like your steak tonight?"

Dickie nodded as he refilled his glass with an overly generous amount.

"What if I could get you steaks like that? And, you'd be the only place in town serving those steaks." She failed to add, 'at least for a while.' "You'd have an exclusive, Dickie. I know you love steaks, you always have. And, to tell you the truth, despite all our differences, no one, and I mean no one…" She leaned forward, reached over, and squeezed his hand. "…can give me better meat than you. You said yourself they were the best steaks you've ever had, and that's high praise coming from you." She sat back and drained her wine glass, relieved. There, finally, win, lose or draw, it was out there on the table.

Dickie pursed his lips and swirled his glass a little before taking a swallow.

"How did you get involved with this? You've never been into the restaurant thing."

She refilled her wine glass. "Well, it's complicated. I heard about this meat company looking for distribution, and I was mildly interested. Then, as soon as I tasted their product, I thought of you. I mean, who loves steaks more than you? And, you own a restaurant. I honestly didn't know things weren't going well, but maybe in a way, that's good." *And not surprising,* she thought.

"Yeah, right."

"We could help each other. I'd get the account, you get the steaks, along with all the benefits that come with them."

"So tell me about this company," he said.

"Okay, they are new in the U.S. Actually out of China. Don't interrupt," she instructed as his head shot up. "They've got a farm and a small processing plant somewhere out in Washington County. They're using ancient Chinese methods to process these steaks. It's a whole Zen philosophy thingy, I think."

"Zen philosophy?"

"Yeah, and they have all the USDA stuff and approvals. They don't have a sales force here. Well, except for me right now, and I just thought it might be a great opportunity for you. Now, after what you told me, it looks like the timing couldn't be better. You don't have to change anything. You can still do cheeseburgers and fries if you have your heart set on that." She shuddered. "But I think these steaks would be something people would drive across town to eat. You'd be the only place serving them, almost like having your own cattle ranch. I mean, just think, Dickie, what do you have to lose?" she asked and drained her wine glass.

"Look, if you're interested, I've got some brochures in the living room, price lists, just take a look. If you don't like what you see, don't want to take a little chance, like I said, the door is open, Baby."

The further down the bottle of Jameson Dickie got, the more sense Rae Nell's steak idea seemed to make. They were sitting a discrete distance apart, facing one another on the couch. Rae Nell was going over a calendar, deciding that Wednesday and Thursday of the following week would allow just enough time to send out invitations announcing his open house and menu change.

"Now, just remember, you butthead," she giggled, "we're not serving dinner to all these people, just samples. They're still going to pig out, so don't worry. I'll make sure we'll have plenty on hand. But, we'll have bread and sauces too, so they don't break the bank just eating these really good samples. It'll work, Dickie. I'll take care of everything. Hey, you want some wine?" she asked, taking three attempts to rise from the couch. "I'm getting another bottle."

"Nah," Dickie said, pouring more Jameson into his glass. He spilled across the polished wood coffee table before adjusting his aim. The near-empty bottle made a hollow sound when he set it back down on the oak floor.

Eighteen

Marti Cullen was just pulling into the parking place when her cell phone rang. She had cruised the giant mall lot for the past twenty minutes looking for a spot. There were plenty she passed, just none of them quite close enough to the door. She planned to do some shopping, then maybe drive over to her spa for a massage and wait for her husband's petulant call. *'Probably him calling now ready to grovel,'* she thought when she heard her phone ring.

"Hello," she said briskly, attempting to sound interrupted.

"Hey, baby, how you doing?"

"Terry!" Marti jumped at the sound of his voice, absently touched her hair, and turned the rearview mirror so she could examine her makeup. "I didn't expect to hear from you for at least another week. You're in town?" she asked hopefully, working to contain her excitement.

"Yeah, seeing a damn specialist 'bout my shoulder," Taggert lied. "They're going to be doing some more tests. But that don't mean me and you can't get together. Sorry and all for the short notice, but I just found out. Besides, it'll give me time to pick up the little gift I got for y'all."

"A gift? Really? For me? Well, it's certainly not necessary, but what girl doesn't like the sound of that? I've never been one to turn down a gift. You know that," she said, more intrigued by the second.

"Great, I'll call you back a little later, let you know where to meet me."

"I'll be waiting," she said, *and getting a wax,* she thought, backing out of her parking spot and racing across town to her spa.

She was too flustered to remember to call her husband Craig and find out why he hadn't returned her earlier calls. She'd had to wait a good hour before they could fit her in between two appointments, and then her clinician had been none too gentle with the waxing. Marti politely suggested they might do a bit better with their procedures, amazed the woman could even understand English. But after the assault, she suffered with the waxing, she decided to forego a massage.

Instead, she'd gone home, applied a mask of ground cucumber and essence of coconut oil, drawn a hot bubble bath, and promptly fell asleep, soaking in the tub.

Terry's phone call woke her, the water barely tepid, the bubbles gone, and her skin pruny. She would meet him in the penthouse suite of the Braxton at eight.

After doing her hair and makeup, trying on a half-dozen outfits from casual to formal, she settled on a pair of comfortable linen slacks and a gorgeous jade top. She slipped into her shoes, and waltzed out the door, forgetting all about Craig.

In the elevator up to the Penthouse, she smoothed her linen slacks, put on her little girl smile, and forced a look of innocence into her eyes, then stepped into the hallway.

"Hey, there, good looking," Terry Taggert said when he answered her knock on the door. He was barefoot, wearing jeans, no shirt, and carrying a champagne flute that he promptly offered to her after a lingering kiss.

She loved the look and feel of his sculpted upper body and let her hand drift lazily across his muscled stomach, sampling thirty-something flesh. Eventually, she stepped into a massive two-story sitting room with a bar at the far end, sporting a gigantic flat screen, tuned, unfortunately, to the sports channel.

Fresh-cut flowers graced a long conference table, and beyond that, a cozy alcove harboring two over-stuffed couches and a fireplace. A half-round side table again mounted with a vase of fresh-cut flowers, guarded the entrance to a darkened bedroom.

"God, it's gorgeous, absolutely gorgeous," she said, twirling around, taking it all in.

"Check this out, sexy," Taggert said, grabbing a remote off the conference table and clicking. Immediately, curtains two-stories tall began to part, revealing a breathtaking view of the Mississippi River. The St. Paul skyline with the final bit of sunset reflecting off the downtown buildings gave way to lights blinking up and down the river.

"Wow, that is really fantastic! It's beautiful," she said, staring at the spectacular scene.

"Thanks for coming on such short notice. Here's to us," he said, clinking her champagne flute with his own, topping up her glass once she finished sipping.

They sat for a while in the cozy alcove, Taggert never bothering to put on a shirt. He chatted on about nothing, asking if she ever thought about pursuing her modeling career again. Marti shuddered, draining the rest of her champagne at the memory of her idiot husband Craig's suggestion she model senior items. *Next stop Depends,* she thought to herself. They talked about a lot of things, most of them having to do with her likes and dislikes. If the topic veered too far off-course, she deftly returned the discussion to herself.

Taggert probed three or four more times to the issue of her modeling and then suddenly asked, "Say, sexy, would you be interested in a modeling gig?" He took another large pull of champagne and wondered how anyone could drink this shit on a regular basis.

"Well, I don't. I mean, well—"

"See, Marti, I've done me an investment. It's paying off very, very nicely, as a matter of fact," he said.

"Oh?"

"We're looking for, actually we need, a spokes-model. A woman who is elegant." He gave her a knowing nod. "Gorgeous." He nodded again. "Has a look of innocence, with just a hint of doing the old nasty laying right below the surface. I think you're that woman. By the way, this here has nothing to do with us, you and me. I think you're the gal. Before ya' say anything, I've taken the liberty to present my idea to the other partners. They're all interested and would like to see some photos if that's okay with you? Now—"

"What, oh my God, Craig. I mean, Terry, oops, sorry about that." She sipped heavily, washing the taste of Craig's name from her mouth. "This is so out of nowhere. I just don't know. What's the product, anyway?"

"Well now, sexy lady, I don't know how you feel about this. Leastwise, you never mentioned anything to me, so I'm going to take a chance."

Oh, God! It's some old lady thing, she thought and got ready to scratch his hillbilly eyes out.

"It's fur coats!" Taggert blurted.

"Fur coats?"

"Yeah. Now, I don't know how y'all feel about fair treatment of animals and all that shit, ya know. But, this here's a line of real elegant-like fur coats. I'm in a partnership with some guys, they're importing the things. Since I'm a big name sports figure, I'm more or less the spokesman, but what we really need is a female model, you know, for the ads that'll be running this coming Christmas and winter season. As a matter of fact, the agency we got lined up is telling us we're almost behind schedule. We're late, even though it's still summer, and we gotta get the damn ads placed pronto like."

"Fur coats?" she asked again, looking up. He was no longer sitting next to her but rummaging around in the closet. He came out with a rather elegant looking black garment bag.

"See, here," he said, laying the bag across the couch where he had been sitting, unzipping it as he spoke. "You know how certain things have this person who represents them? That Jason fella does Subway, the bearded guy did dos Equis beer, Jane Fonda did Depends."

"Depends?" she shot back.

"Well, that's maybe not the best example, but you know how they got movie stars and all of them pushing products and such? Well, we wondered, that is, I hoped, if you…" He reached inside the garment bag and removed a gorgeous, full-length fur coat, holding it out for her to see. "If you might consider modeling for us." The coat was a deep rich cinnamon color, and it shone and glistened as he ran his hand across the soft thick fur sheered to a perfect luxurious length.

"Oh, my, God!" she said, clearly shocked, staring at one of the most beautiful fur coats she'd ever seen.

The fur seemed to radiate as he folded it over. He ran his hand slowly against the grain. The rich fur fell back into place without so much as a ripple. Thick, soft, luxurious, and cinnamon-colored, she felt like crawling on top of the thing naked.

"This one's yours, by the way, whether you decide to do the modeling or not. I thought of you the moment I saw it. Here, see, even had your initials embroidered inside," he said, flashing open the coat's black moiré silk lining, exposing her initials in an embroidered white monogram, *MCC*, subtle shadows along the letters in a darker off-white. Even the monogram was elegant. She sat there absolutely speechless.

"Check out this name tag. See, Chow Furs, and your name here, Marti Cullen."

Her first thought was, *The leather strap with the silver studs and a little brass name tag looked more like a damn dog collar than anything else.* Without her glasses, she couldn't read the thing anyway. She guessed it wouldn't take more than sixty seconds to remove it. Finally, she looked at Taggert's grinning face and said, "This is the loveliest gift anyone has ever, ever given me. I just don't know what to say, Terry."

"Yeah, well, don't you think you better try it on? Get your ass over here, girl!" he said, stepping back and holding the coat open for her.

She normally would have never responded quickly to such a crude directive, but he held an exceptional coat, and Marti jumped off the couch, half-twirling in midair and landing in the perfect position to back effortlessly into the coat. It may have been late August and ninety-five degrees in the shade, but elegant fur was just the thing.

She hunched her shoulders inside the luxurious garment, thrust her hands inside the silky pockets, and wrapped the coat even tighter around her. It hung at the perfect length, bare inches from the floor, and she spun around, watching the hem of the coat glisten and shine with her movement.

"I don't know what to say except it's gorgeous, Terry, absolutely gorgeous."

"There ain't another one like it in the world," he lied. "Ain't it great?"

"I love it," she said, grabbing his face in both hands and giving him a long, wet, deeply-probing kiss.

"Mmm, great, so you'd be willing to model for us?"

"Are you kidding? Yes. Yes! I can't wait."

"Well, good, 'cause they want to take some preliminary shots at a studio tomorrow. If that's okay?"

"Oh, this is so exciting. I didn't know you knew anything about furs," she said, jumping up and down.

"Well, I didn't, but these investor guys are pretty sharp. They got me 'cause I'm famous and all. They import these. It's called the Chow Industries, and…"

"Ciao?" Marti asked, thinking *Italian fashion,* not believing her luck.

"Yeah, that's right, Chow. Anyway, they import 'em and want to make a big splash for the Christmas season. That's why we gotta get the photos done right away. We got ads running in these fancy fashion magazines, and they got some deadline or other we're up against. So, it's balls to the wall right now."

"Well, yes, yes, of course. I'll be happy to do the photoshoot for you, but tomorrow?"

"Now, you'll have to bring the coat, of course. As a matter of fact, I was wondering if maybe you couldn't just stay here tonight. We could go over to the shoot together tomorrow."

"Well, I didn't plan on that, so I didn't bring a change of clothes."

"Not to worry, Baby. They got a makeup gal there and everything. Fact, you slip out of those things right now. You can wear that tomorrow."

Marti suddenly found herself in a position where she couldn't say no.

Nineteen

Dickie was more awake than not, though his eyes remained closed. His tongue was thick, and his mouth tasted like a used urinal cake. He couldn't determine if his head was pounding or it was actually thundering outside. A moment later the sound of heavy rain began on the roof, and with his eyes still closed, he attempted to assess the damage. He opened his eyes, instantly recognized the dark oak woodwork surrounding the three windows facing the street, the soft mauve walls, and the king-sized four-poster bed. He cautiously rolled over and stared in horror at a very distinct tan line and a four-inch tattoo of a mooning Minnie Mouse floating on Rae Nell's white rear end.

He silently oozed out of bed, doing his best not to disturb her. Her rhythmic snores served as a cautionary flag to making any noise. He found a sock near the bedroom door, another out in the hallway, and followed the trail of discarded clothing down the stairs. Rae Nell's pink thong hung on the handrail at the bottom of the stairs. Her white shorts were crumpled on the floor of the entryway.

The dinner candles were reduced to piles of melted wax on the table. The front door remained wide open, an invitation to any ransacking pervert who might have wandered past in the middle of the night. As he picked his trousers up off the living room floor, the empty Jameson bottle rolled under the couch. He ignored the ruined finish bubbling on the coffee table from spilled whiskey. He slipped on his shoes, pocketed the sheets of pricing information, and tiptoed cautiously out the front door into the rain.

The duct tape around the windows had once again failed to do the job, and rivulets of water ran steadily down the corners of the dash, pooling somewhere beneath the moldy carpet. A constant drip from the door splashed on the edge of the driver's seat, and Dickie felt a cold puddle spread across his rear when he sat down. His head pounded as he fumbled the key into the ignition, praying for all he was worth that this piece of shit started. It did, on the fourth or fifth attempt, sputtering to life grumpily before chugging him down the street. He could only hope Rae Nell was still asleep.

He stumbled onto the small rear deck of his houseboat and smacked his mouth, desperately in need of several aspirin. Even with the heavy rain, he still picked up the faint scent of dog urine wafting up from the indoor/outdoor carpet. He was cold, wet, horribly hungover, and thoroughly disgusted with himself. He stumbled over something, and his head pounded as he reached down to pick up a gift-wrapped package leaning against the door. He recognized DJ's scrawled *Dickie* on the envelope then cursed himself again for being such an absolute louse.

He left her package on the counter, dropped his sodden clothes in a wet pile, and washed four aspirin down with whatever remained in a half-empty glass. He didn't brush his teeth but crawled straight into bed just as a loud clap of thunder rattled the houseboat. He wrinkled his nose at the memory of the vanilla candles before he drifted off to sleep.

Twenty

A nylon drape was wrapped around Marti Cullen's waist while she sat completely exposed on a hard wooden stool. Katrina, the make-up artist with kielbasa breath, busily brushed a shadow into Marti's cleavage, then sat back, admired her handiwork, and nodded.

This absolutely sucks! Marti thought.

"Is good, no? Yes," Katrina said, answering her own question.

Marti's eyes had been darting around furiously at the nude photo layouts plastering the walls. After sitting on a hard wooden stool for the past hour and a half, she was almost beyond the point of embarrassment. She sat overly exposed in stiletto heels, nipple blush, and a smile. Thank God she'd gotten that wax yesterday.

"Mmm-mmm." Katrina nodded, brushing and blending, all the while breathing last night's Kielbasa into Marti's face. "Up, up, make tummy little," she instructed, smoothing her own muscular diaphragm and sitting up rigidly before exhaling another noxious plume.

Good God, this is awful, Marti thought, holding her breath for the umpteenth time just as the photographer, Bobbi, swished in front of the mirrors in his overly affected manner. He gushed while Terry Taggert leered behind him like some perverted lunatic.

"Oh, yes. Yes, lovely, dear, lovely. Did we get your model's release signed? Yes? Yes. Good, mmm-mmm, excellent. I see we're a bit cold there." He raised his eyebrows and stared at Marti.

Katrina continued to brush shadow below Marti's breasts as she exhaled into her face.

"They look perfect. Hopefully, the lights won't warm you up. Very well then, Katrina. Almost ready, Dear? We'll be shooting in a few minutes. I'll want to take some test shots first, make sure everything's perfect."

"Could we—"

"Would you mind taking a seat over there, Mr. Taggert?" Bobbi cut Marti off and, with an elaborate wave of his hand, directed Taggert to a group of directors' chairs next to a well-stocked bar.

"Gordon? Are we ready for the test shots?" he called, wandering off into the dark.

Twenty minutes later, Marti Cullen, wrapped in her new fur coat, attempted to position herself exactly as Bobbi directed.

"Excellent, gorgeous. Yes, yes, tits up, Darling. You're an animal, wild, free, a big naughty cat. Meow! Meow!" He hissed at Marti, all the while circling around, clicking cameras in her direction.

Twenty-one

E ven with two pillows over his head, Dickie couldn't ignore the phone ringing through a foot and a half of goose down. Whoever was trying to reach him had placed three separate calls in as many minutes. He cleaned his teeth with his tongue, smacked unhappily at the stale taste in his mouth, and stumbled toward the kitchen counter.

"Yeah."

There was an incessant throbbing in his skull. He stood naked and gazed out at a cold, gray, sodden afternoon as the rain continued in a steady drizzle— hangover weather.

"Hello, sleepyhead, we're not sounding too chipper this afternoon. Did I get you up?" Rae Nell bubbled a little too cheerfully on the other end of the phone.

"No, no," Dickie replied, jolting awake, cursing himself once again.

"Well, I've been busy. I've got your invitations designed. Next Wednesday and Thursday are the dates. I figured from seven to ten would work for the official times. That way, people will have a few hours to linger afterward. I'm getting those printed up as we speak, and I'll drop them off to you. I'm presuming you do have mailing lists, right?"

"Mailing lists?"

"Mmm-mmm, I better do those, too," she said half to herself as if she were jotting something down.

"Maybe—"

"I've got your steak order done. Rule of thumb, figure about forty-percent response rate, so I've ordered with the idea of a sixty-percent rate just to be on the safe side. Free food, after all. Don't want to run out. Now, I've lined up a caterer—"

"A caterer?" Dickie managed in his semi-conscious state.

"And she'll loan us staff for two nights. You're going to need staff who know what they're doing, Dickie. To ensure people are served properly. We're going to move you up a few notches from your normal bottom-feeding client base and introduce a little more polished element to your establishment."

"Rae Nell—"

"Now, the first round of meat will be delivered Tuesday. The bill won't be more than two hundred, two-fifty tops, 'cause I'm giving you a discount. I'll call you with a final amount later, so you can have a check waiting when they deliver. Make it out to Chow Meats. That's C-H-O-W."

Dickie fumbled with the childproof lid on the aspirin container, took another four, and washed them down with the remnants from a coffee mug.

"Okay, I better get going on that mailing list, or nothing's going to happen. Bye, bye, bye." Click.

It was one of the many things on an ever-growing list Dickie had come not to miss about life with Rae Nell, that constant sense of just being bowled over.

He squeezed into the bathroom to brush his teeth, returned to the galley for cold pizza, only to remember there wasn't any. He settled instead for a banana yogurt and then ate another.

He answered the phone as he was just about to return to bed.

"Yeah."

"Oh, hi. Hey, sorry, did I get you up or something?" DJ asked.

He suddenly remembered the gift-wrapped package.

"No, I'm just doing a little work here," he lied, tearing open her card and quickly reading, *Call me when you get this. Love, DJ.*

"Did you get my phone messages?"

"No. I mean, yeah, sorry. I was going to call you like your card said, but I figured it might be too early. Then I got involved in something here, and time just slipped away."

He glanced at the clock, three-fifteen. He quietly pulled off the wrapping paper, cautious not to alert her to the sound, and held a bathroom scale in his hands.

"Well, I just wondered if you might be upset. I didn't want you to take it the wrong way, that's all. I'm really proud of you, just so you know."

"You mean the bathroom scale?" he said, silently letting the wrapping paper fall on his pile of wet clothes.

"Yeah."

"I thought it was kind of neat. It'll help me keep track."

"I was going to stop in early this morning, while I was walking the dogs, but I didn't see your car in the lot," she said and then just let that hang out there.

His antenna was up, suggesting extreme caution.

"Yeah, I got up early, went along the river bluff for my roadwork, you know, those running paths. Wanted to do some hills."

"In the rain?"

"It wasn't really raining when I started. More of a little mist. Course, when I got out at the furthest point from the car, then it really came down."

"Oh."

"I ended up trying to wait it out under one of those picnic areas in the park, but finally just gave up and jogged back to the car, completely drenched. In fact, I'm still looking at the wet pile of workout clothes on the floor," he said.

"You want to come over and use my washer and dryer?"

"I'll do them with some other stuff at the Laundromat. Thanks, anyway. How about dinner tonight?" he asked, trying to escape this particular line of conversation. "I still have your computer here, by the way."

"Dinner would be great. We can practice eating sensibly, something that's good for you and tastes good, too. I'll pick a place and surprise you."

"Good, I'll see you about half-past-seven. I'll weigh myself before I come over," he joked. "Maybe even get some more roadwork in if this rain ever lets up."

Twenty-two

Marti Cullen continued to experience severe intestinal cramps, posing under the lights.

"Oh, come on now, honey. It's not that bad. Is it?" Bobbi said, teasing in response to her grimace. He was bouncing around, clicking shots with one of three different cameras hanging from his neck, all the while issuing directives.

"Katrina, more cleavage shadow, lower the coat Marti, lower the coat. Where's Gordon? No, Mr. Taggert, please don't touch her just now."

Despite her growing discomfort, Marti was aware of another individual entering the studio. Awash in the bright lights of the photo bay, she was unable to really see. Bobbi had sensed an arrival, too, and began to primp and pose a bit more than usual.

"And, all right. Now, Marti, we're shooting you on this blue background so we can outline you and drop you into any stock site we have. You'll be in Central Park, at the Eiffel Tower, the Golden Gate bridge."

Marti grimaced with another wave of cramping.

"I know, not as much fun as traveling to those places, but it makes the shooting a lot more affordable for our clients." Bobbi nodded in Taggert's direction.

Taggert smiled and raised his current Bloody Mary in a toast.

"Now, let's have you drop the coat down. No, no, much further, let ourselves hang out freely. Yes, that's right, that's a girl, show them off. You're proud, you're proud, meow."

"Gordon, Gordy, where's Gordon?"

"Back here, with Katrina." Gordon's voice boomed from somewhere back in the darkness.

"Let's use the choker now in these shots," he said, turning back to Marti, frozen in position, arms still in the sleeves, the coat wrapped around her waist, her upper body fully exposed, and her lower tract ready to explode.

"Now, Honey, we're going to add some jewels. Katrina, you had better come too. Do a little touch up on the neck, and can we increase that cleavage shadow?"

"Marti, this choker is diamonds and emeralds, and for this next series of shots, we'll digitally retouch your eyes to match the emeralds."

Gordon stepped from behind a large klieg light, holding a black velvet choker with cheap plastic glued to it. He wrapped it around her neck and closed the Velcro tab.

"Katrina, her hair, and here, let's be careful. We don't want traces of foundation or blush," he said, pointing along the edge of the choker.

Katrina dabbed with a tissue and Q-tip.

"And see, here and here," Bobbi said, pointing to her pubic region. "Let's just groom her pelt, please. Yes, much better."

He continued shooting, all the while maintaining a running dialog.

"Excellent, yes, good, good. Oh, yes, sultry."

Marti glared into the lights.

"Now dear, say before we go any further, Gordon, Gordon! Will you take a lunch order? Find the deli menu. Marti, we're going to break for lunch in about forty-five minutes. Gordon, do you have the props for the pet walk? Let's get those ready once you've taken the lunch orders."

Marti didn't think she could hold on for another forty-five minutes, but she had enough self-respect not to ask strangers if she could use the restroom while kneeling naked in front of them.

"Katrina, we're sweating here. We'll need some touch-up."

Katrina ran a hairdryer over Marti's forehead then brushed a light foundation back over the area.

A delivery person arrived with the luncheon order and then leered at Marti from behind the lights for five minutes. She felt her legs trembling and became power-less to prevent the release she had been working so hard to avoid.

"Oh, I'm terribly sorry. I—"

"Okay, we'll break for lunch," Bobbi ordered, hastily retreating out of the photo bay.

After twenty minutes in the restroom and a ten-minute lunch, Marti went through another half-hour of makeup redo. As instructed, she positioned herself on all fours. Suddenly, she was joined by a very large muscle-bound man with a shaved head, handlebar mustache, black leather boots, chaps, vest, and tattoos covering his upper body.

"Marti, meet Dermot. Dermot, Marti," Bobbi said, looking through his lens. "Okay, Dermot, you're the master. Gordon, the leash. Katrina, her hair."

Gordon stepped out from behind the lights once again, clipped a black leather leash onto Marti's velvet choker, and handed it to Dermot. Katrina adjusted Marti's hair around the leash for a few seconds, then reached back and folded the fur coat up on her back until Marti could feel her entire posterior exposed.

"Yes, excellent, wild, frightened, an animal to be tamed. Perfect, bad cat, naughty. Meow, sweetheart, meow! Yes, yes, wonderful, love that deer in the head-lights look, Marti. That's it, very good, very good, excel-lent, bravo."

"Lean a little closer to Dermot's leg. Yes, yes, good. Remember, you're wild, frightened. Oh, good, good. Dermot, tighter on the leash, heel, Marti, heel."

It went on like that for another hour and forty-five minutes until she was again at the breaking point. Marti was attempting to save a final shred of decency if she could possibly find one when Bobbi suddenly called, "Okay, that's a wrap. Thank you all. Marti, good girl, well done."

He reached down and gave her a nonchalant pat on the head, then stepped past, eyes glowing toward Dermot.

"Say, Dermot, may I talk to you for a momentito?"

"Certainly," Dermot replied, dropping the leash.

He had a high, soft voice. That one word was the only thing Marti had heard him say since he had stepped into the photo bay almost two hours ago.

"Mr. Taggert, we'll have mock-ups for you shortly. Katrina, Gordon, thank you both. Now, Dermot," Bobbi said, waddling somewhere out of range.

Marti remained down on all fours, exposed, and wearing a stunned look on her face. The sudden rumble in her intestinal tract caused her to wonder if she would make it to the restroom.

"Mmm-mmm, you did real good, Baby," Taggert said.

He pulled the top slice of pumpernickel off a thick corned beef sandwich, stared at the corned beef, then crammed a full third of the sandwich into his mouth.

"Hmm-mmm, ya know." He chewed, mouth open, spitting chunks of sandwich in her general direction. "That leash action was hot, Baby, real hot. Might have to get us one of them. When they match your eyes to them emeralds on the collar, whooie!"

Marti grunted as she struggled to her feet. She wrapped the fur coat tightly around her, clamped her arms across her chest, her face now just inches from Taggert chewing in the director's chair.

"I have news for you, Terry. These are not real emeralds. They're fakes, not even good fakes. It's plastic kids' stuff."

"Ain't the only things fake in them photos." He grinned, mustard smeared at the corners of his mouth.

"Well, if you think someone is going to run those ads, you've got another thing coming. You might have enjoyed this little pornographic demonstration today, but you and your investors have just paid a lot of money for something that will never see the light of day. This, this travesty will be completely unacceptable and out of bounds to every fashion magazine in the country."

"Fashion magazine?"

Twenty-three

Dickie waved into the security camera and called, "Hey."

"Be right down," DJ answered. A minute later, she walked across the marble lobby. She was dressed in faded jeans and a white cotton top. Her auburn hair was pulled back casually. He got a dose of perfume when she kissed him.

"So?"

"What?" He racked his brain, trying to remember what he'd forgotten.

"Did you weigh yourself?"

"Yeah," he replied, turning and walking across the sidewalk. He opened the passenger door for her.

"And?" she asked, coming next to him, looking up expectantly for his report.

"Two-thirty," he lied, knocking off fifteen pounds.

"Okay, so that's our starting point. From here on, we're going to make things better. For example, just think how much worse it would be if you had started at two-forty," she said, sliding past him and into the passenger seat. "Oh, my God! What in the world? I'm soaked," she screamed, jumping out of the Jeep. Her jeans were drenched, soaked a dark blue from the water-logged passenger seat. "Look, I'll have to change. God, what a mess. Does this seat always get that wet?"

"I guess so. I mean, I don't really know. I never ride on the passenger side."

"Well, you might as well come on up. You can grab a towel and start to dry that passenger seat, but we're not riding in your car tonight. Hey, I know. We'll walk. Perfect exercise. I know just the place a few blocks from here. It'll do us good."

Over dinner in the Thai restaurant, Dickie attempted to work up both the courage and the right words to explain Rae Nell's plan for an open house. He had no intention of mentioning waking up in Rae Nell's bed.

Amidst the intriguing smells of cooking peppers and exotic sauce, Dickie failed miserably at least a half-dozen times at even broaching the subject. Walking home, the street was relatively quiet. DJ chattered on about something as he felt the opportunity escaping. He feared he would blurt out some idiotic statement at the last moment that would screw things up even more. They stopped in front of her condo building.

"Want to come in for a bit?" she asked.

Dickie sighed in relief as he felt the deadline mercifully extended and the pressure off, at least for the moment.

She lived on the fifteenth floor, and although he had been in her unit numerous times before, he was still amazed at all the computers and screens she had around the place. He knew she did some geeky thing, wrote software or something, but that had always struck him as one of those vague undertakings he never quite understood.

He glanced around at the different framed photos she had of herself, aware she traveled a lot. DJ in Egypt, Vietnam, Australia, China, Korea, even Washington DC, all sorts of strange places.

She opened a closet door where the washer and dryer were stacked. "Humph, jeans are dry, good as new. Want a drink or something?"

"Maybe just some water," he replied as he stared out her window. He could see the bluffs along the river where he had presumably done his roadwork. Office buildings blocked the view of the marina and his houseboat.

"Hey, I'm having an open house at the Emporium next week." He attempted to sound casual as if the thought had just occurred to him.

"An open house?" She handed him a bottle of water, turned, and typed something on a keyboard. "Why?" she asked.

"Oh, I don't know, maybe thinking of changing the menu around. I came across a new line of steaks I want to try, see if I can't get a little more business in there during the week. Things pretty much suck right now on those nights." He drank some water, thinking with relief, 'There, it's finally out there.'

"Makes sense. It's not like you're jammed on those nights. Steaks?" She walked into the sitting area and folded herself onto the couch.

"Yeah, I got a lead on this brand. Nobody else is carrying them, least that I know. It's different and kind of difficult to explain. They're really tender. I'm thinking a limited menu, dress things up a bit, maybe get a little higher class clientele. You know, folks who would drop a couple of bucks for a steak and drinks instead of some guy nursing the same damn beer all night long."

"And you think this new line of steaks is that good? People will come? Make the Emporium a destination for food instead of, umm, I don't know. What would you call it? A pick up joint? A meat market?"

"It could still be that on the weekend," he said. "But, if I could get some business in there the other nights, it would help. Tell you the truth, I was at Fenton's, my accountant, the other day. I'm barely breaking even. Friday and Saturday pay all the bills, but then there's not much left. If I could get things rolling on the other nights, I could do pretty well, I think."

"Where'd you hear about these steaks?"

"Oh, Rae Nell called me. She's their sales rep."

He realized immediately it was too late to get the words back or his foot out of his mouth.

"Really? Your ex-wife? Interesting. The one who had the sheriff camped on her doorstep to serve a subpoena for stock fraud? The ex-wife who got those wrestler guys after you? Wasn't she involved with that container of honey that shut you down for three days? The same ex-wife who had the great deal on the Clap On, Clap Off computer? Hey, wasn't the guy who smashed up your car with the baseball bat pissed off at her? That ex-wife?"

He hated it when she sounded so logical.

"Well, yeah, but—"

"What are you thinking? No, wait, are you even thinking? You know this is going to turn into some kind of disaster. It's a given. She's the one coming up with the plan to turn the business around? Honey, she hates the place. You told me she always has. No offense, Dickie, but just as a woman speaking, she more or less hates you. It's a pretty safe bet the last thing she wants to see is you successful."

"Well, yeah. I mean, I know what you're saying," he said, thinking, *The whole concept sounded a hell of a lot better last night when I had a fifth of Jameson under my belt.*

"For the record, I don't care about her, okay? Don't get me wrong. It has nothing to do with Rae Nell, honestly. But, I do care about you, Dickie. And each and every time she is in the picture, you come out on the shitty end of the stick. Then I get to clean you off and pick up the pieces. I mean, other than your divorce, tell me one positive thing she's done for you. Well, can you?"

"Mmm-mmm no. I mean, yeah, I guess I know what you're saying."

"But, you're going to do this anyway, right?"

"Hey, look, it's not like I'm going to get drunk and sleep with her or anything." He felt the color drain from his face. He couldn't believe he had just let that come out and began speaking very fast. "I mean, okay, she handles this line of steaks. I went to her office and sampled them. They were pretty good, real good, as a matter of fact. Even you have to admit I know steaks, right? So I thought I'd try them. It has nothing to do with her. Well, except that she's the rep for the line, but that's all."

DJ studied him for a long moment before speaking.

"Well, let me warn you again. She would like nothing better than to get you in the sack. If only just to prove to you that she can. So if she comes anywhere in your direction wearing skimpy clothes with skimpier underwear, or with a bottle of Jameson, or suddenly her top falls off when she hands you a box of steaks, you run the other way, okay?"

"Yeah, right, DJ, like I'd be stupid enough to get myself involved like that. I mean, give me some credit."

There followed a fairly long silence during which Dickie tried to maintain an off-handed look.

"My God, Dickie, you look like you just got caught committing the crime of the century. I don't care if you have business dealings with her, honestly. That's your problem. I'm only suggesting you're too nice, and you're going to get burned here, again. And there I'll be, waiting to pick up the pieces, wash the shit off you. What's the name of this company she's working for?"

"It's called Chow Industries. They're from China, I think," he said, hoping the introduction of the world's most populous nation might somehow minimize Rae Nell's role.

"You ever hear of them, know anyone who's dealt with them?"

"Well, no, not exactly. See, that's the beauty of it. I'd be the first."

"How long have you? Oh, never mind. Look, you said this open house thing is going to be Wednesday and Thursday? Of next week?"

"Yeah."

"Doesn't give you a lot of time. Need a hand with anything?"

"No, I've got it under control," he said, followed by another long, painfully quiet gap in the conversation.

"I see. Hey," she said, jumping off the couch, "sorry to kick you out, but I gotta be up and out early. I'm walking those guys tomorrow morning, so I had better hit the sack. Maybe it might be a good idea if we just had a little break here. I mean, it sounds like you, all of a sudden, have a lot going on, and I might be in the way. Okay?" She walked to the door and held it open.

"You're not in the way, DJ, honest. Don't think that. Please don't be like this."

She stood by the open door, and he could see her shutting down, erecting the walls.

"Can I keep the water?"

"You can keep the water, Dickie, good night," she said, closing the door firmly behind him then clicking the lock.

I told her, she knows, and I'm still alive. Things could have been worse, maybe, he thought, driving home.

DJ typed Chow Industries into her computer and hit search.

Twenty-four

Marti Cullen was attempting to relax at home. She was still upset with the photoshoot and the way she'd been put on display. She was into her third lemon drop martini, sipping in her bedroom, lights off, feet up, wrapped in her fur coat, and feeling the beginnings of a hazy calm descending when she checked her phone messages.

"Hi, this is Maureen calling for Dr. Craig at ten-forty-seven. Just checking to make sure everything is all right. I've gone ahead and rescheduled this afternoon's Benson appointment. If you're not going to be in tomorrow, please let me know so I can rearrange your calendar. Thanks. Hope everything is okay. Bye." Click.

"Hi." The second message began. "It's one-forty-five. This is Maureen, calling to check. Dr. Craig, would you please call the office? Just a little worried is all. Hope everything is okay. Thank you." Click.

Oh God, as if I don't have enough to worry about, 'thought Marti. 'Now what has he gone and done?' She dialed Craig's office. *Dr. Craig, indeed,* she thought.

"Hello, you've reached the offices of…"

"Oh, good Lord," she said, hanging up. Craig will just have to deal with this if he didn't have the common sense to inform his staff where he was. Why should she waste her time worrying about it?

Her cell phone rang about forty-five minutes later, waking her from a martini-induced nap.

"Hello," she croaked.

"Free to talk, Sugar?" Terry Taggert cooed.

"Is this your attempt at an apology, Terry? If it is, I have to say it sounds rather less than impressive."

With a headache beginning to pound behind her eyes, Marti was more than her usual irritable self.

"Hey, look, Baby. You're the one who's parading her ass around town in a new, one of a kind fur coat. You're the one who's been handed a national modeling contract. You're the one who has a closet full of very expensive gifts, all of them from yours truly. So don't give me that apology routine, ever. Got it?"

"Well, for your information, I did not appreciate being put on display like some common tramp. And your disgusting comments did nothing to help the situation. If I'd known what you had in mind, I honestly don't think I would have accepted your contract. The only thing that made me go through with your whole ill-conceived project was my sense of professionalism. I knew you and your investors were going to be paying for that studio and staff time. I simply felt compelled to hold up your end of the bargain for you."

She reached for the glass on her makeup table and swallowed the last bit of lukewarm martini.

"And, just for your information, it's August. I'm hardly parading around town wearing a fur coat during the month of August," she snapped, pulling the coat tighter around her.

"Oh, come on, Sugar. You enjoyed it, I could tell. You liked—"

"No, Terry. As a matter of fact, I did not enjoy it at all. In case you weren't listening, I went through with the photoshoot out of a sense of professional responsibility and a sense of loyalty to you and your investors. But no, I did not like being on the end of a leash like some animal. I did not like exposing myself. I did not like being forced into a series of highly suggestive poses. And, for your information—"

"Well, la-te-dah, just listen to you go on. You would have gotten down on your knees and done the whole NFL if you thought it would have helped to get that damn coat last night, and you know it. Now, this could turn into a really nice little deal for y'all, so just don't start looking the old gift horse in the mouth here. Got it?"

"Sometimes you can be horribly crude, Terry."

"Yeah, right, and other times I can be downright generous. Like all them gifts you got. You think I gave you all that shit because I like your conversation? Truth is, honey, you just happen to like your payment gift-wrapped instead of in hard cash. That's the only difference. Now I'm gonna wait to see you until tomorrow night. Right now, you're sounding just a little bitchy."

Marti felt herself flush.

"You're gonna act like this, I'll call tomorrow. Let you know where and when. You just have that ass of yours wearing a smile and acting happy. Got it? Yeah," he said after a pause, "I thought so."

"Oh," she exclaimed once he hung up, and that damn Dr. Craig was still not home.

Twenty-five

Darcy sounded stressed. "Dickie, where are you? Don't tell me you're still home."

"God, just where the hell did you think I'd be?" Dickie rolled over and glanced at the digital clock, not even eight in the morning.

"Yeah, well, I knew you wouldn't be at work. Look, I just got the call from Helen Hardy. Our boy's got another one of his business meetings tonight. You set to go?"

"No, I'm not set to go, Darcy. Where's this supposed to happen? Tonight?"

He sat up in bed and rubbed his face to wake up.

"I don't know where. You're the guy who said he could figure that part out."

"Well, I can't figure it out. Not if I've got to get all the equipment and shit today. You'll have to do it."

"I don't know how to do—"

"It's not hard, Darcy. It just takes a little time. Time I don't have. God, I didn't think we'd be on it this fast.

It's very simple. You just call hotels, find out if he's checked in. Tell them you have a delivery, flowers, something like that. Or you can just ask to be put through to his room. They'll either say they don't have a guest by that name, or he's not in yet, or they might just ring the room. If they ring the room, just hang up. Oh yeah, see if you can get a room number, too."

"How the hell do I do that?"

"It's really hard, Darcy. You have to ask them. Like I said, just tell them you've got a delivery. It's simple."

"What if it's not under his name?"

"Well, you better hope it is, or we're really screwed."

"And you don't have time?"

"No, I told you I'm running right now," Dickie said, snuggling back down beneath the sheets.

"Okay, okay, I'll call you. You sure you can't—"

"No, Darcy, I'll wait to hear from you." Dickie hung up and pulled a pillow back over his head.

"Ugh," he grunted less than a minute later, rolling over to answer the phone again, ready to cut off whatever objection Darcy had.

"What?"

"Hello, Crabby Appleton, get up on the wrong side of the bed again?"

"Hi, Rae Nell."

"What wines are you planning to serve Wednesday and Thursday night? Have you done anything about entertainment? I don't suppose you've given that any thought."

Dickie could tell two things from her tone. First, she was reading from a list, and second, it was probably a long list. Entertainment? What the hell was wrong with the classic rock he had on the jukebox?

"Yeah, Rae Nell, as a matter of fact, I've got the music covered."

"No, Dickie, do not even suggest that your jukebox is going to work. Oh, God, that was it, wasn't it? The jukebox, country-western, and moldy oldies? Are you kidding? No, Dickie, I told you this is going to be a quality event."

"Don't you think you're rushing this just a little bit, Rae Nell? I mean, I haven't even drawn up a list of the guys I plan to invite."

"Exactly why I've already taken care of that. This is not going to be the party you invite the guys to, Dickie. That is exactly why nothing has worked in the past. I was thinking about it earlier this morning, and—"

"This morning?"

"Yes, this morning, someone has to. As I started to say, I was thinking about it earlier this morning, between, I don't know, three and maybe four-thirty—"

"Obsessing is what it sounds like."

She ignored his comment.

"And, I drew up a couple of fabulous lists here. Now, I've already had the invitations printed, picked those up about eleven last night, ran the labels around five this morning, posted them over an hour ago. I sent you one, by the way, so you'll have an idea of what they look like when it arrives in the mail."

"Rae Nell! You already mailed my invitations to my open house?" Dickie half shouted as he bolted upright in bed.

"Duh, hello! Of course, if we're going to have it next Wednesday and Thursday, we have to give people at least a day or two to clear their schedules. Not everyone just does things when it suits them, Dickie. These people have lives beyond going to various saloons around town. Now, who supplies your liquor?"

"Metro. What's that got to do with anything?"

"Dickie, do you want this event to be successful? This is not another beer-guzzling swill-fest for you and all your over-served friends. If that's what you want, you certainly don't need my input. You can do all this work yourself and have it fail, just like everything else you've tried."

Dickie fell back in bed and didn't say anything.

"Yeah, that's more like it. Don't worry. I'll take care of the wine, and for the music, I've got a line on a really great combo. Hopefully, we can still get them on such short notice. Now, what are you doing with staff? Hello? Dickie, are you there?"

"Ahhh," he groaned. "Look, Rae Nell, I don't know about all this."

"Well, it's a little late for second thoughts, Dickie. You should have thought about that before you had me mail out seven hundred invitations."

"Seven hundred!"

"Yes, seven hundred. Relax, they won't all show up. It won't be like your usual freeloading crowd. But, we have to make sure the place doesn't look empty. I mean, who would want to go to an open house nobody wants to go to? Okay, I'm taking care of everything. Now, I want you to get down to a restaurant supply house and pick out white chef coats and hats for your kitchen staff."

"Coats? Hats?"

"Yes, and no cowboy boots. A new tie and sport coat wouldn't hurt, either. You are forbidden to wear a golf shirt. Now let me just go over the rest of these items while I have you on the phone, see if there's anything else you've forgotten."

Twenty-six

Marti Cullen was fed up. "The photoshoot! You mean that pornographic display you put me through the other day, wearing a dog collar with my rear end exposed? That photoshoot? No, Terry, as much as it disappoints me, I'm sorry to say that's not the reason I'm canceling tonight. The truth is, I can't seem to find my idiot husband, Craig. He's missing."

"Missing? What'd ya' mean missing?" Taggert tried to sound surprised.

"Just that, he hasn't been at work for the past few days. I thought he was just off on one of his tantrums, sulking up at our lake place or off to New York. I'm still not convinced he isn't, but it's unusual he wouldn't let his office know how to get in touch with him. He's always done that in the past," Marti said.

"Hmm-mmm, think he found out about you screw, err, about us?"

"No, no. I don't think that's it at all. This is very unlike him."

"How long has he been gone?"

"Well, to be honest, I didn't really miss him until I talked to his secretary. She kept leaving these annoying messages asking him to call. Eventually, I called her back. I was going to give her a piece of my mind, and that's when she told me they hadn't heard from him."

"So, how long do you think?" Taggert asked, shaking his head. She never even missed the poor bastard.

"Well, he hasn't been in the office for the last couple of days. I'm trying to remember if he told me he was going somewhere."

"Well, can you get away? Sounds to me like you're not gonna have to sneak back in tonight. He's probably just out of town. Didn't you say he goes on buying trips, conventions, those kinds of deals?"

"Yes, but no. I'd love to get together, but stupid Craig has just made a mess of everything, Terry. I'm sorry, but until I get this cleared up, I'm afraid I'm just going to have to cancel. That's all there is to it. You do understand?"

"I understand you have a very nice, one of a kind fur coat, a national modeling contract, even if you didn't like the photoshoot. And, I sure could use a heavy dose of that old Marti magic." He made a half-hearted attempt to sound like he was groveling.

"No, sorry, Terry. I just don't think I'd be the best of company tonight. I've got to clean up this Craig mess," she said.

"Think you should call the cops?"

"The police? No, that's just exactly what he would want. I don't want to play into his hands and make a big production out of his stupid little stunt. No, I'll just wait him out. I'm sorry, but you'll just have to take a rain check."

"All right." He tried his best to sound dejected, all the while doing a little victory dance when she told him she wouldn't contact the police.

"We'll talk in a day or two, Terry," Marti said.

He couldn't believe his luck and immediately dialed the next name on his list.

"Just calling to see if my favorite sales rep has time to get together in the next day or two and collect her bonus."

"Bonus? Oh, wow, Terry," Rae Nell gushed. "Yes, yes, of course, I can. I'd love to. Did you get your invitation, by the way? A bonus, wow. What is it? That's so great. I had no idea."

"Well, let me just say I think it's something you'll really like," Taggert said, looking at the fur coat he'd just draped over a plastic lunchroom chair.

Luther was silently laughing while obscenely flicking his tongue in and out.

Taggert gave him the finger in response.

"Just like before, I'll call and let you know when and where. Figured you done real good on this open house deal. I saw the order you emailed in earlier today, and we should celebrate your success, you know?"

"Oh, okay, gee, wow, this is great. Thank you for the call, Terry."

"Yeah, talk to you in a bit. Bye-bye, Baby."

"Man." Luther shook his head. "You ever get tired of bullshitting these women? Ever wonder if you could just get one without having to spring for a fancy room, a dinner, or all the gifts? Time was I could pick a gal up, make her buy her own drinks, and then we'd climb into the backseat of my car."

"Yeah, well, I ain't met one yet who'd be dumb enough to go anywhere with you, and besides, what do I care? Ain't my dough."

"Well, you just better be careful. You'll kill the damn goose that laid the golden egg is all I'm saying."

"Shit, I got this thing all figured out, Luther, all figured out."

Twenty-seven

The salesclerk rubbed his hands together. He'd probably made his sales quota for the entire month between the cameras, recording equipment, monitor, cable, and transmitters piled on the counter. "Can you think of anything else you need?"

Dickie ran through a mental checklist of how everything would hook up. He planned to hide the camera inside a smoke alarm, activate it using a motion detector, and monitor everything from a room next door.

He happily paid for all the equipment with Darcy's corporate credit card then threw in a nice digital camera and extra memory cards just for good measure. It was a little after four when he checked his watch, thinking, *Darcy could call anytime now with the hotel and room information.*

It was almost five when Dickie finally phoned Darcy.

"Hey, you got a hotel for me yet? We're running out of time."

"No, I don't have anything. I've tried every place in town and got a big zero. I'm afraid he might be using an alias, in which case we'll have to move to plan B."

"Plan B?"

"Yeah, meaning figure out something else, 'cause this isn't working."

"No hotel has this guy listed?"

"Not that I've found, and I've tried all the top places. That's his style, Dickie. He's not the 'no tell motel' type."

"I suppose Plan B could be that we follow the guy. That can get pretty tough, next to impossible, to be more precise, and leaves no time to get into his room unless he maybe goes out somewhere for dinner."

"Huh?"

"Darcy, if we follow the guy as he's checking into his room, what's he doing? Checking in, right? So he'll be in the room. Even if he's just watching TV, he's in there. I'll need at least thirty minutes uninterrupted. An hour would be better to get this shit installed. It's not like I can knock on the door dressed as room service with a camera on my shoulder, ask to come in, and record the action."

"Yeah, I suppose I never thought of it like that," Darcy said, remembering his ill-fated attempt a week and a half ago.

Fifteen minutes later, Darcy called back.

"Dickie, it's the Gresham, the Capital City Suite."

"The Gresham? You sure?"

"Yeah, I did the fruit basket deal. They told me to drop it at the front desk, and they'd deliver it up to the room. But, the guy mentioned the Capital City Suite halfway under his breath. You know, like he was reading it off a computer screen."

"Okay, on my way," Dickie said. He drove the Jeep around the block and headed back the way he'd just come. Ten minutes later, he was at the reception desk of the stately Gresham Hotel.

"May I help you, Sir?" The woman behind the reception counter looked to be all of twenty-four. With a peaches and cream complexion, she looked the picture of innocence.

"Yes, I'm hoping you can help out a guy who just realized he forgot an anniversary. I'd like the Capital City Suite if it's available for tonight?" He worked to look the part of a harried, forgetful husband ready to ask for the suite next door as soon as she told him it was already taken.

"Oh, actually, that's amazing. You must be really lucky. We just had a cancellation for tonight. Wow, great timing," she said.

"Oh, gee, that's too bad," Dickie said, not really listening. "Well, maybe the suite next door? See, we honeymooned in the Capital City Suite a few years ago, but I guess we'll have to settle for next door. Serves me right for doing this at the last minute."

"No, Sir, I can get you into the Capital City Suite, no problem. Like I said, we just had a cancellation."

"Mr. Taggert?"

"Yes, Mr. Taggert, just—" She looked up from her computer screen at Dickie, pausing, studying him for a long moment.

"Yeah," Dickie said, cursing Darcy. "I was saying I wish we could take it tonight, but we can't make it now. Just checking to make sure you received my cancellation. That's me, Taggert. Mr. Terrence Taggert. And you've got my cancellation, good. Sorry for the last-minute change. Well, I'd better be off. Thank you." He backed up, slowly making his way to the door, nodding with every step.

"Careful there," a man said, gently grabbing Dickie by the arm before he backed into him. "Better watch where you're going."

"Oh, yeah, sorry about that I had to cancel. Thank you, thanks," Dickie mumbled, then beat a hasty retreat to his Jeep.

"Darcy, what's up, man? They told me your guy canceled," he said into his phone.

"What?"

"Yeah, they said the suite was available because the guy canceled. Man, I had to do some fast thinking before you got hung with a pricey room for the night. I asked for it thinking I'd grab the suite next door, and the chick tells me Taggert had just canceled. Sounds like something must have come up."

"Think he's on to us?" Darcy asked.

"I don't see how. Unless he's monitoring your phone calls. Maybe call around again, see if he comes up at another hotel."

"Oh, I hate doing that. Can't you?"

"No, I can't. Look, if you find out he's landed somewhere, let me know, but we're almost out of time. At least for tonight."

"But—"

"You're breaking up," Dickie said and hung up.

Twenty-eight

The invitation shook in Dickie's hand as he read, *'More than just a menu change.'* She'd told him seven hundred of the damn things had been sent first-class. A four-color card featuring the photo of a large steak on the front side and ending with the plea to *'Come Break Bread, share some wine with your willing host Mr. Richard Mullins.'* *'Christ,'* Dickie thought, 'God damn Rae Nell, *'Break bread'* my ass.' This was costing him a small fortune, and he didn't even have people in the door yet. Shit, seven hundred invites? He didn't have enough placemats, let alone silverware, for that many people.

"Rae Nell," Dickie said, not disguising his displeasure the moment she answered the phone.

"Oh, perfect, Dickie, glad you called," she replied, oblivious to his tone.

"What?"

"Look, I got that little jazz combo we talked about, but they're going to need some extra equipment. Since I figured you didn't have a piano, speakers, and things. Right?"

"What?"

"That's just what I thought. Listen, not to worry, I've taken care of it. They'll even deliver the stuff. I had to rent it for three days, but we were just fortunate to get it. What with it being the last minute and everything. Lucky us."

"Deliver? What in the hell are they going to deliver?"

"Oh! Do not even suggest you were thinking of picking this up! What, you've got room for a piano somewhere in that awful Jeep you use to pollute the atmosphere? Their best Steinway, by the way, and luckily, still available on such short notice. It's Cities Music, off of 280 and Larpenteur. Look, it doesn't really matter. They'll need a deposit in advance, and payment on delivery, so have your checkbook ready, unless you plan to put it on plastic." she added half-scoffing. "Now, the linens and cutlery will be arriving Wednesday morning."

"Linens?"

"Well, you can't use paper placemats. Those dreadful things you have with all the 'Did you know facts.' Facts no one wants to know. Like the weight of the world's fattest man when he died. God, that's supposed to be appetizing? Oh, please! No, Dickie, you're not going to use those awful things. We want people to enjoy the evening, not run out the door completely disgusted. Now, if you haven't done so, it might be a good idea to air that place out today. No offense, but the smell of stale beer and cheap perfume doesn't go very far in the department of appetite appeal. Bathrooms, too, a flame-thrower might be a good start. Oh, and I've got the caterer bringing twelve-hundred wine glasses. Hmmm-mmm…" She sounded like she was writing something on a list. "Better make that fifteen-hundred, just in case. Okay, I think that about does it for now. Look, I've still got a lot to do, plus a meeting with my boss that I just can't miss. I plan to be in early Wednesday morning, so I'll see you then. Oh," she added as an afterthought, "thanks for checking in, bye, bye, bye." Click.

Dickie wasn't exactly sure what had just happened. Whatever it was, it clearly hadn't gone his way.

It was early afternoon before he arrived at the Emporium of Dance. Walking in the front door, he was immediately struck by the large bouquet of flowers sitting on the bar. *'So help me,'* he thought. 'If Rae Nell ordered a bunch of flowers for this God damn open house, I'm going to scream.'

"What the hell's that for?" he growled at Noel, his bartender.

"Jesus, late night? I don't know. They're addressed to you. Just arrived about a half-hour ago. Someone die?"

Dickie opened the card. It was from Patsy at Metro Liquor Sales, his liquor distributor, thanking him for the order. None of it made any sense to him. "Noel, has Patsy from Metro been in here?"

"Oh, is that who sent 'em?" he nodded toward the flowers. "Must be that order."

"Order?"

"Yeah, came in earlier this morning. Everything's still stacked up in the kitchen. I didn't know where you wanted to put it all, not like there's lots of room anywhere. Jose's in there bitching. Of course, who can tell? It's all in Spanish."

Dickie poked his head into the kitchen, unable to see Jose behind the thirty cases of wine stacked five high just inside the door.

"Jose?" Dickie called.

He couldn't speak Spanish, other than to order beer, but he understood the tone of Jose's string of invectives cascading from behind the cases of wine.

"Oh, hi, Dickie. How sweet, you didn't have to call. Got the flowers, did ya?" Patsy from Metro Liquor smiled into her phone three minutes later.

She was a middle-aged woman who wore nauseating perfume, unflattering brown polyester outfits, and looked like she should be teaching junior high instead of selling booze to bars.

"Well, see, Patsy, that's why I wanted to call," Dickie said, holding himself in check. Patsy had always reminded him of his spinster aunt with the cats, and he was cautioning himself to go easy. He tugged absently on the black cord that spiraled out of the phone from behind the bar.

"Oh, you're so sweet, Dickie. You didn't have to do that. Your order could not have come at a better time. My husband's starting chemo at the end of the week. He just finished with the radiation, but they decided they want to be sure, you know? So, well, you just gotta do it. We're taught to fight all our lives, and now, of course, we're in our biggest fight ever. Well, anyway." She sniffled. "I just wanted to tell you thanks, ya know? It means so much to me. You are so sweet. Just know you're in my prayers."

"Yeah, well, Patsy, glad I could help. I just wanted to say thanks for the flowers. Keep us posted on his progress."

"You bet I will. You are such a sweet, sweet man, and Dickie?"

"Yes," he sighed, thinking, *Shit, thirty cases of God damn wine.*

"Not to worry, the rest of the order will be over on the afternoon delivery truck. Thank you, and God bless you, Dickie Mullins. God bless you, you wonderful, wonderful man!"

"Oh, shit!" Dickie swore once he hung up the phone.

"Grab that, will you, Noel?" he said a moment later in response to the phone ringing. He was attempting to gather his thoughts, regroup in the face of the inevitable Rae Nell steamroller.

"For you," Noel said, laying the phone on the bar. "Something about a cleaning crew coming in after close."

Twenty-nine

Luther had just tossed the last case of frozen steaks into their delivery van. "You know," Terry Taggert said. "We still have some room. How about we toss in about fifty-pounds of that special sausage? First-time order and all, it'll make us look like nice guys."

"Yeah, sure, I can do that if you want." Luther thought, *It might just be the perfect way to get rid of some of ground up Dr. Craig Cullen at the same time.*

"Yeah, do it."

"Hey, are you sure that little model gal of yours won't go to the cops?"

"Marti? Our model? Hell no. In fact, I'm sure she will, eventually. It's gonna just be a matter of time. Sooner or later, she has to. But every minute she waits makes it harder for the cops to put anything together."

"As it stands now, about all they know is poor old Dr. Craig left home three days ago and hasn't been seen since. I'm just thinking it might be a good idea to ditch the car. Why risk it? Someone snooping around here, everything's going our way. Just get it out of here to be on the safe side."

Luther nodded his head in agreement. "I'll drive it into town, leave the keys in it, park it somewhere it'll get stolen. Cops may not ever find it. If they do, they'll be on a wild goose chase. It'll look like somebody maybe nailed the guy for his car. We'll be the last people anyone would ever think of."

"I like it, Luther. Don't forget that free fifty pounds of special sausage with this meat order, and don't forget to get paid when you deliver this."

An hour later, Luther rolled the last of the steaks into the Emporium of Dance. "That's ten cases of our top steaks, Mr. Mullins," Luther said. With all sorts of wine cases already choking the kitchen, he had to stack them almost blocking the doorway. "Oh, yeah, and first-time order and all, we wanted to throw in fifty-pounds of top sausage, just because," he added, slapping the box of sausage stuffed with ground Dr. Craig.

"Yeah, thanks, looking forward to giving these a try," Dickie said, edging his way toward the door, trying to squeeze around a stack of boxes. He was hoping maybe this driver would forget to ask for a check.

"Say, before you go, I'll need you to sign for this stuff," Luther said, taking out a bill of lading from his back pocket.

"Not a problem," Dickie replied, thinking, *It was about time his luck changed, a signature being a hell of a lot better than cutting a check.*

"Oh, guess this first delivery is COD," Luther said, trying to sound like he just noticed, hoping the crooked grin he flashed did the trick.

"Hmm-mmm," Dickie said, quickly calculating float time. He was wondering if the twenty-three-hundred-dollar check would take three days to reach his bank before overdrawing his account when he had a sudden brainstorm. "Not a problem. Let's just put it on the corporate account," he said and took out Darcy's credit card.

"We can certainly do that. Let me get the form out of the van, and I'll be right back," Luther said.

Not only did Darcy's credit card pay for the Chow steaks, but by the time Dickie was finished, he paid for all the wine, four cases of eighteen-year-old Jameson, the deposit and rental on a Steinway piano, the catering staff, glass and linen rental. All that plus a three-person cleaning crew from two-to-five early Wednesday morning, and the thirteen-hundred-dollar printing bill for Rae Nell's open house invitations.

Thirty

DJ hadn't returned any of Dickie's calls over the last couple of days, and he was in the process of leaving another message.

"Hey, DJ, look, I know you were mad. I'm hoping you'll calm down enough to come to the open house tomorrow night. I could use your support. Feeling kind of bowled over just now with all the planning and shit. Please give me a call."

Darcy's number flashed on his cell phone.

"Hey, I got another call coming in. Gotta run. Hope to see you tomorrow night, later. Hello, Darcy," he said, expecting an eruption over all the credit card charges and braced himself.

"Dickie, great news, just got a call from Helen Hardy. Our guy is on for tonight, and get this, I called the Gresham again. Guess what? He's there. I mean, he will be. He hasn't checked in yet, but that's the place. That Capital City Suite again, same as before."

"You're kidding."

"Yeah, you should be able to get over there and have the better part of the afternoon to get everything set up. You believe it? Must have some chick lined up who has a hot button for the place. Anyway, tell me you can do this tonight, please. I'm begging here."

"Darcy, I'll be there. I'll get the equipment loaded up and get over there right now. I'll call you once I have everything set up."

"Fantastic!" Darcy exclaimed.

Forty-five minutes later, the recording equipment was being wheeled down the hallway on the top floor of the Gresham Hotel. Dickie tipped the bellboy five dollars and then watched him through the peephole as he retreated back down the hallway to the bank of elevators.

The room he was in was a generously proportioned suite, with a separate sitting room, Jacuzzi, and terry-cloth robes. There was an adjoining door that led to the Capital City Suite, which he propped open using a chair. The door opened into a mirror-image door. All he would have to do was get that opened to access the Capital City Suite.

He unzipped the garment bag the bellboy had hung in the front closet and carefully removed the flower arrangement from Patsy. He'd spied a housekeeping cart in the hallway and hoped his luck would hold.

"Excuse me, I'm supposed to deliver these to the Capital City Suite," he said, holding up the flower arrangement.

The young woman looked at Dickie with large brown eyes that were so dark he could barely distinguish pupils from iris.

"No hablar Ingles." She shook her head.

Dickie nodded at the flowers, reached into his wallet, removed a crisp five-dollar bill, and handed it to the woman, indicating she should follow.

She glanced around cautiously, stuffed the bill inside her bra, and followed him around the corner to the doorway of the Capital City Suite.

"Entora," Dickie said, making up a word he thought sounded Spanish.

She gave him a queer glance, looked down the hall, and then quickly used a pass card to open the door.

"Mucho gracias," Dickie said.

He walked into the suite and placed the flowers on a chest of drawers next to the adjoining door. He coughed heavily as he opened the door, quickly slipped a matchbook in the door frame, and prayed it would keep the door open for the next two minutes. He coughed again just for good measure, smiled, and pretended to walk down to the bank of elevators before quietly scurrying back to his room.

He immediately set about installing the smoke alarm cover with the motion-activated camera, super gluing the whole affair on the ceiling just above the massive bed. He ran a black cable across the ceiling, down the wall, and out the adjoining door. He thought about covering the cable but decided against it, guessing anything he attempted might just attract attention.

Back in his hotel room, he hooked up the monitor and recording device. A matter of two ISB plugs, and he was set to go. The whole operation, from the time he had set the flower arrangement on the chest of drawers to making his test recording, had taken just under twenty-three minutes.

"Darcy Dalton, please," Dickie said into the phone. With his free hand, he began to click the television remote through one-hundred-and-ninety-four different cable channels, none of which seemed to interest him.

"This is Mr. Dalton," Darcy said.

"Darcy, I'm in and all set," Dickie half-whispered in an effort to sound conspiratorial.

"You got the hotel room?" Darcy suddenly sounded excited.

"Better than that, man. I got that Capital City Suite wired. Just fired up the equipment. It's all systems go. Now, all we have to do is wait for this guy to show up with some tramp, and I'm ready to record."

"Man, finally some good news. I'll call Helen right away. No, wait, I better not. I don't want her saying anything and tipping this clown off. Dickie, this is great. Finally, something going my way. I've been arguing with my credit card company for over an hour. They got my corporate account all screwed up."

"Well, don't sweat the small shit," Dickie said, anxious to get off the line. "Listen, anything changes here, I'll let you know. Right now, we're in the wait mode."

"Call me as soon as you got something."

"Hey, that may not be until the middle of the night."

"I don't care. I want to know right away, and, Dickie?"

"Yeah?"

"Thanks for everything you've done."

"Glad to do it, Darcy. Glad to do it."

Thirty-one

Taggert examined his face in the mirror as he talked on the phone. "Everything go okay with that delivery?"

"Not a problem. Kind of a dive joint. You might like it," Luther said.

"You dump Cullen's car yet?"

"Next on the list. I'll leave it on some side street with the keys in the ignition."

"Make sure you wipe it down first."

"Don't worry. You gonna be in tomorrow?"

"Yeah, but I'm out tonight, so don't count on me until around noon."

Taggert finished his facial examination then thought long and hard about which pair of jeans to wear. He slipped on a favorite pair of cowboy boots, the ones with the anaconda skin, chose a short-sleeved, black silk shirt that showed off his biceps, then stepped back from the mirror to appraise himself.

"Come and get it, baby, party time!"

On her way to her meeting, Rae Nell touched base with the caterer. She double-checked with the cleaning service to make sure the crew would be working at the Emporium of Dance after close. She left a couple of messages for Dickie on his cell phone to call her in the next thirty minutes or wait until tomorrow. She was convinced she had everything under control. There was no way Dickie could possibly screw up the open house, even if he tried, which had her wondering exactly what he would do.

Terry Taggert was on his fourth or fifth bourbon when he heard the elevator bell. He ran to the door and gazed through the peephole as Rae Nell came into view. She paused a few feet from the door, pulled out a compact, opened the mirror quickly touching her hair, checked her lipstick, smoothed her blouse, and then knocked on the door. He decided to wait a moment.

Rae Nell stepped back, glanced at the door, and knocked again. This time a bit more forcefully. She nervously pushed her bra up, smoothed her blouse, and waited.

He half-laughed, watched her another ten seconds, and then opened the door.

"Hey, how's it going there, lady? Whooie, don't you just look good enough to eat? Glad you could finally make it."

"Mmm-mmm," she said, kissing him, wrapping an arm around him, slowly letting it slide off his waist. Her fingers lingered for a brief moment along his buckle before striding into the room.

"Wow, this place is really great," she said, stepping into the main room.

"Nothing too good for you, girl. What can I get you to drink?"

In the next room, the door knocking interrupted the Batman movie Dickie had been watching. By the time he peered through the peephole, whoever it was had already stepped inside the Capital City Suite. He was just barely able to pick up the murmur of what sounded like casual conversation. He pressed his ear against the adjoining door, able to discern male and female voices, but not much more.

Taggert refreshed his own drink and waited for a response. Finally, he asked her again, "What are you drinking?"

She had a tough workday tomorrow and wasn't all that anxious to begin it with a hangover.

"Maybe just a sparkling water," she said, settling onto a couch.

"A water? You kidding me? Water? Don't you know fish fuck in it?"

"I'm not sure I'd be able to catch up to you at this point."

"Okay, not a problem." Taggert staggered a half-step as he took another healthy pull from his glass. He spilled a little in the process of slamming his glass down.

Then stormed to the front closet, tore open the door, and stormed back, dragging the fur coat across the floor.

"Had this for ya'. A little bonus. Thought maybe you should see it, know what you're missing out on because you're all of a sudden getting so high and mighty on me. You don't want to party and earn it, what the hell you come for?"

Her eyes went wide, staring at the fur coat, then up at Taggert.

"Oh my God," she said, stroking the rich cinnamon-colored fur. "Are you kidding me? This is, well it's, it's gorgeous. Oh my God!"

"Should be. It's a one of a kind. Feeling a little more like that drink now?" he asked and grinned down at her.

It was well after midnight. Dickie had been checking his equipment, listening, rechecking his equipment. He occasionally picked up a general conversational murmur but nothing he could make out.

Both his ears were sore from being pressed against the door in a futile attempt to eavesdrop. He had been yawning every few minutes and was beginning to fear that the whole effort might be a bust. Suddenly, the conversation grew louder, more animated as the couple moved toward the bedroom.

Dickie was suddenly aware of them, directly opposite the door where he had his ear pressed. He strained to hear what they were saying, picking up every second or third word. Then suddenly, there was a loud thump. His head bounced off the door, and he jumped, heart stuck in his throat as he stared at the door and heard a male voice.

"Hold on there, baby. You want it that bad, crawl in there." The voice faded slightly, hopefully traveling in the direction of the bed, feminine giggling trailing behind.

He rushed over to his monitor and waited impatiently for a few seconds, with his heart pounding just as a view of the room appeared on the monitor. Dickie could make out a naked male, balding, fairly well-built, rolling onto the bed. Taggert. His movements were heavy, his head wobbled. He grinned idiotically and appeared fairly intoxicated. From out of camera range, something fluttered across the screen, a blouse.

Dickie triple-checked to make sure he was recording, then turned off the table lamp for more clarity. He could make out more distinct facial features as Taggert tossed the blouse aside. Slacks came next, hurriedly thrown, followed by more giggling.

"Yeah, yeah, I like that, baby. Go, baby, go." He encouraged his off-camera partner as a bra sailed over his head. "Come and get it," he said, just as a naked female stumbled and crawled clumsily into view. Whoever she was, she was at least as intoxicated as Taggert.

Dickie saw a blonde head, watched the head bob back and forth for a moment as if she were attempting to get her bearings and maybe stop a couple of walls from spinning. She stretched a red thong on her forefinger like a rubber band, pulled it back, and held it a moment before she let go, firing into Taggert's face. She giggled and made noises that seemed to ring a distant bell somewhere in Dickie's memory.

She crawled slowly, cat-like, along Taggert. With her back arched, she growled then tossed her hair in a way that somehow seemed familiar. She dragged her nails across Taggert's thighs. His legs quivered, and he began to moan.

"Think you can handle this pussy cat?" she said and crawled into full camera range, a distinct tan line, and then the white of her shapely rear came into focus. Suddenly, Dickie found himself staring wide-eyed at a four-inch tattoo of Minnie Mouse, mooning.

"Rae Nell?" he whispered.

Thirty-two

Julius was explaining to Dickie, not for the first time, why his crew had carried all the bar stools, a number of tables, and the pool cue rack outside, stacking everything against the rear of the building. "Well, Sir, Miss Rae Nell drew up this plan, showing exactly where she wants everything to go." They were in the process of unplugging the *Trivia-Tease* game that allowed you, with every correct answer, to remove an article of clothing from the attractive video model, your choice blonde, brunette, or redhead.

Dickie was sweating, still breathing heavily after moving the cases of wine and Jameson whiskey to an out of the way corner in the main barroom.

"Hey," Dickie gasped, "what are people supposed to sit on? What if they'd just like to have a beer quietly and play a little trivia?"

"Oh, please. That's the whole idea, Sir." Julius snorted. He sounded just like Rae Nell. He had been calling Dickie 'Sir' for the better part of the morning, the way a cop does. 'Would you mind stepping out of the car, *Sir*?' The word polite but with a double meaning.

"Well, Sir, I'm just doing what I've been told. Miss Rae Nell seems to have everything laid out here," he said, then opened a manila file folder on one of the few remaining tables. It held a two-page sketch of the interior, indicating the exact placement of tables, chafing dishes, and crowd flow patterns— all vintage Rae Nell over-kill.

"To tell you the truth, Julie," Dickie said, putting his arm on Julius' shoulder, "I was maybe planning on just having platters of cut-up steak and bottles of steak sauce sitting around on the bar."

Julius looked up, waiting for the punch line. After a long moment, it dawned on him Dickie hadn't been kidding. "Oh, honestly, Sir, not to worry. Miss Rae Nell has everything organized." Julius referred again to her two-page battle plan.

"Hey, hey, what are you doing there?" Dickie asked, running over to two guys taking down his Razzle Dazzle martini painting. The painting featured a well-endowed woman wearing cuffs and a top hat but otherwise naked and sitting in a giant martini glass. "That stays. It's an original piece of art!"

"Not according to the plan. The lady makes it very specific," one of them said and indicated another manila file labeled 'décor'. "If you wanted this stuff left up, you should have said so in your plans. I mean, we kinda like it, to tell you the truth, but we're supposed to follow the lady's directions."

"You don't think it leaves a big hole there?" Dickie attempted to appeal to their logical side.

"Yeah, but just for the moment. We got this French guy thing to put up there."

"French guy?" Dickie asked as they unwrapped a three-foot by five-foot poster of a rotund, mustached bald man in a long white apron, raising a glass of wine, something in French was scrawled across the bottom of the thing.

"Hey, you work here?" a muscular looking bulldog called from the back of the room. He was standing just inside the backdoor. "According to our instructions, we gotta put the stage and the piano where all these wine boxes are stacked. Someone's gotta move this stuff before we can bring in the piano."

Thirty-three

Dickie was hiding in the kitchen, sipping a beer, not his first, listening to Jose ramble on and on in Spanish.

He occasionally saw someone through the kitchen door he didn't recognize, carrying in a load of one thing or another… wine glasses, tables, tablecloths, candelabras, more wine glasses, silverware, trays. Everything was spinning out of control, and he longed for a time, just forty-eight hours ago, when he sold a few cheeseburgers and a couple of beers in the evening. He'd been steamrolled by Rae Nell, and every time he tried to pick himself back up, it seemed he got steamrolled again.

He was still in shock from last night. He'd told Darcy he got the pictures, too stunned to mention it had been Rae Nell co-starring. Against his better judgment, he picked up his cell phone and called her again. Wondering when she planned to arrive, at the same time thinking, *There isn't enough beer or Jameson behind the bar to fortify me.*

"Yes," Rae Nell sounded extremely business-like. She didn't acknowledge it was Dickie, although she must have known.

"Rae Nell?"

"Who in the hell did you expect to answer my phone? And where in the hell are you, anyway?"

"I could ask you the same damn thing." Then he did. "Where in the hell are you?"

"What do you mean?"

"You've got all sorts of people running around with these damn lists you drew up. Apparently, I'm the one who has to make sure everything gets done. It would have been nice to have a general idea what was going on before I had to do the work. I'm busting my ass down here taking care of everything," he said, then finished with a long pull from his beer bottle.

"Look, Dickie, I've got a touch of the flu or something today. Okay? So I'm not really in the mood for your ridiculous accusations. I've worked my butt off getting nice people lined up to venture into your dingy, dreadful little saloon over the next two evenings. I think they have a right to expect that stripper trivia games and disgusting paintings of naked women won't greet them the moment they walk in the door. And if it were me, I'd be down here, making sure everything was ready when your guests arrived in…" She paused, "Two hours and twenty minutes."

"Humph. I could say the same thing to you. You set all this up, and—"

"Dickie, I've been down here working. Just where in the hell are you, anyway?"

The kitchen door suddenly pushed open.

"Jose," Rae Nell yelled, then rattled off a couple of quick sentences in Spanish.

"Si," Jose replied, shrugging, then inclined his head in Dickie's direction and rattled back a sentence or two of his own.

"Oh, God!" she screamed. Then hung up and stomped back into the main room.

"Damn it, Jose!" Dickie jumped off the stool and quickly followed.

"How long have you been here?" Dickie called, catching up to her in the middle of the floor.

"Long enough to get everything just about ready." She glared. "Look, Dickie, let's not argue. I've picked up some kind of little bug or something, and I'm not feeling at my best just now. So, if you don't mind, I'd really like to get this finished, maybe go home and soak in a hot bath before I have to come back and be on stage for your 'Big Do' tonight."

"My big…listen, Rae Nell, this is all your doing." He waved an arm that encompassed an army of workers scurrying around. "This is just another one of your typical overkill, uptight operations."

"Yes, that's right, Dickie. It is my doing. Because, as we both know, if it wasn't, if we left this up to you, it would never happen in the first place, would it? It would be the same this week, and next week, and next month, and on into next year. Absolutely nothing would get done. So yes, Dickie, you're right. I take the blame. It's all my damn fault. You're going to have a successful open house because of me. You're going to have a successful open house because I'm a bitch. A successful open house despite you!

"Now, unless you have something positive to add, maybe you could just slither back into that corner of the kitchen where you were hiding and have another beer because we're all working out here!" She had raised her voice substantially, pointing to the kitchen door like she was directing a misbehaving dog to his basket in the corner.

Everyone was suddenly giving them a lot of space.

"Okay, yeah, maybe I'll have another beer. Sure I can't get you something, pussy cat?" he said, regretting the comment before the words had crossed his lips.

She stared at him for a moment, blinking back a look of disbelief, maybe shock, maybe horror, maybe all three.

"Julius, no, let's put those glasses back there behind the bar," she said and stormed off.

"Damn it," Dickie said.

Thirty-four

arti sipped her martini, and said, "Yes, I contacted the police right after we spoke." Then
she washed the lie from her mouth with another sip of her martini.

"Well, did they tell you anything? Do they have any
ideas? What did they say?" Maureen, Dr. Craig's ever-
efficient assistant, asked. "This is just not at all like Dr.
Craig. I've had to cancel appointments for him. We've
got all sorts of things we need answers on. I'm, well, I'm
just really worried to tell you the truth."

"No need to worry, Maureen. Actually, it's just exactly like him. He does this from time to time. Usually,
when he's thinking something through," Marti said. She
was ready to strangle Craig, not to mention meddling
Maureen.

"And the police didn't have any clues or anything?
No fingerprints? A ransom note?"

"Fingerprints? Ransom note? Let's not get ahead of
ourselves or jump to any irrational conclusions," Marti

said. She was looking at the outfits laid out on her bed, debating slacks or the dress.

"Well, I mean, do you think it might be a good idea to get in touch with the television stations or newspapers, get the media involved?"

"No," Marti said, suddenly paying attention. "I think that would be the worst thing we could do, Maureen. And I know that is exactly what Craig does not want. He is purposely not contacting us because he wants to think something through. Apparently, he feels he needs some private time. So let's give it to him. Believe me, he'll eventually be in touch and act as if nothing has happened."

"Oh, I don't know. I mean, are you sure? I think—"

"Maureen, no. Let him work through whatever it is. If I hear anything, believe me, you'll be the first to know. And if you hear anything, you'll let me know, too. Right?" she asked, adding that last part, so it sounded like she actually gave a damn.

"All right, Mrs. Cullen. I suppose you know best."

'That damn Craig,' Marti thought. She was still screaming ten minutes later as she modeled her fur coat in front of the full-length mirror, staring over her shoulder at the back of the coat and blushing slightly at her memory of that dreadful photo shoot.

'What better way of moving past the embarrassment of the other afternoon than a night out,' she thought. She picked up the invitation that arrived in yesterday's mail. *"Come Break Bread..."*

The invitation had been addressed to Craig, but since he didn't have the common decency to give Marti so much as a phone call, the least she could do would be to attend in his absence.

Maureen was still worrying, and ten minutes later, she abruptly made her decision and dialed. "Yes, I wish to report a missing person."

Thirty-five

fter wondering over the last three and a half days what he was up to, DJ was finally convinced Dickie wasn't up to anything. At least anything of a nefarious nature. When it came to Dickie, what you see is what you get. For whatever reason, he had ended up in another business deal with his ex-wife. But that was the extent of it. After all, it wasn't like he was going to end up in bed with the woman. Give him some credit.

The dogs, she was walking five at the moment, were straining at their leashes, and she forced them into a tighter bunch. They were walking at a frantic pace across the Wabasha Bridge, aware that once they got to the large park area known as Harriet Island, they would receive a full brushing and some individual attention. DJ looked down from the bridge onto Dickie's houseboat. She was unable to detect the slightest hint of life. She didn't see the Jeep in the parking lot. Next door to Dickie's boat, Vernon, in what she feared might be a leopard skin Speedo, appeared to be passed out in his lawn chair. A number of empty beer cans were scattered on the deck around him.

She guessed Dickie would be working on his open house, getting ready to throw a party as only he could throw.

Despite being upset, Dickie was not beyond realizing that Rae Nell had done some serious work. There were, however, a few things he could do without, two of them being a coat and tie. He was standing toward the back of the room, close to the makeshift stage area, holding a beer bottle, the only open beer bottle in the place.

"You own this joint?" a husky voice asked from behind.

He turned to face three black guys dressed in black t-shirts, trousers, and coats, late fifties. The one who asked the question was maybe closer to seventy.

"Yeah, Dickie Mullins," he said, extending his hand.

"We're your entertainment for tonight and tomorrow," the older guy said. "The Marshall brothers. Be nice to maybe get three of those. Not really the wine type." He nodded toward Dickie's beer bottle.

"Men after my own heart. I'll get you the first ones. After that, you just help yourself."

It may have been Dickie's open house, but he sure as hell didn't know very many people. In fact, hardly anyone at all. Jose had cut the steaks according to Rae Nell's instructions from yet another manila file folder, this one in Spanish, complete with diagrams. The steak was presented on small white plates, garnished with two different sauces, elegantly served by catering staff carrying silver trays.

Dickie thought they were even more tender than the steaks he had eaten at Rae Nell's, and he had to admit things seemed to be going well.

"Hey, Dickie, great party, man."

He turned to look down on Jerry Baxter, all five-foot-four of him.

"Jerry, glad you made it. Finally, someone I know."

Although a regular, Jerry had somehow managed an invitation, possibly because he was a city inspector when he wasn't nursing his solo beer all night at the bar.

"Oh, Jerry, excuse me, there's one of my sales reps, and I've got to give her tomorrow's steak order. Hold that thought for just a minute," Dickie said and quickly rushed off to Rae Nell.

She wasn't hard to miss. It was a suffocating humid, scorching August evening, and she was the only woman in the air-conditioned bar wearing a full-length fur coat.

"Well, don't you look great," he said, checking her pupils for dilation.

"Oh, you!"

"Rae Nell, I have to say you really did it. I'm sorry I was such a jerk this afternoon, just the stress. I guess. This is all going great, all because of your planning and all the work you've done. Hey, those little sauces you had Jose make up are great, and the steaks are absolutely perfect."

"Thanks."

"Now," he said, bending down slightly to kiss her cheek. "It's almost a hundred degrees out. What's with the fur coat?"

"Yeah, I know, but I just got it, and I didn't want to wait for cold weather. Think it's too much? It's one of a kind."

"Rae Nell, I think it's absolutely gorgeous on you, but like I said, it's almost a hundred degrees."

"Well, listen, party pooper, apology accepted, and it could be a-hundred-and-ten, I don't care. I'm wearing my new coat. What?"

He was attempting to banish the images from the night before and gingerly asked, "So, where'd you get it?"

"Do you really like it? It's one of a kind. I literally just got it last night, a gift, actually. Look, it's even monogrammed," she said, opening the coat to show him.

Not exactly the answer he had wanted to hear. He had a big 'meow' on the tip of his tongue but swallowed it back down.

"It's very nice, a lovely gift. I had better go do my job and mingle."

Five minutes later, he felt a tug on his arm and turned to look into DJ's eyes.

"Hey," she said.

"Oh, man, thank you so much for coming. Finally, someone I can talk to. I can't tell you how glad I am to see you here."

"You know, I can't believe I'm going to say this, but I really missed you, Dickie."

"I missed you too, DJ. Can I get you something?"

"To tell you the truth, it's really hot out. Any chance of getting a cold beer instead of the wine they're pouring?"

"God, but you are one fantastic woman," he said and quickly returned with two cold beers.

"What's that you're drinking?" she asked, not recognizing the bottle in Dickie's hand.

"Non-alcoholic beer. The weight thing, still, I guess."

"Oh, I'm so proud of you, Dickie. Okay, just one more thing." She leaned in closer. "Who's the nutcase wearing the full-length fur coat."

Thirty-Six

If Marti noticed the cab driver's questioning look, she didn't let on. She paid her fare, stuffed the invitation for Dr. Craig Cullen and guest back into the pocket of her fur coat, and strutted into the air-conditioned comfort of the Emporium of Dance. She would have preferred showing off her one-of-a-kind gift at the Guthrie Theatre or an Ordway fundraising ball, but this would have to do.

She immediately thought, *Oh, how cute.* Whoever had done the decorating must have really researched to get just the right feel for one of those dreadfully sleazy, working-class bars. This was going to be fun. Looking around, she recognized a fair number of familiar faces from her fundraising and civic events.

Mercifully, the two martinis she'd downed before arriving served to steel her against the obviously jealous looks her fur coat generated. She quickly grabbed a white wine from a passing tray just to provide her with a little additional fortification.

A glass and a half later, she found herself talking with Rachel and Alf Wagensteen. He was a plastic surgeon specializing in facelifts and tummy tucks. She was his latest trophy wife. Marti had never been fond of Rachel or her good fortune, but Dr. Alf was rumored to be booked twelve months out, and she was determined to act graciously since one never knew. She sipped as the two of them droned on.

Marti finished her second, or was it her third glass, and was looking around for the wine tray when she spotted Rae Nell across the room. Or rather, she spotted Rae Nell's coat, an exact replica of Marti's one-of-a-kind. The coat Terry had given her. The coat she had posed naked in, on all fours and over the course of six degrading hours. From this distance, it appeared to be the exact same coat that sported black silk moiré lining and Marti's monogram.

She grabbed two glasses from a passing tray, quickly drained one, snatched another, and began sipping aggressively. After another double-fisted round, Marti abruptly turned and walked in the direction of the fur-covered usurper, storming off just as Dr. Alf was about to deliver the punch line to some inane joke.

"…and so, when Dickie called and asked for my help, well, I just couldn't say no." Rae Nell delicately sipped a little wine and smiled at the small crowd before she continued, "Over the years, I've had the good fortune to be involved in a number of business opportunities. This location was purchased with the idea of tearing it down, starting over from scratch, and creating a destination dining establishment. Tonight is the beginning of the next phase."

She didn't think she sounded that outlandish to warrant the looks of disbelief.

"I think there's someone who wants to talk to you." A woman with purple teeth nodded over Rae Nell's shoulder then drained her glass of red wine.

Rae Nell turned to see a glassy-eyed woman grab a glass from the passing tray then stagger toward her, nightmare-like, wrapped in a full-length cinnamon-colored fur coat, a carbon copy of the one Terry had draped over naked Rae Nell less than twenty-four hours earlier. Suddenly, she was a big wild cat again, only this time, her claws were out.

Both women stared at each other, slowly, cautiously circling, looking the other up and down in undisguised disgust, blind to everything and every individual around them, focused only on the interloper standing opposite.

"Where'd you get that?" Marti pointed with her glass and sloshed wine toward Rae Nell. There was the slightest slur in her speech. She followed with a very large gulp and glared over the rim.

Rae Nell took the high ground.

"Good evening, I don't believe we've met. I'm Rae Nell, Dickie's hostess. And you are?" She extended her hand, eyes dripping insincerity, an icy edge to her smile as she stepped forward.

"Oh, no you don't, sweetheart." Marti circled to her left with a slight stagger. She wrapped both arms around her fur as if she were cold. Wine sloshed down her sleeve.

"I asked where *you* got that?"

Rae Nell angled her head as if to correct a wayward child and looked down with a cold smile.

"I can assure you, this coat is one of a kind. It was presented to me as a gift very recently. It's even monogrammed," she said, then opened the coat to display the monogram, three white letters, RMN, offset by a subtle, darker off-white shadow stitched on black, silk moiré lining. "I've even got this special designer tag. See, dear," she said, flipping the left cuff back to reveal the black leather studded dog collar. "My tag happens to be number one, and then here, if you could read, made especially for Rae Nell Mullins."

Like a gunfighter getting ready to draw, Marti slowly opened her coat and revealed the same black, silk moiré lining with her own MCC monogram, in the exact same script, with the same subtle, darker off-white shadow.

"Well, isn't that interesting. It would appear your coat is monogrammed something like mine." She took two steps forward and flipped her left sleeve back. "I'm afraid I actually have number one, dear," she said, although, without her glasses, she was unable to really see. "Just where did *you* get that?" Marti pointed with her glass and sloshed another wave over the rim.

A growing crowd surrounded the women, straining to pick up the words hissing between them. Dr. Alf Wagensteen repeatedly gave the slit throat sign, attempting to get the Marshall Brothers to cut their rendition of, *'I only have eyes for you.'*

The two women continued to circle one another slowly, Marti glaring, Rae Nell smiling a little too sweetly.

"I can assure you," Marti sneered as Rae Nell deftly dodged more sloshed wine, "this garment is a unique, one of a kind. As a matter of fact, I've been chosen to be the model and spokeswoman for the line. We just kicked off a national advertising campaign yesterday. I was in a photoshoot the entire day."

"The line? And exactly what line would that be?" Rae Nell countered.

"Ciao furs! I happen to know the CEO on a rather *personal* level," Marti added heavily, leaving no mistake, she wasn't just talking an email address.

"Chow? Furs?" Rae Nell repeated, asking herself the question out loud.

"Well, I knew you wouldn't have a clue. You have a lot of nerve wearing that coat here." Marti celebrated her victory by draining her glass.

"Chow Furs?" Rae Nell questioned. "C-H-O-W?" She spelled it out, unable to believe what she was hearing.

"Oh, God, I don't believe it. How stupid. No, of course not. No, C-I-A-O. It's Italian, dear. You've obviously purchased a knock-off," Marti bluffed, suddenly feeling a little unsure of herself. "As I said, I'm a very, *very* close friend of the CEO. As a matter of fact—"

"This very, very close friend of yours, the CEO?" hissed Rae Nell. "He wouldn't happen to be a balding football player named Terry? Likes to holler, 'take me to the finish line,' when the two of you are on that oh so *personal* level?"

The color drained from Marti's face. Her shoulders slumped, arms suddenly limp at her side, and she let her glass fall to the floor.

"You, you know, Terry?"

"He is a very, *very* close friend of mine, too," Rae Nell said. She leaned forward and hissed. "As a matter of fact, as recently as last night. I think it's time for you to leave," she said, sounding neither smug nor vicious. Then she walked into the kitchen, peeled off her coat, and tossed it on a stack of wine cases. When she returned, Marti was nowhere to be seen.

"That was interesting. You sure know how to throw one helluva a party. Now tell me that wasn't staged," the woman with purple teeth said.

"I don't know," Dickie said. "She just seemed to come out of nowhere. Suddenly, there the two of them were, circling in their fur coats, ready to claw each other's eyes out. It was pretty obvious they'd both been seeing the same guy."

"Oh, stop laughing," DJ said, then slapped Dickie on the chest and rolled back on top of him.

"I'm so sorry for getting mad at you, but every time your ex-wife comes into the picture, you end up getting a raw deal. I've just never seen her until tonight, and it was just like you always say, a disaster of her own making. God, I honestly thought at any moment they were going to attack each other."

"You didn't recognize the other woman?" Dickie asked.

"No, never saw her before. Older, classy if she hadn't been so drunk, maybe attractive, in that plastic-surgeon way. I mean, if anyone can look classy and attractive wearing a fur coat in August."

"Plastic-surgeon way?"

"You know, a facelift, Botox, nips, and tucks, that deal. I think some items were fake if that translates."

"Fake? Who cares?" he said dismissively.

"Oh, Dickie, God!"

Thirty-seven

After firing her glass against the pantry wall to make her point, Marti gulped a giant sip of martini directly from the silver shaker, and shouted into her phone, "You can just come over here and get your 'one-of-a-kind' fur coat, you bastard. It's out on my front lawn."

"Look, I told you before. She works for me. She's a sales rep for one of my divisions. Yeah, she has a fur coat, but first off, the coat ain't the quality of yours. Second, she really had to earn it." Taggert cringed and thought, *That didn't come out exactly the way I thought it would.*

"I'm aware of how she earned the coat," Marti screamed. "She had no problem telling me and everyone else there exactly how very, *very* personal she was with you. Take me to the finish line!" she screamed into the phone. I'm going to have Craig pull out every last dollar we've invested in you, just as soon as I talk with him. You'll wish you never, ever, two-timed me with that tramp, you, you bastard!" She hung up and threw her phone in the general direction of her shattered martini glass.

"Trouble in paradise?" Luther asked, looking up from the flat screen.

"I think maybe I've let this Marti bitch get a little out of hand. We should probably deal with it right now, tonight, before she has a chance to do any damage."

"What can she do?" Luther asked.

"I'm not sure. I don't want to take a chance she starts asking more questions or calls the cops looking for her husband. We just don't need the hassle. Too bad. She could have been a lot of fun, but better safe than sorry."

"Tonight?" Luther asked.

"Yeah, probably the sooner, the better. We get there in the next hour, and she'll let me in, even if it's just to yell. We won't have to bypass any security systems. Just grab her and dispose of her on the processing line like we did with her old man. What are you running tomorrow?"

"Sausage." Luther grinned

Marti staggered to the door after five minutes of pounding, looking worse than Taggert could have imagined. Her hair was limp and greasy looking. She was draped in a ratty blue, terrycloth robe, slightly askew, one side hanging lower than the other. She wore just one slipper with some fuzzy feathers on top of the thing. Her eyes were red and puffy. Thick black mascara had run a good half-inch beneath each eye then tracked down her cheeks. Her skin looked pasty and pale, and her breath was solid 100-proof.

"Well, shit, come on in and join the pity party." She paused, weaving against the door before swinging it open, then staggered back into the kitchen. "If you're lookin' for that damn coat, you can just go ahead and take it." She pointed toward the staircase with her silver martini shaker. As she pointed, an inch-long ash dropped from her cigarette onto the cream-colored carpet. "I dragged it out of the front yard and left it upstairs, somewhere, I think. Too bad, but I already cut the sleeves off. It's August, ya know?" she said, then backpedaled three steps to maintain her balance.

The kitchen lights were dimmed. An empty vodka bottle lay on its side in the sink. Another stood on the kitchen counter, two-thirds full. A plate of scrambled eggs stabbed by a roughly-centered cigarette sat on the granite counter.

The room smelled stale and rank. Everything, including Marti, was in need of a good cleaning. She took a final long drag off her cigarette, blew smoke out her nose, and tossed the butt in the kitchen sink where it hissed. It continued to smolder, and a brown stain slowly crept across the white porcelain.

Taggert stood with his hands in his pockets and attempted to look sufficiently sheepish.

"Make ya one?" Marti took a long sip from the martini shaker, attempting to focus with bleary eyes. "You bastard, how could you do this to me? To me! She younger than me? Is that it?" She unsuccessfully attempted to brush her hair off the side of her face using the silver shaker. "What? You can tell me. The whole damn city knows by now. You and your one-of-a-kind fur coats. Who else has one? You know what you are? You're a liar, and a real bastard, too. Wait 'til I tell my husband when he gets home. Craig will sue your ass off. You know that? Just you wait." She followed up with another long, deep swallow from the shaker.

If Taggert had been under any illusions as to exactly how this scenario was going to play out, her threat quickly convinced him he had no other choice. He tuned everything out, the room, the smell, Marti, her ranting, and he concentrated on the end result.

"… had just one ounce of decency, you, you bastard, just a shred of human decency, you would know what an absolute …"

He had expected her to simply to go down with the punch. But it had been delivered with such force, and he had never hit a hundred-and-eleven-pound woman that hard before. He stood there a little surprised at the sheer physics of the blow.

She didn't go down. Instead, she launched off the kitchen floor like a rocket, picking up speed as she traveled, hitting her head against the cabinet. A misty plume of blood erupted behind her. She seemed to hang there for a moment before tracking a bloody smear down the front of the chrome refrigerator door and settling motionless on the kitchen floor. Her chin rested on her chest.

Blood seeped out from her shattered mouth, down her chin, and soaked into the lapels of her robe.

He looked at her lying motionless for a few moments, then did a little victory dance with his arms raised over his head. He went to the front door and waved Luther inside.

"Holy shit, man," Luther said, checking her neck for a pulse and finding none. He paused to grab her left breast before standing.

"Hmm-mmm, fakes. Man, what'd you use, a baseball bat? Better wrap her up in a couple of trash bags. You touch anything?"

"Just the front door," Taggert said, opening and closing his right hand. It didn't even hurt. He replayed the way she had sailed and marveled at the force he could still deliver.

"Let's get out of here," Luther said, shaking out a large green trash bag. He pulled the bag over Marti's head, then hoisted her up over his shoulder, slapped her across her rear, and carried her out.

Thirty-eight

D ickie shook his head and said, "Look, Darcy, I'm not trying to be a pain in the ass. I'll get it to you, okay? Relax, I told you I got the shot. I just want to make sure it's all professional and everything. Make sure there's no mistaking your boy in this thing."

"When will that be? I need this thing like yesterday. By the way, any idea who the broad is?"

"No, no idea. Actually, you really don't see her face, but I'd put her mid to late thirties. And your boy is really coming on to her. Then there's the money shot. He's groaning something about a finish line. She eventually rolls off and out of range, but he's just lying there, no mistaking him. You got him by the old short and curly's, Darcy."

"Maybe I should just come over and look at it. Maybe she's from some escort service or something," Darcy suggested.

"The DVD isn't here. I've already got it over at the lab being enhanced," Dickie lied, staring at the DVD sitting next to a yogurt container on his kitchen counter.

"Enhanced, damn it, that could be construed as tampering with evidence. I'm not…"

"Darcy, this isn't going into the courtroom. You show your client this, and the guy is out of there immediately. There's no question what's going on, okay? So relax. I'll get this to you as soon as possible, but we want to do it right."

"You sure? Because I could—"

"Yes, I'm sure, and no, you can't. Hey, Darcy, you're breaking up. I'll get to you as soon as I got something."

"Well, just make sure—"

Dickie clicked his phone off and wondered how he was going to eliminate Rae Nell from the DVD. At least the portion where she was identifiable. He couldn't do it himself. Christ, he was barely capable of playing the damn DVD, let alone erasing anything. No, that task would fall to DJ. He just had to figure out how he was going to get her to do it.

* * *

Jerry Baxter slept fitfully that night, revisited by nightmares he hadn't had in years. He was a young soldier again, 1968, barely a week before the Tet Offensive. He was out with two pals and three bar girls they'd paid to entertain them on their weekend leave. They were in a little apartment, eating, drinking, and screwing their brains out. Eating again until, in his dream, that's all they did was eat. Eat until they were stuffed, and then in they came with still more food until Jerry begged them to stop.

That brought another plate of food, only this time, the plate had dog collars on it. Then another plate, this one stacked with piles of little dog ears and little dog noses. He woke, sweating, gasping for breath, getting his bearings. It was three in the morning on his glowing green digital. He licked his lips— dog, that's what it was at the Emporium of Dance, dog meat.

Thirty-nine

Esperonza de Casteon had been cleaning homes for twelve years. She'd been cleaning Craig and Marti Cullen's for the last eight of those twelve years. She thought it was a little unusual that the front door was unlocked, but it had happened once or twice before. She was surprised to see the cigarette ash on the hallway carpet. Marti was always so fastidious, but then accidents did happen. It was when she got to the kitchen that she knew something was very wrong.

She had just set her purse on the kitchen counter and was going to place her lunch in the refrigerator like she did every Thursday. She looked at the vodka bottle in the sink. Another open bottle sat on the counter. A plate with a mound of half-eaten scrambled eggs sat next to the bottle. A cigarette butt stood upright in the middle of the eggs.

Then she saw the blood on the floor. Not a large pool but enough to give one pause, a crusted, black puddle, smeared, and about the size of a salad plate. In slow motion, she looked from the puddle on the floor to the refrigerator, followed the bloody smear up the chrome front of the refrigerator door, stopping at the spray of dark, congealed blood across the door of the cabinet and the kitchen ceiling.

She stood very still and studied the spray. She cautiously moved her eyes left and right, ears perked for the slightest noise, praying to her lord and savior Jesus Christ that she was alone in the house. She carefully gathered up her purse in both hands, left her lunch on the granite counter, and made a beeline for the front door.

The first police squad responded ninety minutes later. Esperonza hadn't phoned them until she had reached the safety of her own home far across town. Now in the early afternoon, she was sitting in her husband's recliner, legs stretched out, a rum and coke in her hand, telling a female officer for the fourth or fifth time exactly what she had seen.

Forty

ickie arrived at the Emporium of Dance a little before one. The previous night seemed to have been a success, and he wanted to make sure tonight was no less. He walked into the kitchen and stepped around a stack of cases emblazoned with the red *Chow Industries* logo. An invoice taped to the top box stated net payment due in thirty-days and listed a fifty-pound box of sausages at 'no charge.' Dickie had to hand it to Rae Nell. This time, it looked like she had picked a real winner.

The idea of Rae Nell reminded him of the DVD and exactly what tact he would take with DJ to get her to erase the tattoo image for him. He decided he would tell her the client wanted to clean the thing up for the courtroom.

DJ arrived for their late lunch looking happy in cut-offs, a t-shirt, and a Twins cap. She reached up and gave him a big hug, then lingered with a deep, probing kiss.

"You seem in a good mood. The dogs didn't bite any little old lady on your walk?"

"I'd make them bite you, but I wouldn't want them to catch anything."

He had Jose prepare two small steaks and two of the sausages from Chow Meats, so he could see what they were like.

"Mmm-mmm, not bad," Dickie chewed, contemplating the unique flavor.

"I don't know. It just seems to taste a little different to me," DJ said, pushing pieces of meat around her plate. "I thought the same thing last night but didn't want to say anything. It's not bad. It's just, I don't know, different." She pushed the sausage to the side of her plate and set her fork down.

"Mmm-mmm, seems okay to me but definitely unique." He inserted another large piece of sausage into his mouth and chewed.

"Course, how would you know? You've got the thing smothered in sauce. You've crammed garlic mushrooms into your mouth with it. Pretty tough not to like anything under those circumstances."

"Listen, DJ. I've been working on this case for a guy. Apparently, a philandering husband screwing around."

"Isn't that redundant?"

"I suppose so." He considered for a moment, not wanting to look like he was blurting something out. "Can you adjust some images for me off a DVD?"

"Probably, but wouldn't that be considered illegal? Making it look like something that didn't happen."

"Well, it would be if that was what I wanted to do, but it's not. I just want you to erase a small portion, a birthmark, or something in an image. I'm not sure what it is. Anyway, it's still obvious the guy is with a woman who isn't his wife, by about fifty years."

"Is your client the wife?" DJ asked.

"Not exactly. My client is actually the wife's attorney. Same thing, only different. And, I wasn't kidding, the wife is an older woman, and this chick, well, she certainly isn't an older woman. I want to clean this thing up a bit, make it better, but not alter anything. You know?"

"Can you go through it with me, show me what you want eliminated?"

"I can tell you sitting here. There's a point where the guy's in bed, waiting for her. She's just out of camera range, throwing her clothes at him. Then she crawls into bed with him. There's a birthmark or something on her butt. I want that removed," he said like it was no big deal.

"Jesus, nice job. How do you get into these things?"

"Are you going to finish that?" he asked, ignoring her question. He stabbed her sausage with his fork and placed it on his plate.

"I've never tasted sausage like this, really different."

Forty-one

ae Nell could feel her temper rising, knowing she had to keep it in check. "Look, Terry. We're both adults here. If you had or even have a relationship with that woman, it's really none of my business. I mean, I get it, no big deal. I just wanted to know, that's all. We should be able to trust one another and, well, you can imagine my surprise when she showed up with the exact same 'one-of-a-kind' coat as mine, that's all. I mean, maybe she was your earlier sales rep. I don't know. God, she even had that same little leather tag with the number one on it."

Taggert rolled his eyes and thought, *God damn it,* then heard his voice weaseling.

"Look, she's a bit of a flake. Her husband got wind of our line of furs and put some pressure on one of the other board members to get a coat for an anniversary or birthday or something. Let me see now. I think the monograms were done by the same company, same style, maybe even the same colors, but the similarities stop there. Well, except for the damn little tag. Now, yours is actually the first. Hers, well, it's just the first one purchased, that's all. The coat you have is a much higher quality, worth about twice as much. Just don't tell her." He laughed then waited for Rae Nell to pick up on the good news.

She didn't.

"So, when I repeated a line to her last night that you always shout when you're about to consummate our little get-togethers, and she knew what I meant, I should ignore that, too? Was it just a lucky guess? Because she certainly looked like she knew what in the hell I was talking about."

"Jesus, baby," he scrambled, deciding to try another path and cursing all women for remembering such trivial things.

"I really appreciate the work you're doing for me. That's why I gave you that top-of-the-line, one-of-a-kind coat as a bonus. I thought you would be pleased. If you're unhappy with it, hell, go ahead and return the damn thing. I want our business and personal relationship to continue. But you've got to understand. I'm an international businessman. I'm involved in a lot of deals, got irons in a lot of fires, baby. Even if this was the first, it probably won't be the last time you run into someone who's worked with me or someone who wants to pretend they worked with me. I get that all the time."

"Irons in the fire? Work with you? Is that what it's called? Gee, I guess I'll have to update. I trusted you. I thought we had something special…"

He didn't hang-up. He just put the phone down and walked away.

Forty-two

The first of the guests had begun to arrive. Dickie just happened to glance out the front window and watched as the navy blue Crown Victoria took its time and parked directly across the street. The tires were black, no white wall, and a dead giveaway. Two crew cuts emerged, detectives. Dickie knew one of them, Dexter something or other, worked homicide.

Dexter buttoned his sport coat. The coat was an off-green and burgundy plaid and looked like it had been pulled off a sick Scotsman.

The other guy stood a full head taller, maybe ten years younger than Dexter. He wore a coat made up of intersecting black and gray lines. Lean, solid-looking, with an 'S' shape to the bridge of his nose, possibly suggesting occasional past difficulty with interpersonal relationships.

Dickie watched as they dodged traffic crossing the street and then moved to meet them coming in the front door. "Hey, Dex." He extended his hand. "You checking liquor licenses now?"

"Yeah, I only wish. Dickie, my partner Kenny Cosgrove. Kenny, Dickie Mullins. Dickie here used to be on the force. That is until he faked a disability, getting capped in his fat ass. Dickie, how you doing?"

"Dex, if I was any happier, I'd be on welfare. Things are going pretty well. Look, can I get you guys some steak? Come on, you gotta try it. Really good, if I do say so. How 'bout a glass of wine, beer, or something?"

Cosgrove had not done much more than nod and was scanning the crowd as more and more people began to filter in.

"Look, Dickie, maybe just a word. We're on a missing person, suspicious circumstances. Actually, we're looking for your ex. She around, Rae Nell Mullins?"

Dexter said her name as if Dickie had a pack of ex-wives.

"Yeah, somewhere. She in some kind of trouble, Dex?"

"Nah, no trouble, just a couple of questions, mostly just background information on an individual. Like to keep it as quiet as possible. Know what I mean?" He lowered his voice and gave a knowing nod.

Dickie figured he knew exactly what was meant and planned to move cautiously.

"Guys, she's here. I just saw her a few minutes ago. Let me see if I can find her. I can tell you she was here virtually all of yesterday from about noon until sometime well after midnight, working her ass off. Probably a hundred people saw her and spoke with her over that period of time if that helps at all. Look, why don't you guys grab a little steak to sample and let me find her for you? I'll bring her over," he added for good measure before quickly stepping away.

"… well, she had obviously been drinking long before she arrived—"

"Rae Nell, excuse me," Dickie said, aggressively grabbing an elbow and steering her away from the assembled group. A number of women flashed their eyes back and forth.

"Dickie, Jesus." Rae Nell attempted to pull her arm from Dickie's iron grip as he manhandled her through the kitchen door. "Will you let go? Jesus, stop, you're hurting me. Dickie, stop it." She raised her voice and yanked her arm away. She wore a sundress, white with large red polka dots, two of which were positioned precisely over her breasts.

"Take it easy. This is nothing compared to what the two homicide detectives by the front door may do to you."

"What?"

"They're here looking for you, Rae Nell. What's going on? Listen, if you're in trouble, let's get an attorney for you. You got about thirty seconds to make a decision before they come in here for you."

"Oh, please, will you stop being so dramatic, Dickie. What, I'm not paying enough attention to you tonight?

Look, I'm here working your damn party. So stop embarrassing me and let me get back to work. Okay? Good lord." She rolled her eyes.

"You know, Rae Nell, it's times like these you'll never hear me complain about our divorce. What? No fur coat tonight?" he said and immediately regretted uttering the words.

She looked at him for a long moment, shook her head in disgust, gave out an exasperated "Oh!" and then pushed through the swinging kitchen door, greeting the first couple she saw.

"Well, hello, thanks so much for coming…"

Dickie did a slow count to ten, continued on to twenty before looking for Dexter and Cosgrove. He found them, plates heaped with steak and sauces, stuffing themselves.

"Dickie, I gotta tell you…mmm-mmm, this stuff is great, man, and this sausage, really different, but I like it. What do you think, Cos?"

Cosgrove nodded. "Mmm-mmm, Rae Nell Mullins?" he asked with his mouth full.

"Yeah, she was just finishing up with some people, but look, I'm sure she'll be happy to answer any questions you'd have. That's her over there in the red and white polka dot sundress, the blonde, just brushing her hair back. She's all yours. Help yourself. Might as well just jump in. Otherwise, she'll be chatting with people all night."

He caught DJ near the door with a wave, and she joined him, giving him a peck on the cheek, then asked, "Who were those two guys?"

"Homicide Detectives. Looking for Rae Nell."

They watched as Dexter and Cosgrove wove their way through the crowd toward Rae Nell.

"Homicide Detectives?" DJ's shriek turned heads in the immediate vicinity.

"Look, now you know as much as I do."

"Homicide? You mean, like murder?"

"That's one of the areas they deal with, yeah. Dexter, the one in the ugly coat, said they had some general questions for her on a missing person case."

"General questions? Suspicious, murder, gee, go figure." Her eyes riveted on the two detectives next to Rae Nell.

"It's probably someone she knows, and they're just trying to confirm employment or next of kin. Maybe a friend of hers who left town to visit a family member and some nosey old bag neighbor had a panic attack," he said, but his tone didn't sound convincing.

"Which one did you say is Dexter?"

"The ugly sport coat."

"Which one is that?"

Forty-three

Darcy had left numerous messages throughout the day with Metro Liquor Sales, wondering just who the hell they thought they were—charging his corporate credit card for over thirty cases of wine as recently as yesterday. He feared some form of identity theft was in progress and had spent the better part of the day changing all his credit cards, personal and corporate bank accounts, not to mention dozens of computer passwords and various security programs.

He was currently on hold with American Express, steaming at the over twenty-minute wait while they checked his audio passwords and searched his account for questionable transactions over the past two billing cycles. He was an hour late for Dickie's open house. He hung up the phone in sheer exasperation and stormed out of his office.

"Darcy," Dickie called twenty minutes later and waved.

"Don't say anything about that DVD you're working on," he said under his breath to DJ.

"Darcy, DJ, DJ, Darcy Dalton, esquire," Dickie joked. His arm was wrapped around DJ's waist, glad for her support.

"Hi." DJ nodded as she shook Darcy's hand.

"Darcy's an attorney I do work for occasionally. How's it going?" Dickie asked, scanning the crowd, not seeing Rae Nell or the two homicide detectives.

"Don't even ask," Darcy said with an animated sigh.

"Problem?"

"I'm afraid all my office, and maybe all my personal systems have been compromised. I've been on the phone all day with about a dozen different banks, my internet provider, a couple of security consultants who aren't worth a shit. Christ, don't even mention the credit card companies. I'm worried about everything from trust accounts to personal identity theft. And no one, I mean no one, can give me a straight answer."

"It shouldn't be all that hard to figure out," DJ interjected.

"You've really no idea," Darcy replied, looking down her blouse.

"Actually, she does. She's a real geek. Writes all sorts of software and shit," Dickie said absently, still scanning the room for Rae Nell.

"God, I could sure use your help," Darcy whined, then in a rare moment of honesty, declared, "I have no earthly idea what in the hell I'm doing. They've got me scanning my systems, deleting things, reinstalling software. Now everything is totally screwed up. I crashed the entire office system and just gave up and came over here. I think someone's stolen my identity. Nothing's working, and my credit cards have all sorts of charges on them. Are you free tomorrow?"

"Well, maybe. Yeah, I guess I could be. What systems do you have?" she asked.

Darcy wore a blanker than normal look on his face before replying.

"How would I know? I mean, I don't have the foggiest idea. I just turn the stupid things on, and they work. I think they're Hewlett-Packard."

"No, what kind of system? Not the hardware itself." DJ chuckled.

"Can't you just come to my office tomorrow?"

"Yeah, okay. I'll be there." She laughed.

"Thank you."

"Listen, DJ, get Mr. Computer here lined up with some steak samples. I've got to check on someone, and I'll join you in a few minutes."

Dickie left to search for Rae Nell. His worst fears seemed to be confirmed when he couldn't find her anywhere. He checked the kitchen to no avail but saw her car in the parking lot, and the Crown Victoria was gone from across the street. He was afraid the detectives might have been looking for a little more than employment confirmation.

Forty-four

Rae Nell poured a little cream into the coffee when Cosgrove nodded then slid the cup across the table. "I'm not sure I should even be talking to you without a lawyer present. I mean, you see how this goes bad for someone all the time on TV. Are you guys planning to arrest me?" she asked.

She sat on the inside, next to Dexter. Cosgrove was directly across the restaurant booth. He nodded thanks to the coffee cup, then shot a quick glance at Dexter to continue while Rae Nell seemed preoccupied with sugar packets.

"You see, Miss Mullins, we aren't considering you as a suspect."

They watched for any kind of body language from her.

"God, wouldn't you know they don't have the sweetener I like," she said.

"Do you know a man by the name of Craig Cullen?"

"No, that doesn't ring a bell."

"He's an investor at Chow Industries."

"No, I really only know Terry. My boss, Terry Taggert."

"How are you paid?"

"Hmm? Oh," she said, taking a sugar packet. "To tell the truth, right now I'm really not getting much more than expenses, but I'll be getting ten-percent of sales. That's based on monthly sales, payable the tenth of the following month."

"Is it working?" Cosgrove asked.

"I really just started at Chow, so I can't tell you. In fact, this open house is my first event. It's funny, my first order came from Dickie."

"Your husband?" Cosgrove asked, slurping coffee.

"He's my ex-husband," Rae Nell said, quick to correct. "I thought if we could turn around his dinner business, well, it could be a great testimonial for Chow Industries."

"So, that's why your ex-husband had the open house last night and tonight?" Dexter asked.

"Yeah, we're introducing our steak as a menu change, hoping to upgrade both the clientele and the food. Of course, it's a little like which came first, the chicken or the egg. Speaking of the open house, I really should be getting back there. See, not only did I bring in the steaks, but I ordered the wine, got the jazz combo, not to mention put the guest list together. You should have seen the place before we shoveled it out. I mean, what a dive."

"How well does your husband, sorry, ex-husband, know Mr. Taggert?"

"Terry? I don't think Dickie has ever met him. In fact, I'm sure of it. Terry's very busy. He's in and out of here with all his traveling and football team and everything. I'm lucky I get to see him at all," she said, thankful she hadn't worn her fur coat. *First, that dreadful drunken woman and now the police. What next?*

"Football team?" asked Cosgrove.

"Yes, the New Orleans's Saints or Sinners. I can never remember. Terry's the quarterback. At least he was before that injury. Now he's been back and forth between doctors, getting x-rayed, and all sorts of therapy. Nothing short of amazing if you ask me."

"Quarterback? For the Saint's, the NFL football team? He told you that?" Dexter asked, unable to hide his surprise.

"Told me? He showed me his jersey." She scoffed, not adding she'd slept in the jersey more than once. She knew these cops wouldn't believe her even if she told them, so why bother? God, the two of them, no imagination whatsoever.

"What is all this about, anyway? Is Dickie in trouble?"

She didn't add '*again.*' Leave it to Dickie to do something stupid just as the open house was going to turn things around for him, not to mention kick-start her sales. God, she felt like strangling that idiot.

"No, he's not in any trouble."

"How about Marti Cullen. Do you know her?"

"No, I don't think I've ever heard of her."

"We have reason to believe she was at the open house last night. I guess you had words with her."

"No, I'd remember something like…wait a minute, was she the woman in the fur coat?"

"Fur coat?"

"Yeah, she was wearing this fur coat. Started accusing me—"

"A fur coat, last night? It was ninety-eight degrees out, and she had a fur coat on?"

The detectives looked at one another.

"Yes, I think she was pretty intoxicated. I just chalked it up to that. She left shortly after we spoke. I'm sure she's probably very nice when she's not drinking. Hey, I really should be getting back."

"Look, Miss Mullins, we'd like it if this conversation was just kept between us, okay? No sense in getting anyone upset," Dexter said.

"Yeah," added Cosgrove, "one of the things we do is make sure big football stars, like your Mr. Taggart, aren't dealing with any undue pressure. You know, gambling or whatever. We're just looking out for everyone's welfare."

"Gambling? Do you mean like horse racing and betting? No way. Terry has been nothing but honest and generous with me," she said, thinking, *That idiot Dickie somehow put Terry and me together.*

"Look, if you gentlemen don't mind, I really must get back. I've got a restaurant full of people I have to deal with. Do you have any other questions?"

Dexter looked at Cosgrove, working at holding back his grin.

"No, I don't think so. We'll give you a ride back. Thanks again for taking the time and for being so honest."

"Yeah, thanks," added Cosgrove.

They drove her back to the open house and then watched her from the car as she hurried inside.

"Do you think she's really that dumb?" Dexter asked.

"Just the way you like them, pretty and stupid. Quarterback for the Saints, Jesus," Cosgrove chuckled.

Forty-five

Dickie was rubbing shoulders with at least three hundred people, the privileged and pompous of Rae Nell's sanctified strata, and he had no idea who any of them were. They were happily inhaling pound after pound of free food and lapping up gallons of expensive wine Dickie had charged to Darcy's credit card. DJ had wandered off with some computer geek she had introduced him to earlier, but he couldn't remember what the guy's name had been.

He had dodged Jerry Baxter twice already, pretty sure he remembered dodging Jerry last night as well. He was looking around for Rae Nell, wishing he had his hands around the neck of a cold bottle of beer. Suddenly, there was a tug at his shoulder.

"Hoo-rah, locked, loaded, and ready to go, Chief," Jerry Baxter shouted into Dickie's ear, then gave him a sloppy salute that left a smear of meat sauce on the right side of his forehead. He was weaving and wild-eyed, a complete contradiction to the quiet, mild-mannered city inspector who showed up three nights a week to nurse the same beer for two hours.

"Say, Jerry." Dickie looked around, smiling while everyone within fifteen feet stared back. "I think you better take it a little easy there, buddy. How about we get you a nice spacer, maybe a coke or a coffee or something?" He attempted to steer Jerry past the bar.

"They'll be coming over the wire, man. Lock and load, baby. Lock and load." He glanced around at the crowd. "You better get these civilians out of here. It's gonna get heavy. Shit's gonna hit the fan."

"Here's some coffee, Jerry," Dickie said, quickly pulling the plate out of Jerry's hand, steering him by the elbow out the back door and toward the large green dumpster.

"Maybe finish your coffee out here, Jerry, and try to cool down. You know, it might be a good idea if you head home once you're finished. Been a long day for all of us, okay?" He handed a mug to Jerry and didn't wait for an answer but went back inside to the air-conditioned comfort.

Rae Nell was suddenly there, directing the catering staff to replenish the meat trays, looking more nervous with every step Dickie took in her direction.

"Rae Nell, can we talk for a minute? I want to—"

"No, not now, Dickie. No, we can't talk. And, for your information, 'Mr. Pry-into-my-personal-life', I don't think it was very nice of you to send two of your old cop pals out to steer me away from Terry."

"Huh?"

"Huh?" She mimicked. "Yeah, that's always the way it goes, isn't it? 'No problem. I'm Dickie. I'll just play dumb. Who'll know the difference?' Well, I got news for you, Buster. I'm not going to Stand. For. It." She spit the words through clenched teeth, emphasizing the last three with a violent shake of the food tray.

"Huh?"

"Oh, that's right." She drew up close, eyes flashing, hissing just loud enough so only he could hear. "Go ahead and continue to act dumb because you know what? You are dumb. Stay out of my private life, you! And you can just forget about whatever scam you've got cooked up! I've got half a mind to tell Terry to pull the plug on you right now, and you can go back to your dreary little pick-up bar, and your shitty houseboat and your— oh, never mind. Just get out of my way!" She barged past him, attempting to slice his arm with the edge of the catering tray.

Forty-Six

Helen Hardy had narrowed her decision down to two. Her eyes flashed, her pulse quickened, and her face flushed ever so slightly. Her breathing grew a bit more rapid. She eyed the German, looking sleek and classy. In fact, almost tasteful were it not for the perverse act she wanted performed.

The American, clearly heavier, a more vicious or savage appearance, but then that was what she was looking for. The American suited her mood perfectly. Forget the deft touch, that had its time and place to be sure, but just now, she needed one capable of giving a real pounding.

She made her decision, dismissing the German for another time with a simple shake of her head. She grabbed the crosshatched grips of the American Colt .45. It was like gripping some fossilized, prehistoric, scaly reptile. The weapon's heft left no doubt to the damage it was capable of inflicting, and she seemed to remember one of her late husband's comments.

"Accurate up to fifteen feet."

Barely beyond handshake distance, although Helen had no doubt she wanted to be a lot closer than fifteen feet when she pulled the trigger.

She wanted to hear the round hit. She wanted to see the fist-sized hole where muscle and tissue had been a nanosecond before she fired. She wanted to be purified in the blood mist of his wound. Wanted to be close enough to hear his final gasp for air. Close enough to watch through the gun smoke when Terry Taggert dropped to the ground at her feet.

"I'll take this one," she said to the clerk on the other side of the counter.

Forty-seven

Dickie crammed a large foil-covered container of steak into his refrigerator and held a beer bottle over his shoulder toward DJ and asked, "So, did you like it?"

"Umm-mmm, thanks."

"Well, did you like the food or not?"

"Yeah, it was okay," she said, twisting the cap off her bottle.

"Okay? That was about five-grand worth of 'okay' we went through in the last two nights. It was just okay?"

"Well, like I said this noon… to be honest, the meat had a bit of funny taste, not unpleasant actually, just, I don't know, different. Maybe gamey?"

"Maybe gamey? But not unpleasant? That's helpful. Would you go back for more?"

"I don't know." She gulped some beer. "I'm obviously in the minority here. A lot of people were eating a lot of steak."

"Yeah, but it was free. Would you pay for it and want to come back again?"

"Probably not, but then I'm not a steak person. Would you go back?"

"Yep. I liked it from the first bite I had," he said, shaking his head as the dinner at Rae Nell's flashed across his mind. "I thought it was pretty good. You got to give it an 'A' in the tender department. I suppose I need to contact Rae Nell and see what's next."

"What did she say?"

"Oh, last time I talked to her, she was stressed out just working the party. Not making that much sense. You know, it's one of the many things I don't miss about her."

"Speaking of not making sense," DJ said, retreating from anything to do with Rae Nell. "What was the deal with your little friend with the beard? I saw you steer him out the back door. Is he some kind of old burnout or something?"

"Yeah, that was weird. Jerry Baxter, he's in about three nights a week, nurses the same beer all night. He's never any trouble. He keeps to himself, doesn't ever say much. He was wigging out. I don't know, maybe flashbacks or some damn thing from Viet Nam the way he was talking about lock and load and stuff. Of course, the poor guy works for the city. That's bound to drive anyone nuts." Dickie shook his head, dismissing Jerry.

"Are you walking those dogs bright and early, or do you feel like hanging around tonight? Maybe you could give me a little back rub. I must have lifted something wrong." He rolled his shoulders, fixing a pained look on his face, groaning from a newly perceived backache.

"I could maybe do that. I might have another beer first." She laughed.

"Here," Dickie said, crossing the room in two strides, opening the refrigerator door, and quickly grabbing a beer.

"Maybe I could finish this one first. Relax, mister. You're going to get your back rub."

"And?"

Forty-eight

Taggert filled Rae Nell's champagne flute and asked, "And that's all they asked you about? How long you worked for me?" He was trying to make some sense out of what she had just told him, but it wasn't adding up. "They didn't ask you about the fur coat or the meat? Did they say anything about a doctor?" he asked, regretting the question before she even had a chance to respond.

"No, no, nothing like that. I told them about you being injured in a game and having to go to the doctor if that's what you mean?" She sipped more champagne, trying to remember if she had forgotten anything. "I bet they're looking at stupid Dickie for some gambling angle. God, it would be just like him."

She shook her head in an attempt to chase Dickie out of her mind. She had been so exhausted by the end of the night, she had forgotten to tell Dickie he could forget about ordering Chow steaks from her ever again in his miserable life. She half-curled on the couch of Terry's hotel room and slid close enough to put her hand on the back of his neck. Her blouse was open, and she was wearing a thong, attempting to set the mood.

"You know, it was a very successful open house, nothing but rave reviews. But now I'm just not sure the Emporium of Dance is the venue that would best serve *us*," she said.

Taggert didn't pick up on the 'us.'

"You know, virtually everyone at the open house these past two nights was due to my contact. But, I may have been a little too hasty in suggesting this opportunity go to that creepy ex of mine." She wedged the champagne flute between her thighs and began to massage Terry's shoulders and upper back.

"Oh, that's nice."

"Mmm-mmm, mmm-mmm," she moaned in time to her kneading hands, hoping Terry would get the idea.

"How did they even know about you? I mean, who you were? Or me, more importantly?" he asked.

"Well, I, I guess I told them. I mean, I—"

"Told them?" he screamed, leaping up, causing the champagne flute to dump onto Rae Nell.

"Ahhh, eeek!" she screeched, jumping off the couch, at first thinking, *God that's cold and fizzy,* then quickly coming to her senses and thinking, *That damn Dickie!*

Forty-nine

Darcy stormed back and forth across his office. He held five pages of receipts in his right hand. All emailed to him by his credit card company. "That damn Dickie better answer his damned phone,"

"Answer the phone, jackass!" he screamed and kicked a chair out of his way.

"Yeah," a sleepy voice eventually scratched into the phone.

"Dickie, how nice of you to answer, you lowlife jerk!" Darcy screamed.

"Hello, my precious," Dickie said, hoping humor might save the day.

"You should be so lucky, you prick! What the hell do you think you're doing? Do you realize the problems you've caused using my credit card for all this shit? You should see these damn receipts, you idiot!" Darcy threw the fistful of receipts in the general direction of his desk then kicked the desk for good measure. "I've been argu-ing with my credit card company for two days now, and at the end of all this, you're the one who paid for close to ten-grand worth of food and liquor with my stolen credit card! What the hell!"

"I did? Relax, Darcy. I'll take care of it. I must have given them the wrong card, that's all."

"That's all, the wrong card! Are you kidding me? Listen—"

Dickie set the phone down on his pillow, rolled over DJ, and waddled into the bathroom. When he eventually returned, he didn't see the phone. DJ kept her eyes closed, groped under Dickie's pillow, and tossed the phone toward him.

"This guy sounds really pissed off about something," she said, never opening her eyes. She pulled Dickie's pillow over her head.

"…intend to prosecute you to the fullest extent of the law. So if I were you, I would obtain competent representation at your earliest damn convenience."

"Anything else?" Dickie asked.

"Anything else!"

"Hey, calm down, will you? I know you're pissed off, but remember, I have that image you want. Okay?" Dickie walked over to his kitchen counter and lifted a beer bottle off the DVD. For the briefest of moments, the DVD stuck to the bottom of the bottle before dropping back onto the counter.

"I've got it in safekeeping for you, and I'll have it over to your office later today. I have some computer geek working on it and making copies for you." He glanced over at DJ, naked on his bed. Her head was buried beneath two pillows, and she was giving him the finger.

"What do you mean working on it?"

"Nothing, just making backup copies," Dickie said, not adding he was going to make sure Rae Nell couldn't be identified.

"I need it today," Darcy yelled, not quite as loud as before.

"You'll have it. Look, I gotta go, okay," Dickie said. He tossed his mobile into the kitchen drawer and leered at DJ, rolling onto her back. Her head remained under the pillow, and she had kicked the sheets down around her ankles.

"Man, what a crab," she groaned beneath the pillows, then stretched her arms and rotated her ankles.

"Coffee?" Dickie asked as he dumped yesterday's remnants down the sink.

"Sounds wonderful."

"I'll put some on. That'll give us ten minutes."

Fifty

The weight of the Colt .45 had initially felt a little awkward to Helen Hardy, but she quickly adapted. Tucked snugly into the side of her large black patent-leather handbag, she would feel somehow unnatural if it weren't there. She was watching Terry fumble for an excuse as he raced to get dressed and dash out the door.

"Look, Hell." He always called her 'Hell', although she had told him countless times she took exception to the moniker. "I told you before, Luther and I were working late, very late. I was so tired I just thought it might be better if I grabbed a quick nap out there at the office rather than risk driving back here, maybe falling asleep behind the wheel. If that's a problem for y'all, okay. I'll just haul my ass back here exhausted, and we can see how that works."

"I would think you could at least have had the decency to phone, Terry," she said, knowing full well he was anything but decent.

"Well, Hell…" He dragged the name out, a little razor cut of insolence, another slight bruise of disrespect. "I meant to call, but like I said before, I guess I was just too tired. I'm one of them entrepreneurs." He pronounced it 'an-trap-an-oors', seriously suggesting he hadn't the foggiest idea what he was talking about.

"Terry, you're not—"

"Hey, you seen my, oh, never mind, here they are under the bed," he mumbled, sitting down on the bed with his back to her as he dragged his cowboy boots out and pulled them on. "Look, I'd like to chat some more, but work's a-calling." He blew her a kiss as he sailed past and out the bedroom door.

Helen clutched her purse and reached inside to feel the cool steel of the heavy pistol. Fortunately for Taggert, she was fond of the carpeting, not to mention the silk brocade wall covering in her bedroom, and so had no intention of shooting him here or anywhere else in the house for that matter.

No, there would be a time and place better suited. She needed to have her evidence, as well. There was no doubt in her mind, but she intended to follow her plan, and for that, she needed evidence.

Fifty-one

Dickie was standing behind DJ, massaging her shoulders while she erased the digital image of Rae Nell's Minnie Mouse tattoo. After a minute or two, he began to gradually work his way over the crest of her shoulders and down her chest, deciding a little verbal encouragement might be just the thing.

"Thanks for last night. It was really great."

"Oh, it must have been. I've been in pain ever since that creep on the phone woke me up," she said, deftly moving both his hands back up onto her neck.

"Really? We didn't do anything out of the ordinary…"

"Not that kind of pain, dopey. My head, oh my God!"

"Oh yeah, sure, just kidding." He continued massaging her shoulders, watching as Rae Nell's tattoo gradually disappeared on the screen.

"God, what kind of a butthead would get Minnie Mouse tattooed on her ass? This girl must have a couple of screws loose. Nice tan line, by the way," she said, finishing up the retouching.

"Got drunk on spring break in college," Dickie answered absently. He paused, massaging her shoulders for the briefest of moments, then quickly recovered. "Or, maybe she did it on a dare or has a thing for cartoon characters, or something. You ever see those guys who get tattoos on their faces? I mean, talk about idiots."

"Hey, ouch! Dickie, watch the massage. You're going to strangle me here. You know this chick, don't you? Who is she?" She glanced back briefly, appraising him. "Oh, don't tell me, not that Barb woman you had the torrid summer fling with sometime back? Dickie, please tell me you aren't into some weird voyeur thingy here. You're not, are you?"

"Voyeur thingy?" He mimicked, glad the questions hadn't gone in Rae Nell's direction. "I don't know who that woman is, honest. Nope, I told you this is for Darcy. Darcy Dalton, you met him last night. He's the high-buck attorney who hired—"

"That nutcase ranting on the phone this morning? That jerk who woke us up, right? That guy obsessing over identity theft? You're doing this for that self-absorbed fruitcake? Great, just great. My God, and I thought walking dogs was way out there. That guy is certifiable!"

"Oh, he's all right. He's just a little excitable and"

"Excitable? You were in the bathroom playing with yourself. You left me in bed with him on the other end of the phone. I thought for sure the guy was going into cardiac arrest. God, all that ranting and raving, the screaming, He's an absolute nutcase. That bozo deserves the kind of woman who would get Minnie Mouse tattooed on her butt."

"Now who's excitable?"

"Nice clients. You better stick with the crazies at the bar."

"Oh, yeah, no weirdos in the bar business."

"You mean like your flashback pal with the beard, mumbling to himself all last night?"

"Oh, poor Jerry? Yeah, I wonder what was up with him."

"Hey," she said as she ejected the disk from her computer. "What did you do to this thing? It's all sticky." She was holding the DVD at an angle to the light. "Look at this crap," she said, cleaning the disk with a silken cloth. "You soak this in beer or something?"

Fifty-two

Rae Nell slowly rolled over and smacked her lips together a few times, then ran her tongue back and forth over fuzzy teeth. She worked at ignoring her breath. She blinked her eyes open, and a half-finished champagne flute came into focus.

"Yuck." She swallowed, keeping her stomach down. Her head pounded as she gingerly made her way to the bathroom. She had no recollection of Terry leaving the hotel room and only the sketchiest memory of late last night. Why was it that things always seemed to get so complicated whenever she attempted to make life better for Dickie?

She sat in the bathroom with the lights off. Her head throbbed as she worked her way through an extensive list of golden opportunities she had presented to Dickie over the years. All for naught, not a one had worked out. Somehow Dickie had managed to screw up each and every opportunity, and maybe, she concluded, it was just as simple as that— because Dickie was a screw-up.

Make that a jealous screw-up after the stunt with his cop pals asking about Terry.

Well, she sighed, so be it. Dickie had no one to blame but himself. Once again, she had handed him a potential pot of gold, and Dickie's response was to piss in the pot. Okay, fine, two could play at that game. It made her decision to cut him out all the easier. She'd make him pay. Oh, God, her head throbbed. She'd make him pay, the jerk.

Fifty-three

Dickie didn't have much time to worry about Jerry Baxter. On his way to Darcy's, he made the mistake of stopping by the Emporium of Dance, where he was greeted by a white mini-van sporting very official-looking crests. Both front doors were labeled City of St. Paul Department of Health.

"Now, what's going on?" he yelled as he stepped into the dimly-lit barroom.

Noel signaled him from behind the bar to keep his voice down, indicating with a movement of his head that whatever was going on was happening back in the kitchen.

"Damn city inspectors, Dickie," Noel half-whispered.

"What the hell do—"

"Said they had some complaints and needed samples. I don't know. They just barged in here about an hour ago. Didn't you get any of the messages I left on your mobile?"

Dickie absently touched his empty pocket where his phone should have been. "Damn it! Okay, don't say anything. To anyone."

"Oh, really?" Noel replied.

Dickie was already pushing through the kitchen door. Four individuals attired in white hazmat suits were crowded around the refrigerator. Department of Health was stenciled in black letters across their backs. They wore white caps, pullover booties on their shoes, and each wore a white mask covering nose and mouth. Blue surgical gloves covered their hands. One of the four, a heavy-set guy with a rip up the back of his hazmat suit, operated a video camera.

"Can I help you?" Dickie asked, then reminded himself this was probably not the best time for a temper tantrum.

"Excuse me, Sir, you've just entered a secured site." A nasally female voice in a distracted tone came from somewhere in the middle of the group. "I'll need you to leave the area immediately. Please don't touch anything on the way out." An arm suddenly extended from the massed group and pointed in the direction of the swinging kitchen door.

"Hey, I own this place. What the hell is going on?" As he took a step forward, Dickie felt his face flushing and heard his voice rising.

"Then we'll definitely want to speak with you, Sir. Now would you please leave the area immediately and wait for us in the other room?" She turned from the open refrigerator and carried a chrome tray filled with last night's steak samples to one of the industrial kitchen tables.

"Get this, Stan," she said to the guy with the video camera. "Murray, bag all of this. We'll want to send some to the state, and we might as well copy CDC down in Atlanta as well. Better document sample temperature in four locations."

"Sir." She looked up, blinked icy blue eyes, magnified behind coke bottle glasses. "I'm only going to tell you once to wait for us in the other room. If you do not comply with my request and leave this area immediately, you leave me no choice but to cite you for interfering in an ongoing investigation. That carries a fine, Sir. A very hefty fine."

"Look, I'm not trying to interfere, but I do own this place. Maybe I can help. What's going on?"

"Sir!"

"Okay, okay, I'm waiting in the bar area."

"Thank you, Sir, for your…" she paused ever so slightly, "cooperation. I'm sure we'll have questions. Murray, label these one alpha. That second tray, the sausage, I'll want to use the same sample mechanism, two alpha. Stan…"

'Oh, Christ,' thought Dickie, settling onto a barstool. He was scanning his memory, wondering where he had met her before. He was unable to recall but relatively sure it had been unpleasant.

'What a complete jerk,' Dickie thought forty-five minutes later, watching patiently as the woman from the Department of Health took her sweet time and carefully placed a brown leather satchel on the bar next to him, sliding it back and forth ever so slightly until it aligned exactly with the edge of the bar.

"Very well, Mr. Mullins, is it?" Coke-bottle-glasses was stepping out of her hazmat suit, rolling it up, and placing it into a yellow plastic trash bag labeled 'Bio-Hazard' in large black letters.

She had a slight upper figure, devoid of any real semblance of curve other than her sloped shoulders. Her close-cropped gray hair was just long enough to accommodate a sharp part gelled into place on the left side of her head. She wore gray slacks, a dingy off-white blouse, no jewelry or makeup. The only color seemed to come from the cold blue eyes magnified behind her glasses, well, and the large brown mole on the left side of her face sporting a slight tuft of gray hair. He guessed she might be in her late forties, but the butch hair, mole, and shapeless clothes easily added another twenty years.

"I'm Dr. Eunice Hazzard," she stated, clearly impressed with herself.

At the mention of her name, his memory jogged, and he remembered her from the Thai honey incident a few years back, compliments of Rae Nell, again. She had attempted to shut down the Emporium of Dance back then. He had managed to dodge that bullet by the skin of his teeth.

"I'm with the City of St. Paul Department of Health," she announced, briefly lifting the I.D. card hanging around her neck. She made no attempt to extend a hand or sound pleasant.

"Nice to meet you," Dickie lied, trying his best to sound sincere. He let his outstretched hand hang in mid-air for an overly long moment before withdrawing it.

"You are the owner of this establishment?" she asked accusingly, opening the leather satchel and placing a recorder on the bar in front of Dickie.

"Yeah, like I told you before. I… what's that?"

Dr. Hazzard held her hand up for silence. "Test one, two, test, test," she said before pushing a button and re-playing the line. "Yes, I remember, contaminated honey the last time we had to investigate this establishment. Very well," she said, blinking in Dickie's direction. "You are the owner of this establishment?" She phrased the question to sound as though *owner* may be a step or two below pedophile.

"Yes, like I said before, I own the place. Now would you please—"

"State your name for the record," she interrupted, adding "please" as a chilly afterthought.

Dickie thought for a long moment before deciding he had nothing to lose. "I tell you what. Dr. Hazzard, is it? I would like to know why you're here, and I'd like to see by what authority you were in my kitchen. Then, since you've begun taping this interrogation without in-forming me of my rights or what in the hell you're doing,

I'm not going to answer any questions or give any further comment without my lawyer present."

"I can assure you, Sir, you are not under arrest. At least at this time," she added icily.

"I need to know under what authority you're here. This is a place of business and—"

"I, or rather we, are here under the authority vested in me by the City of St. Paul, and it would be in your best interests to cooperate with our investigation."

"Let the record state," Dickie said, leaning toward the recorder and glancing at his watch, "that at two-fifty-seven on Friday afternoon, this interview was concluded since Dr. Hazzard has refused to show me either identification or anything granting her authority to barge onto the premises of this establishment. I have requested the same a number of times before and during this interview. So now, the damn interview is over!"

"Now you listen—"

"No, you listen. You're out of here. I'm calling my lawyer, and then I'm calling the cops to get you out of here."

"Well, I have an—"

"Get out," Dickie yelled, interrupting her from pulling out what he assumed was the order from the Health Department.

"Your interference and lack of cooperation is duly noted and does not bode well for the immediate future of this establishment, Mr. Mullins. There have been a number of individuals who were forced to seek medical attention in the early morning hours. We have at least one individual, Mr. Gerald Baxter, an inspector for this very department, I might add, displaying signs of severe psychological trauma. Believe me, you have not heard the end of this nor seen the end of me. It will give me intense personal satisfaction to make absolutely sure this establishment is closed, once and for all."

As she spoke, she returned her recorder to the leather satchel, then picked up her yellow biohazard bag, turned sharply, and stormed out the door.

"Smooth move, ExLax!" Noel said from behind the bar. "Any idea what was going on? Kind of heavy-duty just because somebody got the shits or something. What'd she mean psychological trauma? Who's that Baxter guy?"

"I have no idea what in the hell is going on. But I'm guessing she's right. This isn't the last we'll see of her. I wonder what the deal is with Jerry Baxter. You know who I mean, Noel? he's in here a couple of nights a week. He has a bushy beard and nurses the same beer for about three hours."

"Quiet, spooky kind of guy, always sits over there?" Noel indicated a distant corner.

Dickie shuddered, thinking of the various times he had gotten involved with Rae Nell's schemes. *Please, don't let that happen again, please,* he prayed. *God, he was such a dumbass.*

Fifty-four

Darcy was shaking his head as they both watched Rae Nell crawling across the bed and onto Helen Hardy's husband, Terry Taggert. "Wow, nice ass on the blonde! I'll give this idiot that much. He's got good taste in female flesh. You believe that tan line? Take a good look, Dickie," Darcy said. "You are watching one real stupid son-of-a-bitch in the process of losing a fortune. Hope it was worth it, pal." Darcy hit pause, and the image of Rae Nell's naked rear end, minus Minnie Mouse, froze across the screen.

"This is better than I could have hoped for." Darcy half-chuckled, leering a moment longer before shaking his head again. "Man, that's nice. Okay, I've got to confirm my meeting with Helen for later this afternoon. This will be great. Stand by for some additional requests tonight or tomorrow morning."

"What kind of requests?"

"How should I know? I'm guessing she may want a tail on him. Maybe ID the woman so I could subpoena her to testify. Man, wouldn't mind meeting her," he said, glancing back at his screen. "Who knows what she might want to do? Now, about this other matter." Darcy slid five or six previously crumpled pieces of paper out from under a file. "My corporate credit card, which you have completely hosed up. What the hell were you thinking?"

Fifty-five

Rae Nell's eyes were flashing as she shouted, "What do you mean, what was I thinking?" She had just finished putting on her lipstick and spun around from the hotel mirror to face Terry Taggert. She wielded her lipstick case like a weapon, thrusting it just inches away from his nose. She was battling her hangover and now Terry.

"Terry, we haven't got anything to hide from the police, and certainly not from those two idiots. I already told you they're just two stupid pals of scum-bag Dickie's. He knows about our relationship, and he's trying to insert himself between the two of us. Believe me, I know how his stupid one-track mind works. This isn't some official police investigation. It's not like you committed a crime or anything, for God's sake. Can't you see that? Right now, you're reacting just the way he wants you to."

"Well, just how in the hell did they know there was anything going on in the first damn place?" Taggert asked, ignoring her term 'relationship,' making a mental note to bring his sexual romps with this chick to a close and quickly.

"Oh. My. God," she said, drawing each word out as if to ask, 'are you so dumb you can't see the obvious?' "Honey," she began in an overly patronizing tone, "just for starters, he purchased all those steaks from *us*. *We* put on that open house for two consecutive nights at that tacky, dreadful, Emporium of Dance place. *We* invited everyone who's anyone in town. He has a stack of brochures on *our* business that you instructed me to give him. Is any of this ringing a bell with you? Hello?"

"What else does he know?"

"What do you mean? What else does he know? How would I know what he has in that thick skull of his? God, I can only imagine. They suggested something about a betting scheme he might be—"

"I thought y'all just got done telling me you knew how the son-of-a-bitch's mind works. Think he knows we was getting it on together?"

Rae Nell exhaled loudly then answered barely above a whisper, "I'm sure he has no idea. At least, *I* haven't discussed *our* personal relationship with him or anyone else for that matter. Why? Have you?"

God save me, if I had half a chance of getting away with it, I'd strangle her right here in the damn hotel room, he thought. He envisioned his hands around Rae Nell's pretty little neck, increasing the pressure, her eyes starting to bulge, maybe saying something to her like

'See ya later, Minnie Mouse.' Make her wear one of those Disney hats with the mouse ears, strangle her with that stuck on top of her dumb blonde head. Kiss her goodbye and—

"—any of my questions?"

"Huh?" He shook his head, coming back to reality.

"I said, why aren't you answering any of my questions?" She pronounced each word slowly, sounding overly patient, just in case he wasn't getting the point.

"What the hell, baby?"

"Oh, that's perfect, Terry, just perfect. I'm so out of here," she said, grabbing her purse. She stormed out of the hotel room, paused out in the hall a moment, giving him plenty of time to catch up. He never did.

"Jesus, what a bitch," Taggert mumbled, rummaging for a cold beer in the minibar. "You got no idea how out of here you are, honey."

Fifty-Six

Darcy thought, *'Wouldn't it be funny to use that image as a screen saver?'* but then wisely decided against it. He would have killed Dickie over the credit card fiasco were it not for these fantastic smoking-gun images delivered for Helen Hardy's divorce. With the steamy bedroom images, Darcy felt confident he could get rid of old Terry Taggart without even entering a courtroom. Helen's divorce was going to be an incredibly simple, not to mention a highly profitable undertaking.

"Helen," he cooed moments later into the phone. "Darcy Dalton. I've just had the images delivered to me from our operative. I'm sorry to say there is no mistaking the circumstances. I'm afraid I have to report that your husband, Mr. Taggert, is most definitely unfaithful."

"I see," replied Helen. She may have had strong suspicions, but it was still shocking to hear Darcy's confirmation. "And you're sure, Mr. Dalton? There's no mistake?"

"I'm afraid there's no mistake. I've had the distinct displeasure of having to review the whole tawdry episode. Disgusting, absolutely disgusting," Darcy said. As he spoke, he was clicking the directional keys back and forth, dancing Rae Nell's rear end across his computer screen.

"That's the bad news," he continued, tucking the phone between his shoulder and ear, using both hands to click the keys faster. "I think the sooner we can meet and formulate a plan, the better. The good news, Helen, is that this leaves nothing to the imagination. Once we submit our evidence and I introduce some additional character references, we can be reasonably assured of an open and shut case."

"Very well, let me check my schedule, and I'll get back to you," she said.

"All right, Helen, I'll be waiting for your call. And may I just add my sincere apologies. I will never become used to the fact that, when I represent people I genuinely like, good decent people I respect, I sometimes have the burden to deliver a message, inform them of something that is truly painful. I'm very sorry. If there is anything I can do, at any time, you need only ask." He turned his head sideways, clicking the keys, making Rae Nell's rear continue to bounce faster and faster.

Helen hung up her phone, then looked around for her purse with the Colt .45. She was going to need it when she met with Terry.

Fifty-seven

Driving into St. Paul, Luther smiled, planning to kill two birds with one stone, laughing out loud at his incredible sense of humor. *Get it? Kill. Of course, he got it. He had come up with it in the first place.*

Occasionally, in the Chow litters, there was a pup with a pelt that clearly was not able to lend itself to the fur line. Usually, Luther disposed of these pelts once the meat had been harvested, but he had been busy with other things of late. Specifically, he had been studying a stack of pornographic magazines, a handful of kinky DVDs, processing first Craig Cullen and later his wife Marti through the sausage maker, and suddenly he found himself out of time. He'd promised Terry days ago he had disposed of Craig Cullen's BMW.

So he tossed some sausages, a spicy blend of ground Chow and ground Marti Cullen, into the trunk of the BMW and coaxed puppies with flawed pelts to pile in after the sausages. He drove into the city, where he planned to let the pups loose on the street and leave the keys in the unlocked car for the first joyrider who came along.

He had been humming the chorus of *"Do It All Night,'* and it wasn't that he didn't see the Honda Civic. Actually, he did. Who could miss the thing? After all, it was bright red, with a three-foot-long 'St. Paul Drivers Training' sign on the roof. But Luther had the green light and, therefore, the right of way. He expected the bright red Honda to stop at the intersection.

The fifteen-year-old Drivers' Training student was now apologizing to his instructor, Clarence Gunderson, saying how sorry he was for running the light and broadsiding the BMW.

After being hit, Luther, the BMW, puppies, and sausages had spun through the intersection before screeching to a stop against a billboard encouraging safe sex. Luther deflated the driver's side airbag with a pocketknife and then squirmed out the passenger door.

"Don't say a damn thing," Clarence Gunderson growled at the young driver trainee, adding as an afterthought, "You dumb shit."

Meanwhile, Luther attempted to quietly fade into the crowd.

"Hey, no, man, sit down. Let me get you some water or something," a helpful bystander offered.

"Get that poor man to the bus bench," directed a heavyset woman, who was unfortunately clad in bright yellow shorts.

"Get the hell away from me," Luther growled. He lurched through the crowd and escaped down a trash-littered alley. "Bunch of damn do-gooders, nothing better to do than stand around all day and try to help."

"What's that fool got going on? It sounds like there are babies in here," Yellow Shorts announced, placing her ear and a plump cheek against the trunk of the BMW.

Luther quickly ran down the length of the alley, limping ever so slightly, his hip and shoulder a bit banged up. He took a sharp right at the far end of the alley, glanced back to make sure he wasn't being followed, then slithered into a dingy tavern. He walked to the back of the dim room, mounted a stool, and sat facing the door.

"Tap beer," he wheezed to the anemic bartender, then attempted to catch his breath before he started to sort out his dwindling options.

"Oh, for God's sake!" Rae Nell screamed, slamming her mobile shut, thinking, *Since Dickie was acting irresponsible and not answering his phone, maybe she would just go over to his dreadful, dreary, sleazy little bar. Tell him in person that she and Terry were looking for something with just a little more class and a lot more promise than a pick-up saloon.* See how that went down after getting those phony detectives to waste her time yesterday.

"Two can play this game, Mr."

She finished applying more lip-gloss and smacked her lips in the mirror. Dickie simply was not going to be allowed to ruin her successful business opportunity nor her relationship with Terry. She should have expected as much.

Fifty-eight

Dickie finally found the nurse on duty. He was up on the sixth floor of Regions Hospital. He leaned on a counter, maybe a foot and a half higher than her work surface. She was wedged between stacks of thick manila files, entering information into a computer.

The antiseptic spray in the hospital corridor smelled like a restroom. Fifteen feet behind the nurses' station, a set of double doors were labeled,

'Lock Down Area, SECURE.

No admittance without a staff badge.

No unaccompanied visitors! Immediate Family Only.'

The Psyche wing.

"Hi, I'm looking for Mr. Jerry Baxter,"

"Are you a member of the family?" she asked, not looking up. She closed a file and set it on top of the stack on her left. Then pulled another file and opened it.

"Family? No, just a friend," he said to her white-blonde hair. A half-inch worth of dark roots ran along either side of the part down the middle of her head.

"I'm sorry." She glanced up quickly before continuing to input information and pointed over her shoulder. "No visitors allowed except immediate family members."

"I see. Can you tell me why he's here?" He indicated the general area with his hands.

"I really can't. Data privacy and all that." She leaned back in her chair, causing it to squeak.

"Carol?" he asked, suddenly recognizing her once he read her nametag. A casual friend of DJ's and a sometime Saturday night regular at the Emporium of Dance, Johnny Walker Red with a splash of water and a twist of lemon if he recalled.

"Dickie? Gee, sorry, didn't recognize you. All these files to input, and well, you're just a little out of context here."

"Jerry's a pal of mine. I just wanted to make sure he was okay. He seemed fine earlier in the week," Dickie said, remembering Jerry innocently nursing his beer a few nights ago. He decided not to mention Jerry's ranting during the open house and thought better of telling her about the coffee out back by the dumpster where he told Jerry to go home.

Carol looked up at him, held his gaze for a moment before returning to her computer screen. "Look," she said, making three or four quick entries on her keyboard.

"Baxter, Gerald, Caucasian male aged seventy-four?" she asked, eyes not leaving the screen.

"Yeah."

"Well, I can tell you he is most likely resting comfortably. Wow, do they ever have him sedated? He arrived in the middle of the night, intoxicated and in an agitated state. Only answers to Sergeant Baxter, note here about PTSD, thought to possibly be brought on by a food reaction. Hmm-mmm."

"PTSD?" Dickie asked, wondering why they locked you on the Psyche floor for having a sexually transmitted disease.

"Post-Traumatic Stress Disorder. We see a lot of that." She looked up. "I think he was part of a larger group I heard about down in emergency. I'm not really sure what was going on, but a lot of sick people, stomachs pumped, all that icky stuff. If you'd like to leave a note, I can give it to him at a time when it would be appropriate. Or, maybe I could pass something on to his family if you want, Dickie."

"No, that's all right, just worried about him is all." Dickie wondered what this had to do with Dr. Hazzard's visit earlier, not liking any of the scenarios he was coming up with.

"Well, don't worry. He'll probably be okay. It looks like there was an incident report filed with the police. I don't know what that would be. Most likely, there was something that triggered a flashback reaction. It could have been as simple as fireworks or a stressful situation, maybe a car accident, even a movie or something. Usually, after a few days' rest, they're okay. Sure you don't want to leave a note or something?"

"No, thanks, Carol, you've been very helpful. I'll check back in a day or two," he said and walked to the elevators.

Fifty-nine

Rae Nell was reading the official-looking red notice fastened crookedly across the front door of the Emporium of Dance.

CLOSED

By order of the City of St. Paul

Department of Health.

It went on from there in smaller type, citing city code and amendments. It ended with a warning in large letters about removing the notice under penalty of fine followed by an official signature she couldn't make out.

Well, she had to give this much to Dickie, it even looked real, and as she ripped it off the door, she cursed Dickie because he had really glued the damn thing on. She had just finished peeling the better portion of the notice off when she heard the unmistakable groan of Dickie's disgusting Jeep wheezing up against the curb.

"Ugh, God, I hate that awful thing," she snarled. She cringed and held her breath as a large blue cloud of exhaust drifted across the sidewalk and enveloped her.

"To what do I owe the pleasure, slumming?" Dickie asked. He forced the driver's door shut with a hip check.

"You only wish. Too busy to take my calls? Nice try, but it won't work," she seethed, then crumpled up the notice and threw it at him. It sailed through his open passenger window and into the back seat.

"Huh, missed." He snorted. "Hey, Rae Nell, it's already been kind of an upsetting day, even before your visit. Can whatever this is wait?"

"Upsetting day? Look, Dickie, for your information—" She pushed the door to go inside and stumbled forward a half-step before she realized the door was locked. She turned to confront him. "You know, maybe if you weren't closed in the middle of Friday afternoon, right after my open house, you might just find that business would be a little better. It's after four," she said, glancing at her watch. "And you're still closed?"

"What?" He moved Rae Nell to the side and tried the door himself.

"Don't push me," she growled.

"Hey, Rae, just be quiet for a minute, will you? This isn't about you right now," he said. He fished his keys out of his pocket, unlocked the door, and stepped inside.

"Noel, hey, Noel!" he called. Everything looked in order, except that the door had been locked, the lights were off, and Noel was nowhere to be found.

"Noel, Jose," Dickie called, looking into the kitchen and then behind the bar. He didn't know what to think.

He dialed Noel's home number, hoping he would answer.

"Oh, Jesus, Dickie, you've really got the inmates running the asylum this time," Rae Nell scoffed.

"Hello," Noel answered on the third ring.

"Hello, yourself!" Dickie half-shouted. "Hey, what's going on? You okay?"

"I don't know, Dickie. They came back just before three, told me to lock up, said they were shutting us down, gave me about ten minutes. Told me, if I didn't close immediately, they were going to have me arrested. I didn't know what to do, so I just threw shit in the dishwasher, locked the doors, and left."

"Who the hell are 'they'?" Dickie asked.

"That witch with the gray hair, the one who was there earlier. She said the City Attorney would be in touch and that you had better get a lawyer. Didn't you get any of my messages? I've been calling you on your mobile every ten minutes. They stuck some health department notice on the door. I was planning to sneak back tonight and maybe at least get that thing torn off."

"Just a second, Noel."

"Rae Nell, darling, what did you throw into the backseat of my car a few moments ago?"

"What do you mean, what did I throw? That bogus thing you had—"

"Yeah, I should have guessed," Dickie said, shaking his head. "Hey, Noel, thanks. As soon as I learn something, I'll get back to you."

"You want me to come in?"

"No, take the night off. I'll find out what this is all about and get it straightened out. I'll give you a call tomorrow once I know what in the hell is going on here. Rae Nell, what did that 'bogus thing' happen to say?" he asked, disconnecting the call to Noel.

"What do you mean, what did it say? The Department of Health, closed until further notice, and after all my work. Jesus, your stupid idea of a joke," she muttered, sounding less convinced.

"Shit."

"Dickie, do you mean to tell me that, after working my butt off for the previous week, not to mention the last two nights at your open house, you've now made me the laughingstock of the entire city by getting shut down by the Department of Health? What will everyone think of me when they find out?"

"You know—" He didn't finish. Instead, he walked out to his car and retrieved the crumpled notice from the back seat. He was still standing on the curb, sweating in the late afternoon heat, rereading the notice for the third time when he was interrupted.

"Hey, Dickie, how's it going?"

Looking up, he saw an old friend from the police force.

"Hi, Donny, what brings you to this side of town?" he asked, then noticed Dr. Eunice Hazzard climbing out of the Department of Health van across the street with a television cameraman behind her. Two squad cars were parked behind the Department of Health van, the officers hurriedly getting out of the vehicles.

"Is that really necessary?" Donny asked the cameraman as Dickie instinctively covered his face with the Department of Health notice.

"Dickie, better come with me and climb in the back of the squad car. Quick like," Donnie suggested, an eye on Dr. Hazzard storming across traffic.

"Officer, aren't you going to handcuff that monster?" Dr. Hazzard screamed from the middle of the street, pointing an accusing finger at Dickie. The cameraman turned to film her as she stopped traffic.

"That maniac is interfering with an ongoing investigation. He has endangered the good citizens of this city."

Donny closed the rear door, hurried around to the drivers' side of his squad car, and climbed in behind the wheel.

"Jesus, what in the hell did you do to that old bat? If she had her way, you'd be looking at the SWAT team taking you out instead of me asking nicely. Obviously, you still have a way with the ladies." He turned and checked for traffic before pulling away from the curb and past Eunice Hazzard screaming at them as they drove off.

"I don't even know what's going on."

"Well, it was supposed to be a little more low key, but no one can keep a damn secret nowadays. I tried to call you on your cell phone to warn you, but it just rang. I probably got an old number. They got you on that meat deal, Dickie. All hell's breaking loose. I mean, what the hell?"

"Meat deal?"

"Did you have some big party at your place last night? All sorts of the right people eating your food and drinking your booze?"

"You mean the open house?"

"Hey, call it whatever in the hell you want, Dickie. Just for the record, a couple of us old-timers think it's hilarious. All those judges and high rollers getting sick after eating dog meat. Course, right now, a lot of folks seem to be taking a bit of a dim view. Then again, it don't bother me none what you do to get your kicks! I guess the emergency room over at Regions was jammed with folks getting their stomachs pumped last night. Some old Nam vet from city inspectors started having flashbacks. I mean, it's funny, maybe." He laughed as he looked at Dickie in the rearview mirror. "But, of course, it's not. I mean, little puppies, Jesus, Dickie. I guess that's what's got that old gal, Doc Hazzard, cranked up and yelling in the street. But puppies? Jesus, Dickie, what the hell were you thinking?"

"Huh?"

Sixty

Luther's options hadn't improved much after his fifth beer. He'd attempted to pace himself, take his time, and hope things eventually calmed down at the intersection before he went back outside. He had been worried one of those jackass do-gooders might wander in the bar and recognize him, but after more than an hour, his fear on that score had been put to rest.

He thought about calling Taggert but then remembered he had left his phone in the BMW, and that gave him something else to sit and worry about. He sat stewing, quietly nursing beers beneath a muted and somewhat dusty TV running an old episode of Malcolm in the Middle.

For the next twenty minutes, he kept an eye on a woman sitting four or five stools away. His antenna went up the moment he first heard her speak. "Double Jack Daniels on the rocks," she said.

He cautioned himself, always a sucker for women who got absolutely wasted in the middle of the day, or any time of day, for that matter. She was a dishwater blonde. Broad-shouldered, with a stomach that oozed out beneath her strappy t-shirt and over the waist of her jeans. She sported a blotchy blue, homemade tattoo on her left forearm, a primitive-looking heart surrounding the name Lionel. At least a half-dozen silver studs pierced her right eyebrow, and a small blue stone sat like a wood tick on the right side of her nose.

She was about to finish her latest drink when he nodded toward the anorexic old stork behind the bar and slid a twenty forward.

"Give her another, me too. Okay?" He nodded as the blonde looked over at him.

She had flat blue eyes, the left eye slightly off-center so that he wasn't quite sure which one he should be looking at as he spoke. "I never like to drink alone," he said to her.

"Never really bothers me," she replied with a shrug. She drained her glass with practiced timing and pushed the empty aside just as the fresh drink arrived. She took a healthy belt, slid off her stool, and walked around the corner of the bar to where Luther sat.

"Thanks," she said, holding her glass out for a toast.

Luther clinked glasses with her, then leered down over the rim of his beer mug as she took a large mouthful of bourbon, closed her eyes, and swallowed. She'd probably had a nice figure at one time, maybe fifteen years ago. As she stood close, he became enveloped in a cloud of perfume covering the smell of too many cigarettes and too few showers.

"Hey, I'm Sandy," she said, wiping her mouth before holding out her hand.

"Lou," he said, shaking her hand.

She gave his hand another squeeze and raised her metal encrusted eyebrow.

"Thanks for the drink. I seen you in here before?" she asked, climbing onto the stool next to him.

"Probably not. I was just driving past after a business meeting and decided to stop."

"Yeah," she snorted. "That's what I was doing, too, coming from a business meeting. Let's hear it for business," she said, holding her glass up for another toast, draining the better part of the bourbon without so much as a blink.

"So, Lou, what is it you do? Hey, that rhymes, get it? Lou and do."

"Yeah, great. I got a lot of businesses. I own stuff, a silent partner, investments, stuff like that. How about you, Sandy?"

"Mmm-mmm," she said again with the raised eyebrow. The pierced rings seemed to wiggle ever so slightly. "I'm between things, you know, thinking about maybe getting my act together or something next month. Right now, I don't know, just partying around, doing what I want. Whenever I want."

"Sounds fun."

"It can be." She glanced up from her glass.

Luther nodded in the direction of the bartender, standing just far enough away to hear every word.

"Thanks," Sandy said, again demonstrating her perfect timing, draining her glass just as the fresh drink arrived.

They talked for the next half-hour, Sandy inhaling two more drinks until she looked up at him, her good eye beginning to glaze over.

"Got any plans for later?"

"I don't know, nothing special," Luther said, thinking, *'Finally about time, God knows I've certainly put in the effort.'*

"I got a place not far from here. You know, if you wanted to stop over for a couple of drinks, we could party or whatever."

"Yeah, that might be nice. Got anything special in mind?"

She paused for another sip, slammed the glass on the bar as she set it down, her movements suddenly heavier.

"You a cop?" she half-whispered.

"No." He chuckled, thinking, *'That was really funny after the afternoon he'd had.'* He noticed her left eye had drifted into a normal position, no longer wandering. Both eyes appeared a little glassier than before.

"Sure you ain't a cop?" Her head weaved side to side slightly before she looked around the bar then returned to gaze into his face.

"Yeah." he chuckled. "I'm sure why? What did I—"

"Forty bucks for an hour or a hundred for the night. I'll do anything you want, long as it don't hurt. I'm not into the whole pain thing," she slurred.

"Okay," he said, never one to haggle over price, not that he intended to pay anyway. "You got a car?"

"Thought you said you drove here?" she asked, tilting her head, suddenly looking and sounding a lot more sober.

"Yeah, but I left it in the shop up the street. That's why I came in here," he replied, amazed he sounded that credible.

"Okay, but you better drive. I ain't got a license," she said, sliding off her stool. She took a half-step or two, steadied herself with a hand on the bar before she gave him a single car key.

Overhead, a commercial for the evening news came on the dusty television. A red banner with white copy ran across the bottom of the screen, hyping a breaking news story with the headline *Little Shop of Horrors*.

Sandy's car, a battered, gray Geo Metro minus a muffler and left taillight, was parked halfway over the curb. Along with some fast food wrappers and old newspapers, the backseat held half of a grease-covered plastic wheel cover and a pair of jeans. The neck of what looked like an empty Jack Daniels bottle peeked out from underneath the passenger seat. There was a persistent moldy smell, although the windows were rolled down. The front windshield on the passenger side sported an impact blow the size of a softball that radiated out in a spider web pattern.

"Buckle up for safety." Sandy chuckled.

Luther attempted to do just that until he realized there was no buckle on his seatbelt.

"Ha, ha, got ya'." She giggled. "Okay, okay, I'll direct you. Just go straight ahead to the light and take a right. Left at this corner," she said a minute later. "Third one on the right side. Yeah, honey, perfect." She waved her hand to indicate a grimy looking split level four-plex with a crumbling white-stucco front.

There was no concrete curbing in front of the place. A good portion of the burned-out boulevard had been chewed up by cars driving back and forth, grinding the soil to a powdery dust. A dying tree sporting a bruised trunk that was no more than six inches in diameter cast an anemic shadow across a cracked sidewalk.

"I keep the key right here," Sandy said, weaving up the sidewalk and grabbing a key from beneath a broken brick next to the front door. She steadied herself against the cracked stucco until she regained her balance.

"Jesus, is that safe? I mean, don't ya' worry about someone finding your key and just coming in?"

"No," she said, sounding as though she'd never considered that option.

"Came home one night without my jeans. This is better than breaking another window." She giggled by way of explanation.

A moment or two later, Luther closed the door to her unit behind him, attached the chain lock, and slid the deadbolt into place. Judging from the cracked molding around the doorframe, the door had been kicked in more than once.

Chaos clearly reigned throughout the little unit. A small kitchenette flowed off a sitting room with a tiny hall leading to what he guessed was the bedroom. Open pizza boxes sat on a coffee table next to the stained couch. Judging from the clothes on the floor and dirty dishes piled on every flat surface, it was the maid's day off.

"How 'bout a little something?" Sandy said as she staggered into the small kitchenette area, not waiting for a reply. She drained the remnants from a glass on the kitchen counter. An open bottle of Jack Daniels stood half-hidden behind dirty dishes piled in the sink. She filled the glass, not wasting time on ice or water.

"Mmm-mmm, okay, so, what'd you have in mind, Sweetheart?" she asked, undoing her belt with her right hand, gulping Jack Daniels out of the glass in her left, multi-tasking.

Sixty-one

Darcy cautioned Dickie over the phone, "Hey, watch what you say in there," Darcy was still absently working the keys on his computer, moving Rae Nell's rear back and forth across his screen.

"I'm trying to get some answers, but I've got to warn you, one news station had it on at six, so everyone is going to be all over this thing by ten tonight. And be prepared for this to go national at least. They're calling your joint The Little Shop of Horrors. Kind of clever, actually."

"Darcy, I need to get—"

"Just hold on. I'll get you out of there as soon as I can, but there are a lot of questions right now. Did you know you were— No, never mind, don't answer that. Don't say a thing."

"Look, Darcy, I'm the victim here," Dickie pleaded. He was phoning from a monitoring desk within a secure area in the city jail. He could look out the reinforced glass window of the holding cell and see his houseboat moored in the marina across the river. What he assumed to be police officers were crawling all over the thing. There appeared to be two uniformed officers talking to Vernon on his rear deck.

"God, Dickie, don't use the word victim right now. I'm not kidding. Don't say a thing. I'm working on getting you out. Okay? I know it's tough, but you're going to have to be a little patient. You just hang on. I'm doing everything I can, but right now, jail might be one of the safest places for you," Darcy said.

"But I didn't—"

"No, not a word. Now, I'm on my way down there. Hang on. I'll get you out, I promise. Not a word, Dickie. I'm hanging up and coming down there. Okay? Goodbye."

Dickie listened to the cold 'click' from Darcy's end. After a long moment, he handed the receiver back across the counter. He had to use both hands due to the handcuffs.

"Thanks, Arthur," Dickie mumbled. He'd never, ever liked Ramsey County Sheriff, Arthur Mooney, for even one day of the man's miserable life. Dickie had always referred to him as 'Arty Farty' for the better part of fifteen years.

"Not a problem, Mr. Mullins," Arthur replied, working to sound overly polite, having never, ever liked the man handcuffed across the counter from him.

"Time to return you to your holding cell, Sir," Arthur said, speaking in a soft voice, enjoying every blessed moment and trying not to grin too much. He could only hope he might be lucky enough to let Dickie be the first to experience the effects of his newly-issued Raptor 750 Taser, seven-hundred-and-fifty volts of love, compassion, and understanding.

Normally, Dickie would have reminded Arthur that he hadn't seen his feet in years. That he was nothing more than a worthless desk jockey delivering clean underwear to lowlifes. Maybe throw in the term toilet sniffer just for good measure. But he was too shattered with the events of the past few hours to enjoy such simple pleasantries.

"Thank you, Arthur."

Sixty-two

DJ had been working on a software program ever since Dickie left with his retouched DVD image earlier that day. She was still shaking her head, wondering what self-absorbed idiot would have Minnie Mouse tattooed on her rear. She had the television on, more for background noise than anything else, and she wasn't really paying any attention until she heard the newscaster, *"St. Paul nightclub owner Richard 'Dickie' Mullins..."*

Her immediate thought had been, *'Nightclub'?* But that was quickly erased when they referred to the city's own 'Little Shop of Horrors' then proceeded to describe how potentially a thousand to fifteen-hundred people had been eating dog meat and possibly something even worse.

"Unconfirmed and anonymous reports suggest that something far more sinister may have been served to unsuspecting guests." Pause for effect. *"Human flesh."*

From there, the report launched into a brief history of cannibalism, revisiting Ed Gein and Jeffrey Dahmer before ending with the suggestion that *'Well-known nightclub owner Richard 'Dickie' Mullins may be the Capital city's very own version of Hannibal Lecter.'*

Blurry footage of Dickie being helped into the back of a squad car, his hands up hiding his face behind a piece of red paper flickered across the screen. A vicious-looking gray-haired person, DJ thought it might be a woman, stood in the middle of the street, screaming and pointing a finger as three or four police officers swept past her.

DJ stared at the TV with her mouth open, stunned. She blinked a few times in an attempt to clear her head. She picked up her remote, jumped from station to station to see if she could pick up the story again.

She punched in the numbers on her phone. "Answer, Dickie, come on, answer," she pleaded. Knowing full well, there was a good chance his phone was still resting in the kitchen drawer where he had tossed it that morning. She half-ran out the door, deciding to check the houseboat herself, redialing and listening to his phone ring over and over.

She never made it to the houseboat. She learned all she needed to know watching from the Wabasha Bridge. She stood on the downtown side of the bridge while, across the river, five squad cars and a large crime scene van were parked in the marina parking lot. A beehive of activity seemed to swarm over Dickie's houseboat. In short order, there were two, possibly three, separate news crews arriving to film the police while they tore the place apart. She heard a chopping sound from overhead, then looked up to see a helicopter from a news station begin to gradually circle and film all the activity.

Sixty-three

Leave it to Dickie, Rae Nell steamed as she pulled the bottle of chardonnay out of her refrigerator. She was still replaying the scene in her head. Dickie led away by the police for God only knew what, once again not giving a damn if she became collateral damage! Well, just in case she had any doubts before, and she didn't, this erased them all.

Her decision had been simple. She was going to cut Dickie out of the Chow Meats action. And then she was going to eliminate that creep from her life, again, and this time forever!

"What in the hell was I thinking?" She sniffled on the couch and refilled her glass. It just never failed. Every time she tried to make things better, tried to offer him a taste of success, another golden opportunity, he screwed it up.

Well, here was the lesson. Again. No good deed goes unpunished. He tried to ruin her relationship with Terry. Had those two idiot cop pals of his ask her questions in the middle of the open house.

"In the middle of the damn open house. Oh, God, why do I always try to help him? Is he really that stupid?" She wailed in her empty living room. She knew the answer to her question and took a long sip as if to confirm her assessment.

Now what? She wondered, gambling, prostitution, serving minors, some licensing thing, or even worse? Well, this just settled it. She was going to call Terry and tell him Dickie had made a mistake, again, and they would have to move on in another direction.

'Finally,' Taggert thought, hearing his phone ring. He'd been trying to reach Luther since early this afternoon.

"Well, it's about damn time," he answered, distracted by the three shirts he had just laid out on the bed.

"Hi, Terry, miss me?" Rae Nell said cheerily into the phone, conveniently forgetting she'd stormed out of his hotel room earlier in the day.

'Not really,' Taggert thought.

"Hey there, Rae Nell. Can I call you back, baby? I'm in an owners' meeting here."

"Sure, how long do you think it might be?"

'Not long enough,' he thought, quickly choosing a shirt, half-pulling it on as he fled out of the bedroom and down the staircase. "Maybe just an hour or two. Look,

gotta go. We're talking numbers. See ya'." He quickly hung up and dialed Luther again to find out just where the hell he was.

Sixty-four

The tow truck driver had gotten the reroute call on his way to the impound lot. There had been an alert on the license number of the BMW he had winched out of the intersection. He'd just finished dropping it off in one of the auto bays at the Criminal Analysis Lab. He'd had to wait at the accident scene for over an hour before animal control finally arrived and pulled a bunch of puppies out of the trunk. In the meantime, probably upward of a hundred people, including him, had touched and smeared their sweaty hands and fat asses all over the BMW. He laughed when he saw the crime lab guys dressed in surgical garb and gloves. Whatever they were looking for would be worse than trying to find a needle in a haystack, unless of course, the bad guys had left a note, but then who would be that stupid?

Dexter and Cosgrove had received a call an hour earlier that Craig Cullen's BMW had been recovered and was being towed to the Criminal Analysis Lab. They had just finished confirming the license plate number and the vehicle identification number. Other than being broadsided at the intersection, not much else was known.

At the moment, they had eyewitness accounts describing the driver fleeing the scene. Unfortunately, the accounts went on to contradict one another, describing him as either a heavyset, middle-aged white male with a receding hairline and a limp or a tall, thin black male in his early twenties, limping. They did know one thing for sure. There was a lot of dog shit smeared around the trunk of the car, an awful lot.

"Jesus, were they breeding the damn things back here?" Cosgrove asked, remembering his own backyard last spring after the snow melted, leaving behind a winter's worth of German Shepherd.

"What the hell's that?" Dexter asked, following the sound to the front of the BMW, tracing the ring tone under the passenger seat.

"Hmm-mmm." He winked at his partner, picking up the phone with a gloved hand. "Hello?"

"Just where in the hell y'all at? Been calling your ass all damn day," Taggert shouted. He looked in his rearview mirror to make sure Helen wasn't following him.

"Mmm-mmm," Dexter said.

"Look, just get your ass out to the farm. A couple of things coming down we might have to deal with, okay? Luther, you there?"

"Mmm-mmm."

"Hell, think I got me a wrong number here or something. Sorry to bother y'all." Taggert clicked the phone off, knowing he hadn't misdialed. God damn Luther!

Sixty-five

Luther thought about drowning her in the bathtub, but that old bitch of a bartender might be able to place them together, so he waited, patiently, he thought, while she drank herself into a stupor. It took the better part of an hour before she finally passed out.

He figured there was a better than average chance she would be out for the night, and he only needed thirty minutes to get back to the farm. He rifled through her purse, came up with twelve dollars and her car key. He left her on the grimy floor, snoring beside her litter-strewn coffee table.

As he pulled away from the curb, he had the passing thought of driving through the intersection where he had been broadsided, just to see what telltale signs might remain. Then, almost as quickly, decided it would be wiser to stay as far away as possible and get back to the farm.

Taggert heard Luther arriving before he actually saw him. He stood in front of the building as blue exhaust wafted over him, waiting for Luther to climb out of the sputtering car.

"Where in the hell did you get this piece of shit? And who the hell was that on your damn cell phone?" Taggert asked.

"Cell phone?" Luther replied, looking sheepishly over the roof of the Geo Metro.

"Yeah, been calling all afternoon. Someone answered, didn't say jack shit. I knew something wasn't right. You lose the damn thing again?"

"Yeah, 'fraid so. Must have left it in a bar." Luther shook his head.

"Jesus H. Christ. What's with this?" Taggert inclined his chin toward the car while waving his hand to disperse the lingering blue-gray cloud.

"Oh, this, borrowed it from a friend," he said, implying anything but.

"Best get it in back before anyone sees it. We better start doing some planning here. I got a feeling the shit is about to hit the fan."

"How so?" Luther sounded unconcerned.

"Nothing we can't handle, just a couple of woman problems. My damn wife for starters, and that bitch Rae Nell. She's apt to not leave well enough alone, and I got the distinct feeling she'll be sticking her nose where it don't belong. We may as well deal with the both of 'em together."

"You talking eliminating both of them?"

"It's worked pretty well for us this far, wouldn't you say?"

Sixty-six

ickie could feel his blood pressure rising. "Look, I don't know what to say. I don't know anything about any of this, other than I purchased these steaks from a place called Chow Meats. I've got receipts in my office. Their staff helped me put on an open house over two separate nights this past Wednesday and Thursday. I didn't know anything except that the meat was tender and tasty. At least the sample I had."

'God damn Rae Nell,' Dickie fumed. If he had told this story once, he had told it a hundred times by now. He didn't know how long he had been sitting with Darcy in an interview room, answering questions. He just wanted to go home, take about a hundred aspirin, and go to bed.

"Gentlemen, my client, Mr. Mullins, has answered each and every question you've asked for these past hours as truthfully and as honestly as he possibly can.

You've searched his home, his place of business. It's obvious he's an innocent party here. Don't you think it's either time to charge him or let him go?"

'Charge me?' Dickie screamed to himself, glaring wild-eyed at Darcy.

With a subtle movement of his hand, Darcy signaled Dickie to stay calm. They were seated in a gray cinderblock room, beneath a fluorescent light that flickered haphazardly and was giving Dickie a throbbing headache. Although the air conditioning kept the room a clammy cold, Dickie had been sweating and sticking to the bright orange plastic chair for the past three hours.

"Gentlemen?" Darcy asked.

"I think we've heard enough for now," the interviewing detective said, rubbing a hand down the length of his face, sounding about as tired as Dickie felt. His last name was Gruber, and Dickie knew of the man but didn't know him personally.

"Mr. Mullins, we're going to let you go. It's been a long day for all of us. I would caution you to remain available should we have any further questions. And I'm sure we will. Let me thank you, gentlemen, for your cooperation, and we'll be in touch. Mr. Dalton, thank you. Mr. Mullins, you can retrieve your personal items at the property desk. I'll remind you not to leave by the main entrance. It seems the news media have taken a special interest in some of the more bizarre aspects of this investigation. Gentlemen."

Detective Gruber extended his hand, indicating the door. Dickie stood, stretched quickly, felt his back snap, crackle, and pop, then followed Darcy out the door.

Dickie's voice was muffled as he hid beneath a wool blanket on the rear floor of Darcy's dark green Jaguar. "Look, Darcy, I'm telling you I had absolutely no idea. Do you think I intentionally served dog meat to every mover and shaker in town? Does that sound like a plan that would improve my business?"

"Jesus, look at these vultures," Darcy said absently, easing the car through a crowd of cameramen and news people. A number of people bent to peer into the car for a brief moment but turned away when they didn't spot Dickie.

"You oughta see this, Dickie. Hey, on second thought, stay there. Where do you want me to take you? I'm thinking the Marina may not be the best idea for tonight."

Dickie thought for a moment, then gave DJ's phone number to Darcy.

"Hi, is this DJ?" Darcy asked a moment later. "Please hold for Mr. Mullins. Here, Dickie," he said, dropping his mobile over the seat onto Dickie, still hiding beneath the blanket.

"DJ?"

"Dickie, my God, are you okay? Where are you?" She sounded genuinely concerned.

"Look, I'll tell you all about my day from hell. I need a place to stay tonight. Can I come over?"

"Yes, of course, please, please, come over."

"Okay, see you in ten minutes. Thanks."

He gave Darcy directions but remained on the floor at Darcy's suggestion, not quite sure what they would find when they pulled up in front of DJ's building. They needn't have worried. As Darcy pulled up, the only person waiting was a concerned-looking DJ, standing behind the security door, ready to let Dickie in.

"Okay, the coast is clear, but you might need me up there," Darcy said, appraising DJ in a short, white silk robe.

"Thanks, but I'll call you tomorrow," Dickie said, exiting quickly out of the car and into the building.

Sixty-seven

Rae Nell had turned her phone off hours ago and was now sitting in the dark, working her way through her third chocolate bar. The first phone call had come through a little after six, just after the initial *'Little Shop of Horrors'* newscast. Her oldest sister, Rae Jean, was screaming into the phone, and at first, Rae Nell was afraid her sister might be having a heart attack.

"What in the hell are you trying to do, kill me? What in the hell were you thinking!" Rae Jean screamed.

"What in the hell are you screaming about?" Rae Nell shrieked back.

Rae Jean was halfway through her tearful, screeching explanation when another call came through.

"Rae Nell? Dennis Brennan here. Say, obviously, we're a bit concerned about the news report we just saw. What's going on, Rae Nell? Are we at risk? Christine, as you know, is diabetic. Whom shall we contact regarding legal recourse? You? This monster that owned that tawdry establishment? Christine tells me you were in a relationship with him at one— What's that, honey? Oh, you were married to him! My God!"

She quickly clicked back to her sister's call.

"Rae Jean?"

"You little bitch!" Rae Jean screamed and hung up.

Things quickly went downhill from there until Rae Nell turned off her phone. She turned off all the lights and sat in the dark, curled up on her couch, drinking Chardonnay and eating every last bit of chocolate in the house.

Four different people rang her doorbell, although she never answered. Each time the doorbell rang, she cautiously crawled to the window and peered out from behind the drapes to see who it was.

One man she didn't recognize stood out on her front lawn and yelled. "I know you're in there. Answer the damn door!"

The fifth time the doorbell rang, she looked out and saw a police car at the curb. They knocked, not gently, and she was sure they would hear her heart pounding. They walked around to her back door, pounded on that, jiggled the handle, then pounded on the front door again. They finally left after another ten minutes.

She had to find somewhere safe to go. Terry must still be involved with his owner talks because he wasn't answering her phone calls, and it seemed as though eve-

ryone else she knew was joining the lynch mob and looking for her. *That creep, Dickie, 'she suddenly thought. *He
got me into this. He can just get me out!*

Sixty-eight

D J asked. She was giving Dickie a back rub, trying to get him to relax. "How do you plan to get out of this mess?"

"Get out of this? I'm not even sure what I'm in. I have no idea what I've done wrong," he said, face down on her living room rug. "God, except of course, to get talked into a menu change and that damn open house bullshit by Rae Nell. I thought I was serving steak. I mean, that's what she told me. I'm the damn victim here. My business is completely ruined. I mean, after this, I couldn't give steak away, much less anything else. I should have known the moment she suggested this that I'd get screwed."

"You've got to get hold of her. The police have to get hold of her. I know you don't want to hear this, but she might be just as innocent as you. Maybe she's in trouble, too, Dickie. She doesn't strike me as the sort of person who would do this. At least, not on purpose."

"You're right. I don't want to hear that," he groaned.

"Here, use my phone. She probably won't accept a call from you, but she might just answer one from my phone, give it a try."

"Not accepting calls," he said, handing the phone back to her a moment later.

"You mean she didn't answer and—"

"No, a recording said the subscriber is not accepting calls at this time."

"It might mean she's got her phone turned off, or maybe her message box is just full."

"Now what?" he groaned.

"Bed, that's what. Come on, honey. We're not going to solve anything tonight. Let's sleep on it."

Sixty-nine

Taggert and Luther had come up with a pretty good idea of what they were going to do, eliminate Helen Hardy and Rae Nell Mullins. They just had to work out a few minor details, like how they were going to accomplish it and not get caught.

Luther was replaying a pornographic DVD featuring women with clown face makeup when Taggert told him to turn it off.

"Y'all watched that damn thing at least a dozen different times. Christ, I can't think straight with all them little guys jumping around. Listen up. I think I got a plan here, maybe."

"No one has any idea we got rid of Dr. Craig and his wife, right?" Taggert asked, leaning back, staring up at the lunchroom ceiling. "We could just grab Rae Nell, grind her up, feed her to the dogs out there. Nothing left to find, simple as that, problem solved."

"Now that old bat Helen is gonna be a little more difficult. She might have to take a fall down the stairs, or maybe her brakes go out, and she has a car accident. Whatever it is, you'll have to be the one to do it," he said, sitting up, looking directly at Luther.

"Me? Why me? I'm not married to her."

"Yeah, you. I'm going to have to be in some public place, seen by a lot of folks, so I have my alibi established. Hell, you know what might even be better is if I left town, came back, reported her missing. Do the worried husband act for a day or two. You know, plead to the newspapers, offer a reward and all that kind of bullshit. Folks eat that stuff up."

"What if she has a fall, breaks her neck? You come home and find her. None of that suspicious shit about 'Where's the body?' She's dead for a couple of days. You've been out of town. She's an old gal and just took a fall," Luther said.

Taggert tried to find something wrong with Luther's idea. Other than he wouldn't get to watch Helen tumble down the stairs or go on the news and make a public plea for her safe return, it seemed perfect. But first, they would have to get Rae Nell Mullins out of the way.

Rae Nell slid down and hid in the driver's seat as a car drove past, heading out of the Marina parking lot. She had been parked back in a dark corner, watching Dickie's houseboat for the past thirty minutes. Either he wasn't there, or he was already sound asleep. She gulped directly from one of the Chardonnay bottles she brought along and then stuffed another mini snickers bar into her mouth. She tossed the wrapper onto the pile in the back seat and grabbed another candy bar. She couldn't see Dickie's dreadful Jeep anywhere.

It was well after midnight before she staggered down the steps to the dock. She continually scanned the area for anyone lurking around. She was almost on his houseboat before she saw the yellow and black plastic tape crisscrossing the rear deck and galley door, 'Police Line Do Not Cross'.

"Not sure I'd do that if I were you," a voice said from the darkness.

"Jesus!" Rae Nell screeched and jumped.

"Sorry, honey, didn't mean to scare you. Relax, it's me, Vernon, over here next door."

"Vernon, damn it! What are you doing?" she stammered.

"Minding my own business, having a beer," he replied, not asking what Rae Nell was doing, tiptoeing around her ex-husband's houseboat after midnight and drunk.

"Is Dickie home?" she asked sweetly, as if to suggest she might not want to knock and wake him at this hour for just a social call. She steadied herself on the railing surrounding the rear deck.

"No, and you missed all the excitement," Vernon said. He wore swim trunks and sat amidst a number of empty beer cans.

"Excitement?" she asked, seemingly oblivious to all the police tape wrapping Dickie's houseboat like some freakish Christmas present. There was even a length of the yellow and black tape running at an angle across the little cat door.

"Hey, you want a beer?" he asked.

"No, thank you, maybe a glass of Chardonnay? You wouldn't happen to have any chocolate, would you?"

Vernon was back in a flash with a full wine glass and a bag of chocolate kisses he had leftover from Halloween almost ten months ago.

"Here, Rae Nell, always good to see you. Sit down. It's certainly been a while."

"Ughhh, God, what is this?" she asked, feeling the wine scorch her esophagus before causing a nuclear reaction in her stomach.

"Oh, yeah, sorry, I didn't have any wine, so I gave you some One-Fifty-One Rum. It looks about the same. Want a beer instead?"

"No, this will do." She set the glass on the deck and opened the bag of chocolate Halloween kisses wrapped in black and orange foil.

"Yeah, like I was saying, you missed all the action. Police, news cameras, helicopters. Them news folks even interviewed me."

"Really? About what?"

"'About Dickie. General stuff, the usual thing, you know? Had I seen anything going on? What was he like? Had I heard the news reports? Did he have any dogs? Keep strange hours? That kind of deal. I suspect they'll be using it for background information. I talked to the cops, too."

"The police? God, what did they want to know? Did they ask anything about me?" She took a large gulp from her glass. It burned on the way down. "Oh, wow," she gasped.

"You? Nah, they didn't get that far. I wouldn't have told them about you, Rae Nell, unless it was good." He raised his eyebrows, indicating anything but good. "Cops wanted to know the same stuff. How long I'd known him, their usual fascist inquiry. Course, I never like giving the cops too much info. Never know when it'll come back to bite you in the ass. As if they don't have all the information they need on each and every one of us, anyway. You know?"

"Yeah," Rae Nell swallowed more rum and gasped. It didn't burn quite as much, and she quickly followed it with another chocolate.

"Cops didn't come and talk to you?" Vernon slapped at a mosquito on his thigh, and for the first time, Rae Nell realized he was wearing boxers and not a swimsuit.

"No, they didn't talk to me. What do you make of all the news reports?" she asked, forcing down another swallow and a chocolate chaser.

"News reports? Hell, honey, I haven't watched the news in years, not since Nixon, and I'm better for it. I just get along, like that river flowing behind us, just on and on. Why, now what's happening?"

"Well, it's not exactly clear. I just know the police picked up Dickie at that wretched, dumpy bar of his."

"Let me top that off for you," Vernon said, leaping to his feet, quickly grabbing her glass.

He returned with the glass filled to the rim and two beer cans wedged between his wrinkled arm and ribs.

"Here you go. So old Dickie made the bedtime news. Here's to him." He chuckled, raising his beer.

Rae Nell suddenly became aware of a strange pulsating sound, maybe even animal noises, and she looked between Vernon and Dickie's boats to see if there was a boat in distress out on the river. "What the hell's that sound?" she asked, having some difficulty concentrating.

"I made a CD. My own invention. It sets the mood, helps me to meditate and focus. You like it? Combination of steel drums and loon calls. I call it 'Vernon's number four.' See, four has always been a special number to me. It takes four tokes to get me high, four beers to relax. I've had four wives. I've been arrested four different times. Life is all about the pattern, Rae Nell. You just have to focus and find your pattern. After that, it starts to get really easy."

Seventy

elen Hardy was choosing an appropriate outfit for her meeting with her lawyer, Darcy Dalton. She was going to view the evidence he had obtained incriminating her cheating, philandering husband. Once viewed, she planned to sit down with Mr. Dalton, discuss a legal strategy, and then begin divorce proceedings. Not that a divorce would be necessary; she planned to shoot that cheating fool Terry Taggert long before she incurred any legal bills.

She chose a light blue ensemble, similar in color to the blue silk brocade on her bedroom walls. *'How fitting,'* she thought, sitting in her attorney's office wearing this blue outfit, watching her husband rut like some dog in heat. Then find the sniveling, disgusting, little vermin and blow out what few brains he had left in that thick skull of his. All the while clad in a garment of soft blue, sporting the subtle hint of off-white undertones, reminiscent of the room where she first became suspicious of Terry's betrayal.

Darcy watched out the window as Helen Hardy parked her black Mercedes in the space reserved for clients. He checked his screen for the third time to make sure he hadn't paused the 'dancing buns' as he now referred to Rae Nell's less than discrete image.

"Helen Hardy, Sir," the receptionist's voice came across the intercom a moment later.

Darcy adjusted his suit coat, double-checked his tie in the mirror, and waited a long moment so as not to look too eager in his groveling.

"Helen," he oozed soothingly, patting her hand. "May I have Denise get you a cup of coffee? Maybe a pastry of some sort?"

"Coffee would be fine. Black, please," Helen answered, doing her best to look the part of the stoic, rejected spouse instead of the vindictive gunslinger she had become. Denise sprang up in an instant as Darcy escorted Helen, his gravy train, into the office.

Once Denise had delivered their coffees and closed the door, Darcy took a sip, exhaled deeply, and began.

"Now, Helen, I'm going to state again that this is not necessary. In fact, as I mentioned the other day, I recommend you do not view this assault on the sanctity of your marriage. I've had to sit through this, and I found it rather difficult to view. I can't imagine the pain you must feel now nor the pain and contempt you will feel afterward. So, I'm going to ask you once again to please forego this ordeal. It's not necessary. We have everything we need right here, and your watching it will do nothing but add to the heartache you already carry. Please."

"No, I intend to watch this, if only to prepare myself for what may lie ahead. Let's get it over with," she said.

She knew Darcy might take this route, and she had practiced her response at least a dozen times in the car driving over, just in case. What she wanted to do was scream, 'Oh, for Christ's sake, show some backbone for a change, and let's see the damn thing.' Before going out and shooting that slimy little toad she made the mistake of marrying.

"Very well, as you wish," Darcy said, then came around the desk to stand next to her. He turned his laptop to face them, clicking on the play icon. Immediately, a white rear end burst across the screen.

"Oh, oh, what happened here?" A flustered Darcy suddenly jumped forward, clicking another icon. "Computers," he babbled red-faced. "All right, here we go."

Helen Hardy watched the image of her drunken, naked husband crawling across a bed. Various articles of feminine clothing were tossed his way until Darcy's favorite scene appeared on the screen.

Great ass, Darcy thought.

"Well, I suppose I should be grateful this blonde creature at least has a nice figure and apparently finds time for the sun," Helen commented staring at Rae Nell's tan line.

Darcy refrained from answering. once the DVD was finished, he quickly turned off the laptop, closed the screen, and exhaled heavily.

"Well, there you have it. First, let me say I'm sorry. Second, if you'll pardon my language," he paused, "Now, let's get the son-of-a-bitch. By the time I'm done with him, he won't have a leg to stand on. He won't get one red cent. And, he will be gone from your life forever. Helen, allow me to be your white knight!"

"I don't care what this will cost, Mr. Dalton. My mind is made up. I want him eliminated. What is it they say in the movies? Pursue with extreme prejudice." She quickly ran through her practiced lines again. "Oh, yes, and I'll need this to be handled as discreetly as possible. I'm sure you understand, once this tawdry news breaks, it will simply be all over the papers."

Darcy hadn't really heard anything beyond, 'I don't care what this will cost,' but he nodded anyway as she rose from her chair, clutching a large patent-leather handbag. He jumped to his feet, fawning over her all the way out the door.

"I can make it from here, Mr. Dalton," Helen said, trying to distance herself from his dramatics. "I'll be fine. Thank you. I would like to review any documents you draw up before they're served. I'll wait to hear from you." She extended her hand for Darcy to shake, which he promptly ignored. Instead, he gave her a long, hard hug.

"I'll be in touch soon. This shall not go unanswered," he whispered, then mustered a dour frown on his face, stood back, and nodded solemnly.

Helen couldn't stand another minute. She just nodded quietly and hurried out the door.

Darcy watched from his office window as she drove out of the parking lot, the unbelievably sweet music of her voice saying, *I don't care what this will cost* bouncing around inside his head.

"Yes! Yes! Oh, baby, thank you, thank you, thank you, Jesus!" he exclaimed, then played Rae Nell's image back and forth a few more times before Googling 'Cabin Cruisers'.

Seventy-one

Dickie had no better luck attempting to phone Rae Nell the following morning. So, at DJ's insistence, she accompanied him to Rae Nell's home. DJ suggested he really didn't need anything else going wrong right now, and it would be better to have a witness present just in case a problem developed, like Rae Nell going ballistic.

"Well, her car's gone, mail's still in the mailbox, so she's been gone since at least nine this morning," he said, exiting the backyard and walking along the side of the house.

"And you used to live here?"

"Yeah, and still pay the mortgage and most of the bills."

"Nice place. Any idea where she might be?"

"If she has any brains, she's left the country. If she were in any way involved or tried to pull a fast one, it would be just like her to be hiding inside and peeking out the window through the curtains."

"She can't be that dumb."

"You kidding? She has this incredible ability to convince herself the things that happen are never her fault. I'm sure she saw all that crap on the news last night and is wondering right now why I would do this to her."

"Ugh, blick!"

Rae Nell smacked her lips in an unsuccessful attempt to get rid of the sickly taste of chocolate and too much rum. There was a sharp pain in her head. She couldn't see, then realized her eyes were still closed. She opened them slowly, squinting, gradually adjusting to the glaring sunlight and the unfamiliar surroundings.

"God," she groaned, carefully sitting up and trying to keep her stomach down. She didn't recognize anything in the room, although there was a vague, familiar sense she may have been here before. The bed, small kitchen area with dirty dishes, a round window, just like Dickie's boat, only it wasn't, and she suddenly groaned.

"Oh, God, please, not Vernon!" That caused her stomach to explode, and she leaped out of bed, dashed to the kitchen sink, and was sick over a pile of plates and last night's rum-coated wine glass.

After finding most of her clothes, she only got sick once on the way back to her car. At that point, there really wasn't much left to come up anyway. Vernon's note, written in orange crayon, had promised a speedy return with more rum and chocolate.

She needed a hot bath, aspirin, and an ice pack for her head— God, a night in bed with Vernon. Rum, chocolate, and Vernon, thinking of any one of the three, would make her gag, and she suddenly had to slow her car, open the door, and get rid of the final remnants from her stomach.

"Ugh, ugh, damn you, Dickie!" she cursed and then spat.

Seventy-two

Taggert was beside himself. "Damn it, Rae Nell, where in the hell are you? Another one of them spoiled little girl tantrums. Well, we're about to get that problem solved."

"She answer?" Luther asked.

They were parked in front of Rae Nell's house. After pounding on her front and back door, Taggert returned to his SUV and phoned her, thinking, *Maybe she had fallen asleep, had the TV on, or was just plain stupid.*

"Yeah, Luther, she answered, but I decided I didn't want to talk to her after all. No, she didn't answer. Jesus H. Christ almighty, you think if she answered, I'd be sitting here talking to your fat ass? I must be the only son-of-a-bitch in this whole damn town with any brains left. Did she answer? God. All right, here's what we're gonna do. We have to deal with Rae Nell first before you give that wrinkled old prune wife of mine her all-expenses-paid trip down the staircase. I'll keep phoning Rae Nell and get her to come out to the farm. Whenever she gets there, we deal with her immediately, get her inside and grind her up. Handle her car the same way you did with that jackass Craig's car."

Luther glanced over at Taggert a little too quickly.

"What? You did get rid of his car, didn't you?"

"Yeah, I already told you I left it in town with the keys in it. That's why I was driving that piece of shit around yesterday."

"Okay, soon as we deal with Rae Nell, I head out of town for a few days. You take care of Helen, then I come back and find her at the bottom of the stairs. Cops won't have the slightest idea."

Detective Dexter blew on the mug of coffee in an effort to cool it but only succeeded in dribbling onto his shirt and trousers. "Damn it," he said, setting down the mug, lifting a sheet of paper, and reading to Cosgrove.

"That phone is registered to one Luther Suggs. Fella's got a list of priors about three-feet long. Petty shit, nothing too bright. Driving a car belonging to a missing person would fit. Fleeing the scene and leaving his cell phone in the car fits really well. Amazingly, he works at Chow Industries."

"Now, our caller is kind of interesting. The number is registered to a Mr. Terrence Taggert of Sunfish Lake, a pretty tony area. Owner of Chow—"

"He the guy Rae Nell Mullins works for?"

Dexter nodded.

"Bunch of priors listed here, indecent exposure out of New Orleans pled down to disorderly. A public intoxication pled down. Possession with intent to distribute pled down. Propositioning pled down. He got a DUI in Alabama. Aggravated assault in New Orleans again, this one dismissed."

"Craig Cullen, owner of this BMW, is an investor in Chow Industries. Suddenly, he's reported missing, and all sorts of people got their stomach pumped after attending the open house from hell. Why, you ask? Woof, woof, woof!"

"You mean the dog meat from Chow?"

"Oh, so brilliant! Yeah, the dog meat, and then there's the little item of human remains in the sausage. You see, Detective Cosgrove, this is why we make the big bucks."

Seventy-three

Rae Nell took the ice pack from her head and half-sitting up in bed, told a little lie. "Oh, hi, Terry, I've been trying to reach you." The shades were pulled, the curtains were closed, and her head still throbbed. She wrapped her robe tighter, pulled the covers up under her chin, kept her eyes closed, and hoped her stomach would stay down.

"Oh, really, Rae Nell? Funny, I've been trying to reach you most of the damn day! Where in the hell have you been? Your phone turned off or what?"

"Oh, I've been making sales calls and was probably in an area that doesn't get service. Just below the river bluff," she said, immediately thinking back to last night with Vernon and shuddering.

"Hmm-mmm, well, look, we need to get together. I want to go over some things with you. Can you meet me out at the farm?"

"Sure, I guess I could meet you. When were you thinking? Sometime tomorrow?" she asked, sounding hopeful.

"Nah, today, tonight, actually."

Her headache suddenly throbbed with a vengeance. The afternoon hour glared back at her from the digital clock.

"Tonight?" she whined.

"Yeah, look, I gotta be out of town for a while. I'm flying out early tomorrow morning, so it's got to be tonight. I'll adjust my schedule. What time works for y'all?"

"Well, maybe about eight? Unless that's too late?" she half-pleaded, hoping it just might be.

"No, I'll see you at the farm, in the office, at eight. Thanks, gotta run."

Rae Nell turned off her phone, slumped back under the covers, and felt sick.

Taggert shook his head at Luther. "You know, if that woman was going to be around for much longer, she could very quickly become a major pain in the ass. We'll process her tonight and get everything cleaned up before I'm on that flight tomorrow."

Helen Hardy had always been capable of making tough decisions and then seeing them through, but this was not a tough decision, nor would it be the least bit difficult to complete. She set about planning, running through her mental checklist. Colt .45, ammunition, trash bags, full tank of gas, carving knife, saw, hand-wipes, old slacks and blouse, and her two-fifteen appointment at the hairdresser.

She phoned Terry as she drove, ready to leave a message, thinking, *I will wait up for him later tonight.* Amazingly, he answered her call.

"Hey, Hell, how's it going today?" He sounded rather chipper.

"Terry?" she asked, ignoring his insulting greeting.

"The one and only. Miss me?" he replied.

Not in the least, she thought and ignored his question entirely.

"I wondered what time do you think you might be home this evening?"

"So, you do miss me. Can't say as I blame you. I don't know. We're wrapping up a big distribution deal out here. I should be home, oh, say ten or eleven." He reached for another triangular slice of pizza, tilted his head back, and dangled the end of the slice into his mouth. By ten or eleven, with any luck, old 'Hell-on-Wheels' would be sound asleep.

"Oh, so you're out at the farm, and your distribution deal is going well?"

"Pretty well, but, mmm-mmm, may have to be out of town the next few days. Wrapping up some discussions in St. Louis, I think. Yeah, St. Louis." He swallowed the huge mouthful of pizza, tilted his head back, and crammed the remainder into his mouth.

She wanted to ask, 'Do I really seem that stupid?', but settled instead for a disarming, "Well, I'll most likely be asleep when you arrive home."

"Yeah, I figured." He smacked through the pizza.

"I won't keep you anymore and let you get back to your negotiations. Goodbye, dear," she added as an afterthought.

She made a mental note to phone a friend from home around seven, so her phone records would indicate she was in for the evening. After that, she could drive out to the farm and deal with that snake of a husband.

"That was your date for tomorrow night, Luther," Taggert said, tossing his phone on the table and grabbing the last slice of pizza.

"She got any idea?" Luther asked.

"Christ, she's clueless. Any idea? All she thinks about are her bridge games and her la-te-dah high society charities and the like. Tell you what, we get this last bit wrapped up, and I'm back in town. The first thing I'm taking care of is them high society charities. I'll send each and every one of them do-gooders a nice little note from yours truly, saying, 'Kiss my ass. The free ride is over.' I'll be damned if I'm giving away any more of my hard-earned dough to them bastards. Jesus," he said and wiped his hands on his shirt.

"Mmm-mmm, c'mon, better get things ready for old Rae Nell. I don't want to be screwing around with her till sunrise. I got that early flight," he said and laughed.

Seventy-four

Dickie screamed into the phone, "Darcy! What do you mean you haven't had time to get to it?"

"Hey, calm down, Dickie. I've got it under control. Actually, I've initiated an investigation. That's the first thing we want to do. I want to find out a little more about this Chow Industries organization before I respond to all the various allegations. That's the prudent approach." He didn't add that his investigation consisted solely of leaving a phone message for Rae Nell earlier in the day.

"Who's doing the investigation?"

Darcy turned away from the current cabin cruiser website he had been looking at and attempted to calm Dickie.

"It doesn't matter who's doing the investigating, Dickie. A secondary source I sometimes use, if you must know. Look, this is a complex issue. Let's assemble as many facts as possible. In the meantime, expect some more stupid statements to come from the Department of Health. Hold your fire. Let them climb up on their high horse. It will be just that much easier to knock them off. We can't just jump in and answer these allegations by making a series of rash statements."

"Series of rash state— Darcy, I haven't done anything wrong here, other than trusting my ex-wife, Rae Nell. I keep telling you I'm the innocent party here."

"Of course you are, and that's going to come out in the end, Dickie. But we have to be careful. You've got the media on the warpath, don't forget."

Darcy wrote himself a note to call the local networks and schedule a press conference in the morning. Nothing like free publicity.

"Okay, I'm sure you're doing all you can, but it isn't fun on this end. Christ, that witch from the city, Dr. Eunice Hazzard, has me closed down. I mean, it's not like I'm making any money off this deal. They called the Emporium of Dance a 'Shop of Horrors.' Did you see that? How in the hell am I going to open up again after that? I'm screwed, Darcy, absolutely screwed!"

"Well, for starters, I'll be going after them for defamation," Darcy said, doing the mental math on twenty-percent of a fifteen million dollar settlement.

"That doesn't get me reopened."

"Look, let's not put the cart before the horse here. I know it's hard, but hang on, be a little patient, and things are going to start coming our way, okay?"

"I'm just about out of patience, Darcy."

"Give it a little while longer, Dickie."

"Okay, but I want it now!"

"Well?" DJ asked.

"Well, nothing. You heard. He's got someone investigating, and I'm supposed to wait."

"Do you trust him?"

"Darcy? He's a lawyer, of course not."

Rae Nell had been soaking in a hot tub with the shades down, and the drapes closed in the bedroom. She could barely make out the fuzzy shapes of the porcelain sink and the light fixtures on either side of her bathroom mirror. Despite the aspirin, her head still throbbed, and she had yet to find the courage to put anything back in her stomach.

She was attempting for the umpteenth time to go over in her mind how she intended to tell Terry that Dickie's Emporium of Dance was not the grand introduction into the local restaurant trade she had hoped for. Unfortunately, she couldn't seem to get past swearing to herself every time she thought about it.

As she adjusted the cold compress covering her eyes, it occurred to her that Terry never once mentioned anything about the 'Little Shop of Horrors' news bulletins that had been running for the past twenty-four hours on TV. Was it possible he was unaware? God, if only she could get them to convict Dickie before Terry returned from his trip. She guessed the death penalty would probably be too much to hope for.

Seventy-five

Terry Taggert figured they had everything staged perfectly. Luther was waiting back in the production area with the lights off. Even if she snuck up and peeked in the windows, all Rae Nell would see was Terry sitting alone at the table, presumably going over paperwork. Paperwork was a generous term. He was actually paging through a stack of Luther's magazines.

She arrived stylishly late and spritzed a little of the perfume Terry liked before stepping out of the car. Her stomach rumbled loudly after being empty all day, and she pressed against it to make it stop. She wore stiletto heels, very short shorts, and a blouse more unbuttoned than not, just to ensure she would have his undivided attention.

She planned to listen to what Terry said, then tell him it wasn't all that surprising because Dickie always seemed to ruin everything anyway. The good news was they had a very unique product, and no matter what

Dickie did, Rae Nell was convinced she could make the Chow Meat line hugely successful.

"Terry?" she called from the darkened reception area, looking down the dim hall toward the light drifting out of the distant lunchroom.

"Rae Nell, back here, just finishing up," he called, putting away the foldout image he'd been leering at and placing a sales brochure on top of the magazines.

She snugged her blouse down, absently patted her hair, and walked toward the light.

"Whoa, honey, don't you look tasty. Hot date tonight?"

"We'll see," she teased, raising an eyebrow and taking a deep breath in an effort to stop her stomach from rumbling.

"So, how'd you think your open house went? A lot of them folks thinking they got to have more Chow steaks?"

She couldn't tell if he was setting her up or if he was genuinely unaware Dickie had ruined everything.

"Well, I think the product was a huge success. People loved our product, Terry. But, you know, I'm just not sure that location and its owner are the images we want to ally ourselves with."

She conveniently omitted the fact that working with Dickie, her ex-husband, had been her idea. As she spoke, she took a seat opposite Terry, bending down a little too far, lingering a second or two longer as she set her purse on the floor.

"Yeah?" Taggert said, distracted by the view.

"Well, yes. It just strikes me that the market and venue we're looking for are exactly what the Emporium of Dance is not going to be able to deliver. I spoke to a lot of our guests during and after both nights. Everyone agrees we have a fabulous product. They just raved, said they had never had anything like it. But they weren't wild about the location. And sadly, I'm afraid Dickie just isn't the type of person who can create confidence with the successful individual we want to establish as our customer base."

"Hmm-mmm." Taggert nodded, pretending he understood, all the while thinking, *It is going to be a shame to grind up such hot, Grade A, female flesh. Maybe it might be worth the effort to grab one final piece just for old time's sake.*

"Rae Nell, did I tell you you're lookin' damn good tonight?" His eyes took on a glint.

"Thanks, that's so sweet of you." She laughed, *wondering where in the hell that came from?* "Like I said, I think our customer base would be more comfortable—"

"Customer base? Come on, honey. You kidding me? I sound like I care about some damn customer base? Shit, I'll show you what I'm interested in right now," he said, standing up from his chair. He took three steps toward her, unbuckling his belt as he approached.

"What the— Get away from me. Terry, no, stop." She half-laughed, finding nothing funny. She squirmed away from his aggressive grasp and tried to knee him when he came back after her.

"Whoa, close, but no cigar," he said, dancing back on his toes like a boxer. "Don't tell me this time you're gonna fight it. Come on, Rae Nell. What difference does one more time make?"

He reached for her and grabbed hold of the collar on her blouse. The flimsy fabric ripped as she spun away.

"Don't you grab me. What's gotten into you? Are you nuts? Get away from me before I call the police. This stops right now. You get away from me, Terry. I'm leaving."

As she bent down for her purse, he backhanded her, knocking her to her knees. A drop or two of blood splattered on the floor, but before she could react, he had his hands wrapped in her hair and yanked her up off the floor. He slapped her back and forth across the face then kicked her feet out from underneath her. As she landed on her back, her head bounced off the floor.

"Don't," she gasped, not recognizing the voice that coughed out of her throat. She spat blood down the front of her blouse as she tried to sit up.

"Please," she pleaded, then raised her hands in defense as Taggert faked with his left and punched her twice with his right.

"Oh, we're just getting started, honey," he half-shouted. He slapped her hard and punched a solid right to the forehead that bounced her head off the floor again. Before she could focus, he grabbed her ankles and began to drag her across the white tile floor, out the door, and down the hallway. As he rounded the corner into the dim hall, her body half-rolled, banging her head hard against the doorframe with a heavy thunk.

"Ha, ha, ha, knock before entering." He chuckled. "Come on, honey. Y'all like it a little rough, don't ya?"

He dragged her down the hall by her ankles. Rae Nell desperately tried to dig her nails into the concrete floor to slow him down.

"Whoa, Baby, putting on the brakes? Well then, we'll just have to go a little faster." He rotated her ankles, flipped her over on her stomach, and jogged toward the processing room.

"Here we come, special delivery."

Luther had been napping comfortably next to the industrial grinder. Rae Nell's shrieking in the hallway caused him to suddenly jerk awake. He had just flicked the lights on in the processing room when Taggert ran through the doorway, dragging Rae Nell behind him.

"Well, here we are, one hot piece of grade 'A' ass all ready for our special treatment. What do you think, Luther? Feel like sampling the goods first? Maybe you ain't so high and mighty now, honey, are ya?" he yelled, pulling her up by the hair.

Rae Nell hurt so much she wasn't sure where the pain was coming from. She just knew there was plenty of it and felt woozy.

"Help, help me," she mumbled through split lips as she attempted to focus on Luther.

"Get her over there on the plastic. We've got enough to clean up already," Luther said.

Rae Nell half-attempted to scratch Terry, but he held her by the hair at arm's length. He slapped her hard enough to make her ears ring, then picked her up in a bear hug and tossed her effortlessly onto a large plastic sheet rolled out across the floor. She bounced on all fours and fell forward. She groggily looked up and shook her head in an attempt to clear it. Suddenly, everything went dark with the explosion.

Rae Nell felt as though a heavyweight had landed on top of her, and she waited for her out of body experience to begin. Then she waited some more and wondered when the bright light would appear.

"Help her up," a female voice commanded, sounding far away. The weight was removed, and hands gently helped Rae Nell to her feet.

"I…I was just about to stop him," a male voice stammered behind her.

"Are you all right? Can you walk? Come over here, dear," an older woman in a light blue outfit motioned with the very large pistol she was holding.

"Not you, you disgusting piece of filth. You'll remain right where you are if you know what's good for you." She leveled the large pistol at Luther, standing a foot or two behind Rae Nell.

"Come here, dear. Come on. You're all right." Helen Hardy motioned again with her pistol.

It was at this point Rae Nell gasped, aware for the first time of Terry Taggert lying very still on the floor and missing a large portion of the back of his head.

"No, no, don't worry about him. Just come over here, that's right. And you, you horrid, disgusting man, you get down on your knees and stay right where you are, or you'll end up just like that ungrateful, miserable excuse for a human being and a husband."

"Now, just hold on here. I was trying to help this young lady. I had no idea any of this was going on," Luther groveled, getting down on his knees, holding his hands together as if praying, which maybe he was.

"I'm not sure she was prepared to enjoy your idea of a party," Helen responded. As Rae Nell moved, Helen stared at her blonde hair and suddenly eyed her suspiciously.

"Young lady, let me see your backside."

"W-w-what?" Rae Nell was coming to her senses, suddenly aware that the woman holding the very large gun had referred to Terry as her husband.

"You heard me. Turn around and pull down those shorts." She pointed the large pistol at Rae Nell and sounded deadly earnest.

"But, I don't—" Rae Nell turned and lowered her shorts an inch.

"Further, hurry up," Helen demanded, finger tightening on the trigger once she spotted the crisp tan line across Rae Nell's hips.

Rae Nell whimpered, closed her eyes, and pulled the tight shorts down further.

"Oh, good heavens. Stop. That's far enough. Never mind, pull them up," Helen ordered, spotting the top of Rae Nell's Minnie Mouse tattoo on her right cheek.

"Sorry, dear, just checking. Now you, you're going to move my late husband to the rear of his automobile, climb in next to him, and then we're all going to go for a nice little drive in the country." She leveled the pistol at Luther.

"Dear, you're going to accompany me on this ride, but please don't worry. You'll be safe. While I'm supervising here, you might want to get an ice pack put together. I'm afraid you're liable to have a little swelling on that face."

Luther made a slight movement in Helen's direction, attempting to get off his knees.

"Oh, please, don't be so foolish as to present me with the opportunity. I'd gladly take it. Now, wrap him up in this plastic the two of you so conveniently set out, and we'll get started. Get on with it, move!" she ordered.

Seventy-six

Dickie glanced over at DJ and said, "I don't know what else to do." They were returning to the Jeep after leaving a note on Rae Nell's door.

"Do you think she may have left town?" DJ asked.

"No, that would be the smart thing to do, so she's still around somewhere."

"Does she have family? Somewhere she could go?"

"Yes, she has family, and no, she couldn't go there. Her sisters would scratch her eyes out, just because, and then want to make up two days later after the damage had been done. It's the way they operate. No, that's not where she's gone. I know that for a fact. I just don't know where she would be."

"What about Chow Industries? It's too late now, but why don't we go to their offices tomorrow?"

"Unfortunately, all roads lead back here. I don't have any record of where their offices are. No phone number. The police took all my files. All I've got is a

big, fat nothing. Everything went through Rae Nell, absolutely everything."

"Okay, then, come on back to my place. We're not
solving anything here. You've done all you can, at least
for tonight, Dickie. Come on."

Seventy-seven

When Terry's phone rang Hellen grabbed Rae Nell's wrist and said, "Don't answer that. I can't tell you how sick I am of that awful thing."

"Gee, and I thought it was just more strange noises in my head," Rae Nell said, adjusting the ice pack back onto the bridge of her nose.

"I'm afraid those eyes are going to be black by sunrise," Helen said, not taking her eyes from the road. They had been driving for close to four hours.

"Oh, God. I don't know what I'm going to do." Rae Nell pulled the sun visor down, lifted the cover, and looked in the mirror. Even in the half-light over the small mirror, she looked battered.

"Oh, you're young, for goodness sakes. You'll heal in no time. Take a few days for yourself, go to a spa."

"Well, actually, I meant my job. Obviously, that's gone south." She inclined her head to the rear of the car. Luther, his wrists and ankles taped together, a hood over his head, lay on his back next to Terry's plastic-wrapped body.

"I suspect you're quite capable of doing rather better," Helen replied.

"Oh, I just had such high hopes, and now all this. Damn ex-husband, I should have known."

"That's something we can both agree on," Helen said, exiting off the interstate and onto a state highway. Illuminated by stabbing headlights, the navy-blue ribbon of road wove its way steadily north. Occasionally, the moon revealed a small clearing carved out of the wilderness, but for the most part, the forest closed tightly against the single-lane road.

"Can I ask you something?" Rae Nell shifted her ice pack to her cheek.

"Please do, dear."

"Why did you have me pull down my shorts? What was that about?"

"Oh, ha, ha…at first, I thought you might be someone else I was looking for. I suppose I'll never know, but then again, maybe that's just as well."

"What are you going to do with them?" Rae Nell asked, glancing into the dark rear of the SUV.

"I'm not exactly sure. I have a plan for my husband. I hadn't counted on this second fool coming along, so I haven't made up my mind on him, exactly. Do you have any ideas? It's no secret what they had planned to do to you."

"God." Rae Nell shuddered. "I just can't believe it. All my plans…ruined. And this." She looked back into the mirror.

"Well, we're almost there. Maybe just twenty minutes more, dear. Then we can turn around and go back home. I don't know how you feel, but I, for one, could use a hot bath, my own bed, and some decent sleep."

Seventy-eight

DJ half-rolled over on Dickie and said, "Mmm-mmm, good morning. How long have you been awake?"

"Long enough to study you up close and personal, and I've come to a couple of conclusions."

"Oh?"

"Well, look, even when, not if, but when I beat this thing, my business is done. I mean the 'Little Shop of Horrors' that was just the final nail in the coffin. The whole reason I did that damn open house was to try to get more business in the door. As it turns out, not even the type of business I would have enjoyed. I mean, even if it worked, why would I want a demanding clientele who'll run to the next new place the minute it opens? I've never been very good with the 'beautiful people' kind of folks, you know?"

"Really?"

"Yeah, really, I— Oh, I get it, a joke, right?"

"Yeah, pretty much, but I have an idea. Want to hear it?"

"Yeah, is it any better than my idea of just untying the houseboat and drifting downriver for fifty miles?"

"Umm, yeah, I think so. Okay, here goes, you sell the Emporium of Dance to someone who has a great idea for a new place, maybe play off some of the notoriety and bad press you received. They could make you a silent partner."

"Yeah, great, you know anyone crazy enough to get involved?"

"Matter of fact, I do."

"Who?" he asked, genuinely surprised.

"Me."

"You? Gee, thanks a lot, honey. I mean, I really appreciate it, but we're going to need something besides good intentions to sell this sow. Don't take this the wrong way, but you walk dogs for a living, you know? This is just a little bit more involved."

"Walk dogs for a living? Are you nuts? I do that for exercise, you big dope. And for your information, Mr. Big Business, this building, I own it, and that one across the street, if you'd care to look out the front window, I own that one, too. You know all that computer stuff in the other two rooms? That's what I do for a business. I write software. What? Do you think I'm playing around on Facebook all day? Your accountant, Fenton Larkin? His firm just signed a two-year consulting contract with me for twenty-grand a year, plus four percent of what my software saves them. Dickie, his firm has six offices. I'll clear a hundred and twenty with them, and it's one of a dozen contracts I've got going. That doesn't count ongoing residuals on my software. So, walk dogs? Yeah, that's what I do, Dickie. I walk dogs. Jesus Christ, if I wasn't so damn crazy about you, I'd tell you how stupid you were."

"What?"

"You heard me."

"Why didn't you tell me? Why the hell didn't you ever say anything?" He sat up in bed, clearly in a state of shock.

"Because then, I wouldn't know if you loved me or the bank account. I've been there before, and it never works. I learned a long time ago, I can't buy love. We've never been about money. We've been about us. Look, you run a disgusting bar that is failing, or, according to Fenton, has failed. You drive a dreadful car that's on its last legs. You're overweight. You're broke. But life with you is a real blast. And even when you thought all I did was walk dogs, you loved me. You never hassled me, never tried to change me, you just loved me. I happen to think that's pretty damned great. I think I'm pretty lucky. I think you might almost be as lucky as me, 'cause I love you, too. Okay, I'm going to put some coffee on, soon as I find my thong," she said, getting up.

"Leave it," he said and pulled her back into the bed.

Seventy-nine

Luther sniffled and wiped the tears running down his cheeks. "All right, there. God, please, I promise! I didn't know what he was going to do, honest. He told me he was just going to talk to her."

He had no idea where he was. They made him dig Taggert's grave, and he had just finished filling it in. Christ, he could never find this desolate spot again. Birch trees as far as he could see, that should narrow it down to about ten-thousand square miles. He was probably going to be shot in the next minute or two, die in this godforsaken middle of nowhere.

"What…what are you going to do to me?" he croaked over the lump in his throat, fully prepared to begin digging his own grave. So this was where it would finally happen. *Great, just great, in the middle of the damn sticks,* 'he thought.

"Against my better judgment, I'm going to have you tape your ankles, then place that hood back over your head. This young lady is going to tape your wrists. If you should be stupid enough to attempt anything, anything at all, I won't hesitate to shoot you, and I promise you will slowly bleed to death unless the wolves get you first. Is that understood?"

Luther sniffled and nodded tearfully.

"Very well, step over by the car," Helen directed with her pistol.

He did as he was told. He taped his ankles securely then draped the hood back over his head. He placed his wrists together and stood still while Rae Nell wound the tape tightly around them. He was too afraid to breathe, much less attempt to try anything just in case that old bat with the gun got the wrong idea. The younger one unceremoniously pushed him into the back of the car, where he lay completely helpless.

It might have been an hour, possibly ten hours. He had no idea. All he knew was that the car eventually stopped, and a moment later, the rear hatch was opened. He was pulled by the ankles and tumbled out onto the ground.

"Uff," he groaned, landing and bouncing on the hard prairie.

"We're not going to undo your wrists. I'll expect you to keep that hood on your head until you are unable to hear this vehicle, then I'll expect you to wait a full five minutes before you remove the hood. Is that understood?"

"Yeah, five minutes. I got ya', but where, where in the Hell am I?"

"Hell? Oh, this is much worse than Hell. You're in North Dakota. If you're wise, you'll continue west. Do not think of returning to St. Paul, not even for so much as a change of clothes. And, do not ever think of bothering this young lady or me ever again. Have I made myself clear?"

"Oh, yeah, real clear. Believe me, I promise," he half-pleaded from inside the hood.

Helen bent over, placed the pistol close to his head, and pulled the trigger. Luther jumped from the noise.

"Ahh, Jesus, I promise, honest. I won't ever go back. God, I promise."

"Mmm, that was just a small reminder. Remember, five minutes," Helen said, then calmly walked back to the car, got in, and drove away.

As Luther's ears rang, he decided since she wanted five, he would give her ten minutes, just to be on the safe side.

"Now," Helen said, watching Luther's figure shrink in her rearview mirror. "We had better get our stories straight. Take that mobile and send me a text message from Terry saying he's leaving town."

Luther remained still for what he figured was ten minutes and then waited for another five just to be sure. He eventually worked the hood off his head and looked in all directions. God, it must be North Dakota, not a tree in sight. It took him a while to gnaw through the tape around his wrists. Once that was accomplished, he unwrapped his ankles and began walking.

He followed the semblance of a gravel road, scanning the horizon for some indication of human life, power lines, or, God forbid, a farmhouse. He decided he would cut across the endless fields to save time, although he wasn't even sure which direction he was traveling. He grew tired and hot over the course of the cloudless day. He continued to sweat, knowing he needed water, aware he was beginning to dehydrate.

He tugged throughout the day at his ears, still ringing after that old hag damn near gave him a heart attack firing the gun next to his head. He had to get out of the sun, but the horizon, as far as he could see in any direction, didn't offer so much as a tree.

"We'll see who has the last laugh. Don't return for so much as a change of clothes." It was going to be a lot more than a change of clothes he returned for. See how tough she talked once he was finished with her. The biggest mistake that old witch made—

The snap was audible and was immediately followed by Luther's scream from the intense pain in his right leg. He went down and rolled across the ground in agony. Every time he moved, the pain seemed to ratchet up another notch. Jesus, ground as flat as a pancake, and he broke his leg in the only hole. It just couldn't be. But it was.

After lying there for what seemed forever, the late afternoon heat began to take its toll. The slightest movement caused intense pain, and he tried to remain very still. He could feel his face and arms beginning to blister beneath the unrelenting sun. His exposed skin burned to a painful scarlet. His shirt and trousers were drenched in sweat, and he would have given anything for just a swallow of water.

Despite the pain, he eventually rose up slightly on his elbows. His lower leg lay cocked at an unnatural angle. His trousers were blood-stained below the knee, and he guessed the bone had most likely broken through the skin. The swelling filled the confines of his trouser leg until it looked like the sausage casings he had stuffed with ground up Craig and Marti Cullen just days before. He grew semi-delirious from the pain and lack of water until eventually, he passed out.

When he woke again, it was dark. His face was so blistered and burnt he had trouble seeing anything through his swollen eyes, despite the full moon. He thought he heard something in the brush, a panting and rustling off to his left. Then it seemed to come from the right. A minute or two later, it was back on his left again, circling. He tried to move, but the sharp pain shot through his nervous system and caused him to groan loudly. He heard something or someone moving maybe ten feet away.

"Anyone out there? Hey, you there, I'm hurt here, damn it. Don't go, please." His voice croaked, now little more than a whisper.

There was a sudden howl off to his right, answered by another and then another. Whatever they were, they were close. Dogs, out here? Maybe not. The howl started up again, closer. Then more rustling in the brush, close enough now that he could hear panting. The pain shot up from his leg again. His scream came out as more of a painful groan.

More rustling seemed to be coming from all sides and growing closer, much closer. He could smell them, a scent of 'wild' suddenly in the air. Then he saw the eyes glowing and heard the deep, throaty growls.

Eighty

Cosgrove circled an area on the overhead photo of the Chow Industries farm complex. The enlarged photo was spread out on the hood of his car. "We'll want the last vehicle in to block the drive here."

"This is the only way in or out. We've got warrants for the entire complex. We'll be going in hot. Any questions?" he asked the assembled SWAT team.

Rae Nell gripped her steering wheel as she drove out of the Chow complex and rounded the corner on the paved county road. A half-mile further, she drove past police cars pulled over on the shoulder. She'd seen enough movies to know police cars, surrounded by a dozen guys clad in Kevlar vests with SWAT stenciled on their backs, could not be a good thing. She just wanted to get home and put this all behind her.

"That damned Dickie," she said as she glanced at the SWAT team in her rearview mirror.

Six minutes later, the police vehicles fishtailed off the paved county road and raced down the long drive, splattering gravel and mud before skidding to a stop at the front door of the Chow Industries processing plant.

"Police, stay where you are," Dexter yelled, storming through the unlocked door and into the empty lobby. "Police, stay where you are," he hollered, moving quickly down the hallway. "Clear," a voice called behind him from what must have been a break room. He pressed forward. "Police!" He echoed through the empty processing room. "Stay where you…hey, anyone here? Hello, hello, anyone out there?" The only response was a choir of barks coming from the kennels somewhere in the rear.

"The place looks completely empty. Did they know we were coming? Anyone check the bathroom?" Cosgrove asked the assembled group behind him.

"It's like everyone just walked away, disappeared."

"Okay, treat the entire area as a crime scene. Call the lab guys in to start going over things."

EIGHTY-ONE

Darcy had received a return call from the City Attorney's office the day before. The good news was they were not pressing charges against the Emporium of Dance. The bad news was they could not guarantee the same response for the Department of Health.

"Look, Mr. Dalton, as I've already explained, as far as this office is concerned, at this time, we do not see a need to proceed with any action against your client relative to the Chow Industries situation. I can't speak for the Department of Health. They still seem to be pretty worked up."

"What about the damage done to my client's reputation? His restaurant was described as a 'Shop of Horrors'?"

"His restaurant, yes, I might suggest the 'Shop of Horrors' line is something you could take up with the news media. Certainly, the city didn't come up with that."

Darcy had been checking the cost of boat slips at various marinas on Lake Minnetonka. The list was fairly short given the size of the slip he thought he was going to need, and of course, specific accouterments, the normal fueling, and refitting services, not to mention a decent private club with a restaurant and eighteen holes. He had a growing list of boat names next to him, and as a new name popped into his head, he would add it to his list. He had just finished writing down 'Dog-Gone' right below 'Divor$e' when his receptionist came across on the intercom.

"Mr. Mullin's on line two."

"Darcy Dalton, here," he said after letting Dickie wait on hold for a few minutes.

"Darcy, I have—"

"Dickie," he interrupted, "glad you phoned. I was just on the line with the City Attorney's office. It took some doing, but I got them to drop the charges. I'm going to set my sights on the Department of Health next. Once I'm finished with them, we'll look at the news media, starting with Channel Seven."

"Any chance I can open for business?"

"I'm working on that right now," Darcy said, chuckling to himself as he wrote down 'Tan-Line' on his list of boat names. "But I think it's going to take some time," he said, remembering the cautionary words from the City Attorney.

"Yeah, well, time is the one thing I don't have. I can't make any money if I'm not open."

"Look, I'm well aware of that, Dickie. I'm working on it. You'll just have to trust me on this."

"Yeah, I know that, but—"

"I'll be in touch as soon as I have something." Darcy hung up the phone and clicked on another marina website.

"So?" DJ asked.

"So, it's just like you said. Nothing from the Department of Health, and they're going to take their own sweet time. I'm guessing a month, at least. I'm effectively out of business."

"Unless you officially close and then sell. Then, it's still going to take at least a month or two to refit the place, change everything, but be honest, a month from now, how many people are going to remember you were an innocent party in the story? Or, are they just going to remember you served up puppy steaks and man meat to the cream of the city? The way these things work, even if the media issued an apology, it would just remind people of the original story. I'm really sorry, honey, but I think the Emporium of Dance is screwed. It just might be time to move on to the next phase. Okay?"

Eighty-two

From her living room couch, Rae Nell could see the empty spot where her gorgeous fur coat had hung in the front closet. Those two cop pals of stupid Dickie's, Dexter and Cosgrove, had come and taken it. That was just fine with her. She wanted to get as far away from this whole sordid affair as possible. Just to put the frosting on the cake, Dickie's pals looked like they enjoyed letting her know the gorgeous coat had been dog fur. My God, dog, and not even imported at that.

She sipped her ice tea, picked up the hand mirror, and checked her face for possibly the thousandth time today. The good news was the bruises around her eyes were no longer black and purple. The bad news was they had turned to a disgusting yellowish green.

More importantly, the police had asked her only a passing question or two about Terry Taggert's whereabouts. Again, the more distance she could put between her and that whole sordid night, the better it would be.

She shuddered, thinking, *I escaped the police raid of Chow Industries by no more than five minutes the other morning and had come way too close to being murdered the night before.* She knew exactly who to thank for all of it. Everything always came down to the same problem, that damn Dickie.

Eighty-three

Dickie double checked his notes and said, "I'll have to confirm this with the boss, but I'm thinking two cases each of the four white wines and two cases each of your four reds. That, plus the beer taps, should be enough to get us going. DJ will be in early this afternoon. Oh, hey, Patsy, glad to hear your husband is doing better after the Chemo. I know that's not fun for either of you."

"I'm glad things are working out for you, too, Dickie. We were all just shocked last month when everything happened, and well, you know, we're all wishing you the very best of luck."

"Thanks, Patsy. Hey, gotta run. Here comes the boss."

"You didn't have to get off on my account," DJ said.

"No big deal, just placing your order with Patsy."

"Say, I got a call from a friend of mine, Carol. She's got a problem."

"Like what? She needs a babysitter or her grass cut?"

"She only wishes. No, unfortunately, more like she needs your investigation thingy. Would you mind talking to her?"

"Do I have a choice, DJ?"

"No, not really. But seriously, would you at least talk to her?"

"Is this the woman who's the nurse over on the Psyche wing at Regions hospital?"

"Yeah, Carol. She came in the Emporium from time to time. Shouldn't take more than a minute or two. She just needs a little advice, is all."

"Yeah, have her come in sometime, and we'll chat."

"Good, 'cause she's swinging by once her shift is finished tonight."

Dickie looked over DJ's shoulder as Darcy walked in. She turned at the same time and said under her breath, "Oh, have fun." Then, she gave a wave, said a cheery, "Hi, Darcy," and fled into the kitchen.

"Darcy, how you doing?" Dickie asked.

"Don't even ask. I've been fighting with that damn fancy marina all day. I had to cancel the order for the cabin cruiser since a huge case I thought would come my way just fell apart, and if I don't have a boat, I guess I won't be needing the slip, now, will I? Right now, they're trying to hang me with some bullshit about a signed contract and a golf club membership. I can't believe it."

"Hey, are you really going through with this?" Darcy looked around the redecorated, former Emporium of Dance.

"Yeah, it's a really simple concept. Some guy called this morning about franchising, and we haven't even opened. I got a couple of news stations wanting interviews. We've talked to magazines, both papers, but I'm having DJ handle all that."

"You're calling it the Dog Pound?"

"Hey, I said it was simple. She figures we can build on the negative press I got from the Emporium fiasco, more than enough of that to go around. We'll have about a dozen different hot dogs, with chips, fries, onion rings, all served in stainless steel dog food bowls— more of a family joint. You know, shakes for kids, chocolate covered cookies that look like dog shit for dessert. Plus, even better, DJ owns it lock, stock and barrel. I'm just another employee punching the clock."

"Yeah, right, except you're working for your new wife."

"Yeah, I know, and that's the best part."

The End

Thank you for taking the time to read *Chow Down* the fourth book in the Hotshots series. Reviews are a big help. If you enjoyed the read, I would really appreciate

a review. Even if it's just a sentence or two it really, really helps.
All the best,
Mike

Check out the sample of the next book in the *Moonlight Dance Academy* the fifth book in the Hotshot series.

Sneak Peek

Moonlight Dance Academy

Second Edition

MIKE FARICY

Prologue

It all started back in Blue Earth, Minnesota, in the days before Hub 'made' all his money. Funny thing, there had been all sorts of rumors. You always get that when there's money involved. But rumors usually have some small basis in fact. There aren't any real hard facts where Hub's fortune is concerned. No facts, just rumors. Like the robbery rumor, the sunken treasure off the Florida Coast rumor, the New Orleans rumor, the New York mob rumor. Rumor, it's the fuel that can power a small town.

Everybody who knows Hub agrees he's a hell of a nice guy, but he wasn't doing much back in those days. Truth be told, he was sort of adrift. He was looking for something, but he had no idea what. About the only sure thing he knew was he hadn't found what he was looking for. Up to that point, maybe the only real purpose in his life had been to serve as a warning to others.

The two facts people know are that Hub left town broke, and he came back wealthy. The facts no one but

Hub knows are that, along the way, five people died, none of them very nicely. The mob is still looking for a very large amount of cash, and somewhere, Hub learned to dance, which seemed to get him a very nice lady.

See what you think.

One

Friday afternoon, Hub stood at the receptionist's counter, reading the note for the third time. It was written on a small slip of pink paper with the heading 'While You Were Out'. The note told him to stop in Jim Nelson's office at the end of the day. How appropriate it was pink. He guessed he was going to be fired again. After a couple of times, you just get the sense it's coming. It wasn't going to be fun. The 'F' and the 'U' were correct, but fun wasn't exactly the word.

"Hey, Hub!" Jim Nelson slapped him on the shoulder before Hub could come out of his fog and look up. "Let's you and me go across the street to the Legion, grab us a couple of cold ones. What do you say, son?" It wasn't really an offer to be refused.

"Yeah, sure, Jim. I got a couple of things to wrap up here. I'll meet you there in thirty minutes? You have one waiting for me."

"Marlene," Jim said to the blonde seated behind the receptionist's counter. "You make sure this man gets his tail over to the Legion in thirty minutes, hear? I'm back Monday, 'less I get really lucky tonight. Hub," he said, looking down from his 6-foot-6 height, "see you soon, buddy."

Hubbard Schneider installed home security systems. He was "Hub" to anyone who knew him, built stocky, in a farm boy sort of way, country solid. He stood a shade under six feet with blonde hair worn a little too long but nothing freaky. He had blue eyes, not bright like movie stars, softer, more like a denim work shirt that had been washed too many times. The color the shirt gets when it's really comfortable, just before you have to throw it away.

He was an easy-going sort of guy, laid back at forty-eight, with a failed marriage and a number of less than successful relationships floating in his wake. He didn't really care about the job. There were plenty more like this one, and that was part of the problem. The big picture was, he'd had four jobs already. Work for the boss, make the world safe for him, and then don't let the door hit you in the ass. After fifteen years of being bounced around in the home security industry, he had learned the business was just like Minnesota weather, it sucked. If you didn't like the way things were going, hang on for a minute, because they were bound to get worse. And that seemed to be what was happening now.

Monica was going to be tough. He'd have to tread lightly there. She'd probably be supportive for the first minute or two, at least with the words she used. But, lately, everything with her seemed to be a double-edged sword. It sounded all right, whatever she said, but somehow there was always a trap. He always seemed to find the trap and stumble into the damn thing headfirst.

Of course, one thing about getting let go four times in fifteen years, you get pretty good at grabbing a little extra on the way out the door. He grabbed some extra tools, extra installation kits, meters, clips, wire, manufacturer manuals, and armloads of everything from the storage area. He grabbed a carton of note pads, some pens and four golf shirts, although he hated golf.

He carried it all out the door without raising an eyebrow. He had no idea what he was going to do with it. Maybe start a business for himself. Maybe get out of home security, once and for all, and start a business training bird dogs or something. He dumped all his extras in the back of his black Ford Ranger and drove down the block to the Legion Hall.

"Hub, let's you and me grab a back booth." Jim Nelson didn't really wait for an answer. He nodded to the bartender. "Put it on my tab, Becky." He clamped his paws around two beers and strode toward the back of the room. Hub's only option was to follow.

The room was stale from three hundred and sixty-five days a year of cheeseburger grease and the odd spilled drink. The sort of small-town place where you automatically drank your beer from the bottle. Although this was September, the posters on the wall still touted a

Coors beer St. Patrick's Day celebration from the previous March.

Once they settled into the back booth, Nelson took a half-moment to stretch out and said, "Son, I don't like it, but I've got to let you go, damn it. You've never given me a problem. You show up every damn day. But you're the most recent man hired, and I don't have to tell you that business has been down. On top of all that, I got those damned, dimwitted Hanson twins coming on board the beginning of next month." He drained an inch or two out of his bottle, washing the Hanson twins from his mouth. He'd pretty much said it all right there.

Two

onica Walsh appreciated all the attention she'd been getting from Dave Collins lately. Certainly, it was more than she seemed to receive from her boyfriend or whatever Hub had become. She'd tried a number of different things to light a fire under him, but none of them had worked. All of a sudden, she was forty and wondering how that had happened?

Things had gotten sort of bumpy after high school, Hub being her current bump in the road. She knew one thing for sure, she wasn't going down again. She'd already been through the routine of having to sell a house and put the best spin on things. She wasn't going to take another lousy vacation to visit her folks up north instead of going someplace fun with friends.

She'd felt at the end of her rope for the past couple of weeks. She called Home Tech to tell Hub she was going out with some people from the office. There was no point in mentioning to him that Dave Collins would be there, too.

When he left for the day, Jim Nelson had sent the receptionist an email to post. The email thanked Hub for being a good employee and wished him well with his new opportunity. Marlene figured she could get the word out a lot faster on her cellphone. She made a point of following up the email with a personal phone call to people who would be dying to know exactly what had happened. It was in-between these calls that Monica phoned. Marlene thought it would be a kind thing to do to offer condolences and to wish Monica good luck.

"You know, Monica, about Hub losing his job and all. He's such a great guy. We're all going to miss him. What are you guys going to do?" Marlene asked it sweetly, hoping for a piece of gossip to pass around Monday morning.

That had done it for Monica. She slammed down the phone, giving Marlene her gossip, and stormed out of her office. It was a toss-up whether she would throw Hub into the street or she would leave.

It took her less than an hour to cram Hub's things into a footlocker and musty boxes from the basement. She dragged them out the door and dumped everything in front of the garage. She added a note telling Hub she hated him and wanted him out of her life. Now!

Just in case he missed the note and his pile of worthless possessions, she emailed him the same message at

Home Tech, followed by a laundry list of nineteen separate reasons he was a failure. That accomplished, she hurried back to join the girls from work and Dave Collins.

Tonight could be the night to get things rolling with Dave. She could start working on her own future, do something for Monica for a change. It was finally going to be her time to shine.

To be continued...

Thanks for checking out the sample of Moonlight Dance Academy. It apparently wasn't the best day for Hub. Better grab a copy to catch up and see what happens. . .

Books by Mike Faricy

The following titles comprise the Hotshot series.

- **Reduced Ransom!** 2nd edition
- **Finders Keepers!** 2nd edition
- **Bankers Hours** 2nd edition
- **Chow Down** 2nd edition
- **Moonlight Dance Academy** 2nd edition

Contact the author:

- Email: mikefaricyauthor@gmail.com
- Twitter: @Mikefaricybooks
- Facebook: Mike Faricy Author
- Website: http://www.mikefaricybooks.com

Published by

MJF Publishing